The Other Miss Bates

The second book in the Highbury Trilogy
inspired by Jane Austen's Emma

Allie Cresswell

Contents

Introduction

My story is set some thirty years before the beginning of Miss Austen's novel *Emma*. In the original, Mrs Bates' elder daughter plays an important part. The younger, Jane, is named only once and never appears in Austen's *Emma*. Her only importance in *Emma* is as the deceased mother of the elegant and accomplished Jane Fairfax. In my story she plays a much more central role.

The Other Miss Bates is the second of the three *Highbury* books which trace the pre-history of *Emma* and then run in parallel to it, the first being *Mrs Bates of Highbury*. Fans of Jane Austen need have no fear; I have no intention of deviating from her plot and in the end she and I will be on exactly the same page. For those readers unfamiliar with *Emma*, I hope *The Other Miss Bates* will be enjoyable as a stand-alone novel.

Douglas Fairfax and his brother Angus had the extreme good fortune of being the sons of one of the masters at a highly reputed school. The master's family occupied a pleasant lodge within the grounds and the boys took their first air in the quadrangles of the ancient buildings, learned to totter on the green sward of the playing fields and ate their first mutton in the lofty refectory of that famous and respected institution.

When the time came they joined the boys in the classroom, gaining an education equal to the sons of landed gentlemen, earls and archbishops. Douglas, a gregarious and sturdy child, soon found those boys, and later those men, counted him amongst their friends. *They* might be the future inheritors of vast tracts of grouse moor and fertile farmland, *he* merely the son of a school master, but they took to him nevertheless. He was bright, amusing and bold, the lynchpin of the school rugger team and the originator of many a legendary escapade of mischief and derring-do after lights-out. From school he gained a scholarship to Oxford where he soon won his blue and an even wider circle of well-heeled acquaintance. In this way, by the time he was one and twenty Douglas was intimate at a number of manorial estates and quite at home amongst strings of thoroughbreds and armies of liveried servants. If his parents worried that their son was growing comfortable with a lifestyle with which he could by no means afford to become accustomed, they did not say so. They trusted to their son's good sense and pragmatic character, his easy-going nature and excellent manners. Douglas Fairfax was such a young man as would recommend himself wherever he went. It was no surprise, therefore, that he recommended himself to the Honourable Lady Cecily Whitby to such a strong degree that she agreed to become his wife. Lady Cecily was the only daughter of Lord and Lady Whitby, sister to Viscount Whitby, one of Douglas' closest friends. Lady Cecily was to be very well provided for indeed— there was no necessity that her husband should bring either wealth or title to the union, which was a blessing, since Douglas Fairfax brought neither. What he did have was a large circle of very superior acquaintance, a superlatively excellent education and manners which would pass without the slightest blush anywhere.

Douglas' brother Angus was not so fortunate either in his character, his robust good health or his charismatic appeal. Angus was studious, vulnerable to the ague and without that easiness or affability which so recommended his brother. He was a gentle soul, contemplative and shy but with an honest, tender heart. He preferred the library, long, solitary walks in the countryside or the company of an interesting book on botany to the clash of titans on the sports field or high jinks in the dormitory. The six or seven years which separated him from his brother were a boon—the celebratory reverberations of Douglas' career at school and then at university had virtually stilled by the time Angus made his more timid entrance to those institutions. He was not forced to live too much in his brother's shadow and was saved from unflattering comparison. There existed between the two young men, in spite of their differences, the most affectionate bond.

Following University, Angus opted to apprentice himself to a surgeon and to qualify to practice that profession. The boys' parents had by this time retired to a small cottage but Douglas was able, and extremely willing, to offer his brother both a home and the pecuniary means to pursue his studies being, by this time, the husband of Lady Cecily and she herself having made over to him the absolute control of her substantial fortune.

Mr Fairfax and Lady Cecily owned a number of properties but the commencement of our story finds them, in September of the year 1780, taking up residence at Brighton. Lady Cecily expected to be confined the following Easter and the air at Brighton as well as the diversions of that fashionable resort had been recommended as particularly healthful and distracting to a lady in her delicate health. Angus Fairfax was at that time in the final stages of his apprenticeship with one of the doctors in Brighton and the Fairfaxes depended upon their brother's advice for the most efficacious treatment of Lady Cecily's indisposition. The amusements of Brighton were legion; card tables at the Assembly, carriage excursions, boxing bouts and horse racing all offered the kinds of entertainment certain to appeal to such a man as Douglas Fairfax. He was a man determined to be happy and enjoy himself wherever he went; Brighton, Bath, London, Monaco—it was all the same to him, but Angus' being there was a powerful draw. Douglas hoped that with a little assistance from himself, society in Brighton would provide such a lady as might be beneficial for Angus' future. The Fairfaxes moved into one of the premier addresses on East Street overlooking the pleasure ground known as the Steyne, only one or two houses removed from the Pelhams—the first family of Sussex—and not very far distant from the residence of Mrs Sealy.

Chapter 1

'My dear,' boomed Mr Fairfax to his wife three or four mornings after their arrival in Brighton, as he sat at the breakfast table, 'I wonder if you might have a word with the housekeeper? She seems to have but a very tenuous hold on the management of the house. Our lease includes a full household of staff, you know, but there is much wanting. My shirt was nowhere to be found this morning. The wastrel who purports to be my valet knew nothing about it at all. The cook is very behind hand in sending up the dishes. This toast is cold and so is the tea. I have been waiting these twenty minutes for my eggs. Is a decent breakfast too much to ask? I have been up since six. You know, my dear, I am the last man to complain, but where there are servants one does expect to be adequately served.' Douglas Fairfax was indeed the most sanguine and easy of men, big-hearted and generous to a fault. His liberality manifested itself in every dimension of his character; he was large in every aspect; tall and burly, broad-shouldered, with a loud laugh and a big smile. His round face was distinguished by bright, lively eyes and a broad forehead. He was energetic and forceful, his character quite equal to his frame in size and vigour. Marriage had only augmented these qualities— he was as happy and thoroughly satisfied as it is possible for a man to be; his contentment showed in every gesture and was as apparent to the world as it was manifest to himself.

'I believe the cook is incompetent,' murmured Lady Cecily. She was standing at the bay of the dining room window observing the comings and goings on the street below. She was an elegant, very beautiful young lady with a fine complexion, fair of hair and blue of eye, as petite as her husband was large, as delicate as he was strong, as doubtful as he was decided. She was by nature rather languid, little liking to exert herself, with a distracted air. Marriage, and her interesting condition, seemed to have increased these natural characteristics, her indolence and lethargy increasing in parallel with her husband's energy and verve. It was by no means part of her general routine to be dressed and out of her room at this hour; her breakfast had habitually been taken in her boudoir during the mid-morning. The shock of rising so early had quite taken her breath away. But the exigencies of the Brighton day demanded bathing before the fast was broken and she had, that morning, made her first attendance at the medicinal baths. The experience had left her feeling more listless even than was usual for her. 'Last night's fish was raw—I did not touch a morsel of it—and the sauce was lumpy and the colour of …' she gave a shudder, 'I could hardly bear to look at it.'

Mr Fairfax got up from the table and strode across to the fireplace, where he agitated the bellpull with much vigour.

'I hardly feel mistress of the place myself, as yet,' Lady Cecily went on, faintly. 'At Woodley Court things run very smooth. I never have to give household matters a moment's attention. I will speak to the housekeeper but she hardly seems to have a better understanding of the household than I do; she was quite vague on the subject of linens and my laundry has not been attended to these past three days. Perhaps we should send for Berkley and Mrs Fitz from Woodley. What is your opinion?'

'Oh!' bellowed Mr Fairfax, 'I leave it entirely to you to take matters in hand, my dear. The household falls to your remit, you know, and I have every confidence of you establishing some order once you turn your mind to it.'

Lady Cecily looked very much less certain of her powers but the subject was clearly closed and Mr Fairfax turned his attention to the post which lay on a silver tray awaiting his attention.

'Oh,' he exclaimed, on perusal of the first letter, 'that lady and her daughter are expected today. I suppose you will make arrangements with the housekeeper?'

'Which lady?'

'My father's friend, Mr Knightley of Donwell Abbey, wrote to me about them, you recall my dear,' Mr Fairfax said. 'They are ladies of his acquaintance, thoroughly genteel, you need have no fear, but in somewhat reduced circumstances. The young lady is to be companion to Mrs Sealy. The mother comes to see her properly settled and is to stay with us until she is content. *She* is sister-in-law to Captain Bates. I met *him* last evening at cards.'

'Oh,' Lady Cecily replied, distantly. 'Do they have acquaintance in Brighton?'

'None at all, as far as I know. Captain Bates declared he had never set eyes on the woman when I mentioned her name to him last night, which is why they will stay with us, I suppose. Or at least the widow will—Mrs Bates. The daughter goes straight to Mrs Sealy's. By God!' Mr Fairfax exclaimed, 'after my dip in the sea this morning I could eat a dozen breakfasts. Ring the bell again, will you my dear? If my eggs do not come soon, I declare I shall eat the table.'

Lady Cecily crossed slowly to the fireplace and twitched the bell cord. 'I am engaged to meet Mrs Pelham at the circulating library this afternoon. There is to be a recital. Who will receive these ladies if I am from home? Really, Douglas, life here in Brighton is very different to life in town or in the country. One is *out* all the time. One is never to be *at home* it seems. The ladies at the baths this morning were not even going home to have their hair dressed! They were going straight to a coffee house for breakfast, and then to church, and only then will go home to change their gowns before an afternoon of promenading on the Steyne. The very idea exhausts me. We have been from home every evening. My feet have barely touched the ground.' She paused the train of her observations at the entrance of a liveried footman to the room.

'There you are at last,' Mr Fairfax cried, 'but *still* with no eggs I see. What *is* the cook about? We require eggs, please, coddled, a great many of them, and some dry toast cut very thin for Lady Cecily. And fresh tea.' He turned to his wife. 'Anything else?'

She shook her head and made a moue of distaste.

'Well then,' Mr Fairfax went on, 'some ham, if you please, and a bumper of ale, and *make haste.*'

'*I* can hardly be expected to take a widow-woman, be she ever so genteel, under my wing, when I am so new to the place myself,' Lady Cecily resumed when the man had left the room. 'I cannot introduce just *anyone* to Mrs Pelham, either. I must confess, Douglas, I had rather you had not invited Mrs Bates so early in our sojourn. One is not established.'

'Mrs Bates will be weary after her journey,' Mr Fairfax said, dismissing her concerns, but not unkindly. 'She will no doubt wish to rest. It will be a kindness to allow her some respite before dinner—she may even wish to be excused dinner, or be engaged to dine with

Mrs Sealy. In any event, my dear, *your* enjoyment shall not be curtailed in any way by Mrs Bates. From what Knightley tells me she is the last person to desire any ceremony, hasn't an ounce of self-importance and will wish to be as little trouble as possible. I am certain she will be an excellent guest. Half the time we shall scarcely know she is here at all.'

Lady Cecily sighed. She knew better than to stand in the way of her husband's sanguine nature. 'I suppose we shall have to pay her subscriptions. Only her arriving today is somewhat inconvenient. If I had known, I would not have engaged with Mrs Pelham.'

'Cecily, my love, do not give it a moment's thought. Ah, *here* are the eggs at long last. I thought I would die of hunger. Would you like to go to the theatre this evening? Or do you prefer the Assembly? If you wish to see the play, I shall secure us a box.'

'I hardly know,' Lady Cecily replied, taking her seat at the table again and reaching gingerly for a slice of toast.

'I shall see what the Macartneys are doing. I am to see him this afternoon. He has a fine filly he wishes to sell. If they are intent on the Assembly, we shall join them.

These eggs are quite palatable—almost worth the wait. Let me serve you some, my dear.'

But Lady Cecily's wan expression and shrinking lips stayed his hand. 'No? Very well. Perhaps you are wise to restrict yourself to toast, then, but let me pour you some tea at least. Where is Angus this morning?'

'He spoke of a walk towards Hove,' Lady Cecily replied feebly.

'He was still at his books when I came in from the card room and that was well past one,' Mr Fairfax grumbled. 'I wish he would be more in society and less at his studies. There are several men here with eligible sisters. Miss Poole is not an ill-looking girl and quite cerebral enough for Angus, I should think. She attends the afternoon lectures, I am told. What about your friend Miss Churchill—isn't she due in Brighton? How do you think Angus would like her?'

Lady Cecily shook her head. 'Louisa Churchill is a dear friend of mine but I would not inflict her on Angus. She is wilful and headstrong.' She pushed her plate away. 'The bath did me no good this morning, Douglas. I am as bilious as ever. I had not expected to feel so wretched.'

Her husband made no reply but her paleness and trembling lip did not escape his notice. 'Miss Churchill is rich and can please herself where she bestows her hand,' he demurred, 'but if she would not make Angus happy it will not do.' He reached across the table and enveloped his wife's tiny hand in his capacious palm. 'It is too much to ask that he could be as blessed as me. Now, my dear, let me urge you to take three—no, very well—two more bites of your toast, and to finish your tea. You must take something, Angus says, even if you … if it … a small amount of sustenance will remain. Though he is not yet qualified I trust his medical opinion more than anyone else's. We will be guided by him, will we not my dear? There. Very good. And now you should go and rest. I will speak to the housekeeper about our guests and if you do not feel well enough to join Mrs Pelham this afternoon you must send a messenger. Here, do not exert yourself. Let me carry you.'

He swept her up into his arms. She was as light as a child and almost, against his bulk, as small. He strode from the room and mounted the imposing staircase two steps at a time.

Chapter 2

'Jane, my dear, I have something I wish to tell you,' Marie Bates said, as the Donwell coach left the familiar lanes and byways of Highbury. It was very early in the morning—hardly six o'clock –but they had determined to undergo the journey to Brighton in one day rather than to divide it into two and suffer the questionable accommodations—not to mention the unnecessary expense—at an inn. They were to stop at Hand's Cross to rest, refresh themselves and change the horses and would arrive in Brighton between five and six in the afternoon.

Jane was wild with excitement. She had never travelled so far before and looked with avid attention from the windows at the passing landscape, towns and villages. The journey marked the fulfilment of all her dreams—of adventure, of new surroundings and fresh faces.

'I hope you are not going to tell me that you have forgotten to pack my stout boots, or my spare chemise or my straw bonnet,' Jane said, 'for I dare not ask the coachman to turn back now. He was surly enough at being made to rise and put the horses to at such an unconscionable hour.'

'No, my dear, I believe we have not left a single article behind, everything is in your boxes.' Privately, Marie had viewed Jane's paltry number of trunks with concern. She possessed so few dresses. They were quite numerous enough for a country gentlewoman and eminently appropriate for a poor parson's daughter but they were surely *too* few and those few too *homely* for such a lively, fashionable place as Brighton. Even as an old lady's companion—Mrs Bates assumed Mrs Sealy to be in her mid to late sixties—and allowing for the limited society available to that invalid lady, surely there would be *some* occasions when Jane would need to be properly dressed? Balls she did not expect for Jane—what use would Mrs Sealy have for dancing? But there might be dinner engagements, concerts or other evening entertainments at which Jane, even if she did not shine, certainly must not be allowed to shame her patron. Between Miss Grace, the Highbury seamstress, and herself they had made over Jane's wardrobe as thoroughly as they were able but there remained, in Marie's mind, the nagging sense that, in the affluent society of Brighton, Jane would look dowdy and poor. 'Your closet was quite empty and there was nothing of yours in the press. Hetty will be able to spread her things right out, when she returns from the archdeaconry.'

'Hetty spreads herself out in any case,' Jane observed. 'It explains why she is always losing her belongings. She can never put a thing in the same place twice and consequently never knows where she has left it. And as for the bed! Well, I suppose she will be glad to have the whole of it, at last. She has spent the past months either pushing me against the wall or over the edge, depending on which side she has decided to take. And even that she could not make up her mind about.'

'Your sister will miss you very much,' Marie said quietly, 'and so will I. I quite understand why you are going to Mrs Sealy. I will not pretend that your going will not ease our straitened finances but I would not have you go on that account. We would manage, and in fact …'

'I am not going on that account, Mama,' Jane put in,

tearing her attention from the passing scenery and turning to her mama in alarm. 'We have not much but we have enough, and our friends have been so generous. They have easily made good what we have lacked, have they not? I hope you do not entertain the notion that my going to Brighton reflects in any way on our condition of life since Papa passed away. We have been as snug and perfectly happy in our rooms above Mrs Pellins' shop as we were in the vicarage except for the absence of Papa himself. No,' with a sigh, 'it is not that at all. It is Highbury itself. I feel so confined there, so restrained. We walk the same lanes day after day, and greet the same acquaintance whose news is nothing more than it was the day before—a lamb more, a hen less, the state of Mrs Cropley's bunion, the progress of master John Knightley's teeth—it is all so humdrum and dull. It is not that I do not care for these people—I care for them very much, especially little John—but I fear the education Papa gave me has made me yearn for mental stimulation of a—I will not say higher—but of a different order.'

'I understand entirely,' said Marie, although, in *her* mind, Highbury was all-in-all. Her neighbours' flocks and herds, their ailments and troubles had been the whole of her care and concern for the past thirty years. And now it seemed—it truly was—that she was to be elevated to such a situation from which she would be *more* able to guide and assist, a position of—she would not say authority—but of influence, of honour. She was to marry the squire of Donwell Abbey at Christmas. 'I hope and pray that Brighton will be all you desire, that Mrs Sealy is a kind and fair patroness to you, that the society is as varied and amusing as you could wish. But Jane, I have to tell you that I shall require you to come home at Christmas.'

'At Christmas Mama? But I do not know what Mrs Sealy's plans may be. The season at Brighton does not finish until the New Year. Most visitors, I am told, go back to their own estates or to London to partake of the entertainments there. Mrs Sealy is a permanent resident in Brighton but I surmise she may remove abroad where the climate is more temperate. She was in Switzerland until just very recently. Am I not to accompany her, then?'

'You may go where-so-ever she requires, Jane, but I shall have need of you at Christmas, for a day or so at the very least.'

'Mama you are blushing, and I see you cannot look me in the eye. Something is afoot. What is it?'

Marie found that the joy of the secret she had been holding inside for the previous weeks could not be prevented from escaping onto her cheeks. 'Oh Jane, dear Jane, I am to be married. I know you will be shocked. I am shocked myself. So soon after the death of your dear papa, it hardly seems proper, and yet he—*he*—who is so good, and would do nothing that was not entirely right, says that it shall be so. And if *he* says it, he who will be my guide and my model in all things afterwards, why should I not be directed by him now as I will be then?'

Jane, in a very few moments of surprised but rational analysis of her mother's words and emotions, and making sense of a certain oddness of behaviour over the past few weeks, soon made herself mistress of the situation. 'You are to marry Mr Knightley!'

Marie nodded. 'Yes, yes I am Jane. Are you outraged? I fear everyone will be when they hear of it. It is so soon. I have struggled with my feelings, believe me. For a time, I felt it was very wrong of me to entertain such a strong partiality and yet it would assail me, day after day. I believed him indifferent, or, worse, engaged to another, but then it was revealed … he told me … and, oh! Jane … since then I have come to think that it is not so wrong at all although it remains, to me, a very great amazement.' Marie took one of Jane's hands and looked at her through her tears. 'I have questioned myself very closely, Jane, and asked myself whether my attachment to Mr Knightley is at all related to my grief at the loss of your papa; whether I am using the one to replace the other. But I am convinced it is not so. This is a new plant which has grown independently, with its own integrity and unique beauty. It will not replace what I had with your papa, nor improve it. It is separate. Tell me your opinion honestly, Jane. If you do not approve it—if you think it unwise or find it painful to the smallest degree—I will give him up.'

'Oh Mama!' Jane cried, her own tears beginning to fall, 'oh Mama. How could I deny you such happiness as you clearly feel? And as for my judgement, well it is only your own good sense—and Papa's—which have been instilled in me since I could understand a coherent sentence. If you think it right then it must be so and Papa—well—Papa would wish you to be happy.'

The two women wept on each other's shoulders as women are wont to do and as two such affectionate women—with so much of empathy and innate care and understanding as these two enjoyed—could hardly help but express. The carriage proceeded through the Surrey countryside and presently Jane dried her tears and sat back in her seat. 'You know Mama it is not so very amazing that Mr Knightley should wish for a wife,' she opined. 'He is not a young man and he has his boys to consider. They need a mother as much as he needs a wife. And that he should choose you is a thing as thoroughly natural as it is predictable. Who more suitable, more gracious, more gentle or wise? I am only rather angry with myself that I did not see what was going on beneath my nose. You have informed Hetty, I suppose?'

Marie shook her head. 'No. I thought it better to wait until she returns from Hermia Winwood's wedding. She is likely to let things slip and I do not want the matter to be public knowledge until I give up my mourning.'

'She will go to live with you at Donwell?'

'Naturally she will, and when you come home—if you do, for whatever reason—Donwell will be your home also, for as long as you shall wish. Mr Knightley is all kindness and acquiescence on the matter. You can imagine I was ready to make it an absolute stipulation but there was no need. He would entertain no alternative. He has broached the matter with George. I believe that apart from ourselves he is the only living soul who knows of our engagement. George, of course, was all agreement.'

'Donwell Abbey is large enough in all conscience. George might go a week without encountering Hetty, if he does not choose. Hetty will quite lose herself in the landings and passageways of the Abbey,' Jane laughed. 'She might go missing for days on end! You will have to tie a skein of cotton to her wrist so you can follow her erratic wanderings through the rooms from attic to basement before you locate her half-starved in a dark linen room.'

The idea of Hetty at Donwell was very strange to Jane. As Mr Knightley's stepdaughter she would find herself occupying a higher, wider social sphere. Mr Knightley went quite often to London—he had acquaintance and business there. Under his wing Hetty might find a husband who would not mind her somewhat angular looks and odd mannerisms or her loquacious tongue; for the honour of such a connection as Mr Knightley suitors might find they could overlook these things. He might, perhaps, provide a dowry … Of course, it could not but help occur to Jane that the advantages in store for Hetty would also have been available to her. But did not expect she would ever return to Highbury except to visit. Even at Donwell Abbey, which was certainly the largest house and had the most extensive grounds of any property in the vicinity except perhaps Clayton Park, the same sense of obscurity and restraint would oppress her. Whereas Brighton … She imagined streets crammed with shops, coffee houses and inns. There would be people—the fashionable, the grand; aristocratic ladies and titled men, militiamen and naval officers—but also costermongers and fishermen and market traders, travellers from abroad with sun-burnt skins and strange accents. All would have their tales to tell. There would be concerts, lectures and debates. She hoped Mrs Sealy would be a lady with a lively intellect who would wish to attend these events and discuss them afterwards. There would be libraries—uncounted numbers of books to read—and galleries where art and sculpture would be displayed. The idea of the sea excited her—she hoped to bathe—and all this was hers to explore and observe and even, perhaps, a little, to enjoy. No, she would not exchange it for Donwell Abbey.

Chapter 3

By just after one in the afternoon their coach drew into the yard of the inn at Hand's Cross. A large and very splendid equipage was already in occupation, its doors emblazoned with a family crest depicting a lion rampant argent. Numerous liveried servants busied themselves with a second, more humble, cart which was loaded with luggage.

'Mama,' Jane exclaimed, 'isn't that the Duke of Marlborough's coat of arms?'

'Surely not,' Mrs Bates demurred.

'I am almost certain of it. Papa and I studied heraldry quite extensively. Who else could it be, with all those attendants?'

The Donwell coachman went into the inn and came back with the tidings that the premier parlour was already occupied by the ladies and gentleman belonging to the other coach but that he had secured for them a lesser—but still private—room where they would be served refreshments. Mrs Bates and Jane readily agreeing to this arrangement, the innkeeper's wife greeted them in a narrow passageway and they were shown up a short flight of steps to a room on the first floor.

'You are very kind,' Mrs Bates said, removing her bonnet and looking around the light, bright and comfortably appointed room, 'this room is quite sufficient—indeed more than adequate—for our needs. We will trouble you as little as possible.'

'Not at all, ma'am,' the woman replied. 'Tea will be with you directly and I will get my girl to bring up some fresh bread and cold meats as soon as she is able. I would attend you myself ma'am but the party in the downstairs parlour,' she gave Mrs Bates an exasperated look, 'are all out of sorts. *They* have been travelling for four days—they come from Yorkshire. They rested last night at Crawley and found the accommodations less than comfortable, I gather. The young mistress declares that nothing will induce her to set foot back in the coach but her husband and the other young lady are all for going on.'

'Yorkshire is a vast distance away,' Jane remarked, thinking of a certain Lieutenant who was stationed in that far-off county. 'I wonder whither they are bound?'

'Brighton, miss,' the woman said with a sigh. 'Most of the folks who pass through Hand's Cross are bent there or coming away from it. I do not know what I will do if the mistress prevails, for I have but two spare rooms in the house and can make but scanty provision for the coachmen—such a number of them as there are! I pray you will excuse me. Susan will be with you directly.'

Tea arrived and shortly thereafter a selection of viands and the two ladies had just begun to partake when the door burst open and a gentleman entered the room. He was of slight build and something under the normal height, closer to thirty than to twenty years of age. His face was thin, his jaw rather set and his colour pale, but he had the bearing of a gentleman and his voice, when he spoke, was soft and well-modulated. 'Oh,' he exclaimed upon immediately beholding the occupants of the room, and then, collecting himself, he executed a low bow. 'Pray excuse me. I fear I intrude. The lady of the house directed me to the room at the top of the stairs but I have clearly mistook the door.'

There was rustle of skirts and what almost sounded

like the stamp of an irritated foot on the landing behind him. 'Let me *see*, Charles,' a lady's voice carped.

The man turned. 'We have mistook, my dear, the chamber is occ …', he began to say, but he was summarily thrust aside and his companion stepped into the room. She was young—hardly more than two or three and twenty—and very elegantly dressed with a superfluity of satin in her train and a plentiful froth of lace at her throat. But her bearing was stiff and cold, her expression very haughty. A sharp nose and thin, cruel lips were by no means compensated for by the sophistication of her coiffeur of the array of jewels on her hands and wrists. She surveyed the Bateses with a degree of disdain amounting to contempt before turning to her husband and saying in a voice not at all calculated to make light of his error, 'You have brought us to the wrong room, Charles. I knew you were not attending to the housewife below when she directed you. If only you had allowed *me* precedence on the stairs we would not have been confronted by these persons. *I* should not have mistook the room.'

'Let us make our apologies and withdraw,' the gentleman replied in a low voice, adding, through clenched teeth, 'There was no necessity of you disturbing yourself at all, so comfortably settled as you declared yourself to be in the room below. I think I may be relied upon to inspect a chamber.'

'Manifestly you may *not*,' his wife retorted. 'The rooms you took for us at Crawley were not to be borne. From hence forth I will not set foot in one unless I have examined it myself beforehand.'

'Well, *that* will be a clever trick to pull off, and no mistake,' Jane whispered to her mama.

The gentleman's cheek quivered but he kept his gaze fixed on his wife, who concluded her complaint by saying, 'If we had gone to Blenheim, as I suggested, your great-uncle would have accommodated us in proper style. We could have rested there for a day or so until I had recovered.'

'My *dear*,' the gentleman hissed, his voice lower still but very firm, 'Blenheim would have taken us many miles out of our way and in any case one cannot simply *arrive*, without an invitation or any notice, even at a house like Blenheim, *especially* at a house like Blenheim. My great-uncle would have been outraged and I would not embarrass myself by such an ill-mannered act. But we will not discuss this *now*, these ladies are at table and we intrude.' He threw a look of abject apology at Mrs Bates. 'My sincere regrets,' he said, 'our imposition is unconscionable.'

Mrs Bates and Jane had risen from their seats at the entrance of the couple and remained standing, in some amazement and, on Jane's part at least, some amusement, throughout their discourse. At the gentleman's words they curtseyed and, since the lady declined to notice them, Mrs Bates addressed her words and her smile to him. 'Pray do not disturb yourself sir.' She indicated their scarce-tasted meal. 'We have just but begun, you see.'

The gentleman took a step backwards but his wife walked further into the room and cast her eyes around it. 'The other room had better be a great deal better than this if I am to lodge in it,' she remarked. 'It is west-facing, which is never a pleasing aspect for a bed chamber. You had better hand your card, Charles. I suppose these people will want recompensing.'

Mrs Bates opened her mouth to protest but the lady waved her words away and her husband stepped with resignation further into the room.

'I am Charles Churchill, of Enscombe in Yorkshire,'
he said with another bow. 'I trust you ladies will do me
the great service of arranging matters with the
innkeeper. May I enquire who I have the honour of
addressing?'

'I am Mrs Bates, from Highbury,' Marie said, 'and this
is my daughter Jane.'

'I am delighted to make your acquaintance,' Mr
Churchill declared, adding, with an attempt at levity,
'even in such awkward circumstances. But your tea is
going cold. Eustacia, my dear, let us leave these ladies
to enjoy their repast.'

Far from retreating, Mrs Churchill crossed the room
and looked out of the window into the yard below. 'Is
that your coach?' she enquired, addressing the Bateses
for the first time.

'Not our own, no ma'am. Our good friend Mr
Knightley of Donwell Abbey has been so kind as to
put it at our disposal for our journey.'

'I have not heard of Donwell Abbey,' the lady said,
losing interest.

'I have not heard of Enscombe,' Jane murmured,

taking up her teaspoon and stirring her tea.

Mr Churchill smothered a smile before turning again to his wife. 'My *dear,*' he urged, 'we ought to withdraw and locate the bedchamber, to see if it is suitable. Louisa waits below. She will wonder what has become of us.'

'*She* wishes to continue to Brighton,' Mrs Churchill grumbled, adjusting her trimmings. 'She does not have my delicate constitution. *She* may be thrown around in a carriage until kingdom come and suffer no ill effects whatsoever. She has no care for what *I* might suffer. In that,' she concluded bitterly, 'she is like you.'

'Eustacia,' her husband cried, 'I am wounded that you should think me so unfeeling. Our coach is as comfortable as any. I dare say it is *more* comfortable than many, but we cannot legislate for the state of the roads and Brighton is a great distance from Yorkshire—*that* cannot be altered or got around by any means. If one wants to go to Brighton, one must travel there.' He looked at Mrs Bates as though for confirmation but also, she sensed, for some assistance.

'When I have finished my tea, I intend a brisk walk along the lane and back,' Mrs Bates said. 'I noticed a pretty meadow a mile or so back, with an enticing view of the hills beyond. The vista, the fresh air and some vigorous exercise will restore me, I believe. We have been travelling since before six and it will be many more hours before we reach our destination.'

'You go to Brighton?' Mrs Churchill enquired, addressing herself more to the back of a chair than to Mrs Bates and then, without waiting for a reply, 'Where will you lodge? An inn?' This last enquiry was accompanied by a curled lip and a scornful shudder.

'I am invited to stay with a Mr Fairfax and his wife,' Marie replied airily. 'I believe they reside in East Street.'

Mrs Churchill's demeanour altered so immediately and so dramatically it was as though she had been replaced by another person altogether. She smiled, she positively glowed with condescension and approbation. Her tone, which had been shrewish in the extreme, became quite honeyed. 'Mr Fairfax!' she exclaimed, turning her beaming countenance to Mrs Bates, 'you astound me. What a coincidence! I am intimately acquainted with Lady Cecily. How extraordinary! Lady Cecily has never mentioned any connection by the name of Bates.'

'Has she not?' Jane replied, disgusted both by Mrs Churchill's sudden alteration of manner and her sycophancy. 'That is most surprising. Mama, I see that the fresh horses are being brought out. If you wish to walk, we should not delay.'

'But you have not finished your meal,' Mr Churchill cried, genuinely dismayed. 'Eustacia my dear, take my arm. We must not detain these ladies a moment longer.'

But Mrs Churchill, having scented the whiff of an honourable connection, was not about to leave without instituting it as an irrefutable fact. 'But Charles—there is established acquaintance here—or as close to it as makes no odds.' She turned to Mrs Bates. 'You must forgive me, I fear I behaved rather coldly at first but one can never be sure, can one, when one meets people in these circumstances? The last thing one wishes is to establish unsuitable acquaintance. Charles did it at St Albans—spent the whole evening conversing with a gentleman who claimed—he didn't absolutely *claim*—I suppose I ought to give him that much—but he certainly *implied* he was a Whittle closely allied to Lord Whittle of Whittle-in-the-Forest and it turned out he was no more than a wool merchant—a nobody! And when I heard your name at first I did not recollect … but surely it must be so. You must be related to the Hazelwoods Bateses. I know the Contessa extremely well. How is she? My dear Mrs Bates! But why did you not say so? I must have misheard you. I thought you said Highbury. Of course, you said Highgate—a very desirable locale. You must call on us when you are settled in Brighton. We have taken a house on North Street—nothing better could be got at such short notice but I am assured it is at the east end of North Street, hard upon the Steyne. I suppose your husband remains in town. He is a prosperous lawyer, I recollect.'

Mrs Bates regarded the other woman squarely. 'I am a widow, ma'am. My husband was Frederick Bates, youngest brother to the present squire of Hazelwoods. I *did* say Highbury—it is a village in Surrey. Frederick was the minister there until his death. I would not claim relation where there is none; I regret to say that I have had no intercourse with the family at Hazelwoods for many years. Now I must ask you to excuse us.'

'Upon my word,' Mrs Churchill said, going at first very red, and then very white, 'a parson's widow, are you?'

'A *poor* parson's widow,' Jane amended, but speaking to no-one in particular, 'but we thank God every day that no extreme of poverty or lowliness of situation can sever our blood-tie with the Bateses of Hazelwoods.'

'Indeed,' Mrs Churchill sniffed. The sickly hue of obsequiousness had utterly disappeared from her manner. She was, once more, the proud, self-important person who had entered the room. 'Charles,' she said, languidly, 'you will escort me hence.'

Jane moved across the room and curtseyed to Mr Churchill before taking hold of the door handle. 'Good day to you sir. I wish you a pleasant stay in Brighton, if you ever get there.'

Mr Churchill smiled and this time made no attempt to disguise it. 'Good day Miss Jane Bates. You are a spirited young lady, I will give you that. My sister Louisa will like you. I hope to introduce you. Now Eustacia, come.' He ushered his wife from the room and Jane closed the door.

'What a hateful woman,' Jane said. 'I pity her poor husband. *He* seemed extremely pleasant. You will not call on them will you Mama?'

'By no means. I do not intend to go out into society while we are in Brighton. The sole reason for my visit to is ensure that you are settled. I shall enjoy the sea air and the change of scene, and of course if I can be of any use to Mr Fairfax's wife I shall be delighted, but I shall do no more and, once I am content that you are happy, I shall go home.'

'I anticipate Mrs Sealy's habits to be very retired,' Jane remarked. 'I do not expect to be much in society and, if Mrs Churchill is an example of the type of person who sojourns at Brighton, I shall not be sorry to avoid acquaintance with them. I thought her extremely ill-bred and insolent.'

'I agree with you my dear but it will not do to broadcast our opinion. If asked, we will say that we encountered Mrs Churchill very briefly and found her to be extremely elegantly dressed. It is at one and the same time the most and the least we can say of her. Now let us finish our meal and see if there is time to walk a little way.'

But they had no sooner set to once more when a timid knock upon the door disturbed them once again. The serving girl brought fresh, hot tea with the compliments of Mr Churchill and communicated the information that their coachman had been told to delay their departure a further hour to enable the ladies to complete their disturbed rest and refreshment and take some exercise. She delivered also a hastily written note from Miss Louisa Churchill, who begged the honour of accompanying them on their walk. 'Please knock on the downstairs parlour door when you are ready to set out,' the note concluded, 'and I will be with you immediately. I *alone* will join you. My sister-in-law _declines_' this in heavy script and doubly underlined, 'the opportunity of exercise.'

Accordingly, when they had drunk their tea and made what they could of the dishes, Marie and Jane descended the stairs and knocked on the parlour door. A beautiful young lady joined them directly in the passageway. A ready smile, appley cheeks and a cascade of glossy ringlets were all their immediate impression as they shook hands and left the inn together.

Miss Louisa Churchill was a vivacious and confident young woman, as blessed in physical beauty and perfect openness of manner as she was fortunate in birth and wealth. The Churchills of Enscombe were but distantly related to the house of Marlborough but the connection was incontestable and relations with the more illustrious branch of the family were most rigorously kept up. They were wealthy and well-endowed with land, quite entitled to be considered—and to consider themselves—the very first in the premier circle of Yorkshire society and not so very far from the axis in any other sphere worthy of note. Louisa had been the darling of her parents until their demise quite early in her life, and thereafter the apple of her elder brother's eye. To him had devolved the responsibility and privileges of Enscombe and the Churchill family fortune as well as—more weighty—the duty of his sister's regulation and education. He had diligently attempted both, but her happiness had been his chief concern and it may be said that his desire to ensure *that* had often taken precedence over the rest. Louisa had become used to getting what she wanted, whether it was beneficial or not. She learned how to cajole her brother into acquiescence, finding a pouted lip, a lustrous tear or—in extreme cases—a tantrum could generally bring him round to her way of thinking. Mr Churchill was a young man to shoulder the heavy burden of a vast estate, let alone the care of a small child. His distraction, added to his easy-going character—so compliant and willing to please—meant that their battles were not often of great duration and Louisa usually triumphed long before the lines were drawn. As a consequence, she had been extraordinarily happy in her nineteen years but not excessively well-educated and scarcely ever disciplined to any degree. Whether it had already broken in upon her understanding that where her brother gave way on every point the world at large could not always be expected to do so, was yet to be known. Possibly she had inferred that this might be the case but had determined to oppose such unchivalrous and inconvenient inclinations to the last iota of her power. What *was* certain was that she had taken it into her head to visit Brighton. She had proposed the idea with her usual enthusiasm and forcefulness to her brother and sister-in-law, had smoothed away their objections, countered every doubt and waved away their scruples. She had painted such an attractive and vivid picture of a stay in Brighton—the great social, healthful and marital benefits which would unarguably accrue—that the family had embarked upon the nigh-on three-hundred-mile journey borne along almost solely by her energy and determination.

The exigencies of the journey had by no means dampened her enthusiasm for Brighton. She was as bright and full of anticipation as she had been at its outset; indeed, the closer they got to their destination, the fuller she was of eagerness and delight. But a very few words from her brother relating to the spirit and wit of the girl in the upper parlour had determined Louisa on securing Jane's acquaintance and she had dashed off her note in an instant. Now, she drew Jane's arm through hers as they left the inn yard and took the lane out of the village.

'I thank you most sincerely,' she began, when they were only just out of earshot of the inn, 'for offering me the opportunity of some respite from my sister-in-law. You cannot imagine what torture the last four days have been, cooped up in the carriage with her and listening to her carp and complain at every jolt and shudder. I offered to ride on the dogcart but my brother would not hear of it. I wonder, had I suggested that *she* did so, if he would have been more ready to agree! He is the most patient and easy tempered of men but even *he* has found her querulousness intolerable these past few days, I am sure. He is too loyal to *say* so, but …'

'Travelling in a confined space for long periods can be very testing,' Mrs Bates observed, diplomatically.

'Oh, I do not know, Mama,' Jane said, 'I could travel to the world's end with *you* and I am sure we would never exchange a cross word.'

'You sound like the perfect companion, Mrs Bates,' Miss Churchill said. 'How Eustacia could have got so cross with you I cannot imagine. Or rather, I *can* imagine for she is cross with everything and everyone.'

'She has delicate health, perhaps?' Marie suggested. 'Have they been long married, your brother and Mrs Churchill?'

'Ah, I see the import of your question,' Miss Churchill said, with more directness than Mrs Bates quite liked in a girl so young. 'They have been married two years this coming October. No 'delicacy' has yet been conceived. No,' she concluded, cheerfully, 'she is just naturally evil-tempered and constitutionally out of sorts.'

'They say sea bathing cures all manner of ills,' Jane replied.

'I believe, in Eustacia's case, only drowning would cure her completely!' Miss Churchill quipped, lightly. 'I don't suppose *that* has ever been heard of, has it?'

'Miss Churchill,' Marie said with knitted brows, 'I forgive your jest because you are young and I see your patience has been sorely tried. I am the mother of two daughters and I understand how a young lady's tongue may sometimes run away. You need have no fear that *we* will misrepresent you but not everyone would be so forbearing. Really, such a thing is no subject for humour.'

Miss Churchill sighed. 'You are right to chastise me, Mrs Bates. Of course, I wish no ill to befall Eustacia. In truth I feel rather sorry for her. It must be so tiresome to be always ill-humoured. It is my sincere wish that Brighton will enliven her spirits. I am sure I have no doubt that it will enliven mine.'

'Your spirits seem to me to be already most animated, Miss Churchill,' Jane remarked. 'What particular pleasures do you anticipate at Brighton?'

'Oh,' Miss Churchill effused, 'society, of course—balls especially. I love to dance. There is so little scope in Yorkshire. Fresh acquaintance,' squeezing Jane's hand, 'I have begun with *that* already! The air in Brighton is reputed to be so good, no rain to speak of, balmy warmth and sunshine for week upon week. My understanding is that one is out of doors from morning 'til night. What bliss! Yorkshire, you know, is notorious for rain. One is confined to the house for days together. So, the opportunity and the conditions for excursions, promenading and riding are manifold. And then … but no, it would be injudicious to say too much. You and I will explore Brighton together, Miss Bates. It will be such a delight to have you as my friend.'

'It would be delightful,' Jane said, 'but I must impress upon you that *I* am not likely to have such liberty as *you* will enjoy. I am to be the companion of an invalid lady. She will have the first call on my time and resources. I do not anticipate that she will attend the

Assembly. I expect she lives quietly, reads a great deal and perhaps entertains only a small circle of very old friends.'

'Oh, she will release you to me if I ask her,' Miss Churchill declared. 'My need of you will be far greater than hers. Why, any old woman will suffice to turn the pages of her book or adjust the curtains or tuck her blanket around her. You will be wasted on such tasks.'

'Nevertheless,' Marie cautioned, 'that is Jane's lot. You are very kind, Miss Churchill, but I fear that you and Jane will move in very different circles in Brighton. Now here we are at the meadow I glimpsed from the coach, and very splendid it is too, the hay almost ready for cutting—the farmer will have a fine store for the winter. Look at the hills in the distance! What a truly pastoral scene, is it not?'

Miss Churchill said no more and presently the ladies turned to retrace their steps.

'Do you remain here for the night, then, Miss Churchill?' Jane enquired as they neared the inn. 'Your sister-in-law seemed quite determined that she would travel no further today.'

'Oh no. We shall go on, I am quite resolved. And

when I convince Eustacia of the utter impossibility of remaining—the privations of the chambers, the plainness of the food, the questionable cleanliness of the linen—she will be sure to agree with me and we will not be many miles behind you on the road.'

The Donwell coach was in readiness and there was nothing more for the Bateses to do than to say their farewells. Jane and Miss Churchill parted quite like old friends and as they embraced Miss Churchill murmured, 'Regardless of what your mama says we will explore Brighton together. Once she is gone home, we shall be each other's chaperone and have quite the freedom of the place. I have set my heart upon it!'

At last, the Donwell coach entered Brighton and deposited Jane at the steps of a tall, narrow town house on North Street. The driver unloaded Jane's trunks while she and her mama made their farewells.

'If you have liberty, send me a note at the Fairfaxes before you retire,' Marie said, very conscious of the tears which would rise to her eyes and clog her throat. 'I will do myself the honour of calling on Mrs Sealy in the morning unless I hear from you otherwise—I do not know what time she may rise, what appointments she may have on account of her health—but I will presume her to be at home before noon. By then I hope you will know much more about your situation and duties.'

'Yes Mama,' Jane replied, almost as full of emotion as her mother now the moment for their separation had come. 'I will send a note, or perhaps I will be able to run along and deliver it myself. The streets seem very quiet—I do not suppose there will be any danger in my going out alone. This is not Highbury, I know, but

…'

'You should be guided by Mrs Sealy and your own sound good sense,' Marie cautioned. 'It is past the dinner hour but I suppose people are dressing for the evening. Later, the streets may be much more crowded.'

'Very well Mama. The housekeeper is waiting, I must go in. Goodbye for the present dear Mama.'

With a final heart-felt embrace Jane got out of the coach and mounted the steps to the door where a soberly dressed matron waited to admit her. Marie could make out nothing more of the house's interior than that it was brightly lit before the coach bore her onwards.

Jane stepped with more apprehension than she had expected to feel onto the chequerboard floor of the constricted but elegantly decorated hall, her ears full of the sound of the Donwell coach as it drove away. A sombre lady of middle age introduced herself at Mrs Mallard, housekeeper to Mrs Sealy, and bade Jane mount the stairs.

'The mistress awaits you in the drawing room,' she said. 'Ironside will attend to your things. Is this all of them?' She lifted a doubtful eyebrow at Jane's few trunks.

'Oh yes,' said Jane, 'quite all.'

A burly footman materialised from a doorway further down the hall and busied himself with the luggage while Jane ascended the stairs. A turn at the top brought her to a carpeted landing and two doors. She paused to tidy her hair and smooth her dress before summoning her courage and knocking on one of the doors.

'Come in, come in,' called a cheerful voice from within, and Jane stepped into the room.

The lady within was so much younger than Jane had expected—the same age or perhaps a little younger than Mrs Bates—that for a moment Jane doubted that this could be her new patroness. She was very beautiful; a complexion remarkable for its fineness and glowing with health, her eyes dark and very bright under arched brows, her mouth generous. Her hair was chestnut, lustrous and elegantly dressed, glinting with jewels which shone also from her richly ornamented gown. She lay on a long chaise.

'My dear Miss Bates,' the lady said, holding out a hand,

'Jane. May I call you Jane?'

'I am looking for Mrs Sealy,' Jane stammered, too full of astonishment to speak more decidedly. The lady before her was so very far from the elderly, crooked widow she had been conjuring in her imagination.

Mrs Sealy—for, in truth, it was she—laughed; a delightful, musical sound. 'Yes indeed, and you have found her. It is I. What had you been imagining? A crone?'

Jane smiled through her blushes, 'A much older lady,' she admitted.

Mrs Sealy pulled a face and contorted her upper body into a stiff, awkward pose, 'Like this?' she croaked, 'wizened and bent all out of shape? Bad tempered as well, I'll be bound?'

'Oh no, not *that*,' Jane replied. 'Mr Fairfax reported you to be very amiable.'

Mrs Sealy resumed her normal, graceful posture and gestured Jane further into the room, leaning across to pat the seat of a chair close beside her. 'Mr Fairfax is all kindness,' she said. 'I have had tea ready for you this past hour. Mrs Mallard is very angry with me—

she has brought four or five kettles of fresh boiling water up but I would have it ready immediately on your arrival. You must be exhausted my dear. Please do the honours. It is difficult for me to reach unless Mrs Mallard puts the table right next to me, which she refuses to do, the minx.'

'Minx' was not an adjective Jane would ever have appended to the dour woman who had greeted her at the door, but she sensibly abjured herself to judge no one until she could make herself more thoroughly acquainted with their character. As she made this resolution, she poured herself some tea and a cup for Mrs Sealy also, who took it and drank without any sign of incapacity. Her arms and upper torso seemed unaffected by whatever debilitation afflicted her lower limbs, which lay perfectly lifeless amongst the folds of her dress.

As she drank her tea Jane was at liberty to examine the room. The chamber was a large one; both doors on the landing apparently giving access to it. Its front wall spanned the width of the house, with two tall windows looking down onto the street and at the houses opposite. Its back wall had been knocked away to allow passage through to what must at one time have been a separate room. A French door there suggested a terrace, or steps down to a garden. Though the day had been warm, a bright fire burned in the grate, around which a number of elegant chairs, a sofa and Mrs Sealy's chaise-longue were arranged. The walls were hung with large oil paintings, one of Mrs Sealy herself in company with an older but very handsome man in the uniform of the Navy, much decorated and draped with gold brocade. Altogether the air of the room was one of extreme comfort and style.

As Jane looked around her Mrs Sealy continued to talk, either from a natural excess of spirits or with a view to giving Jane some moments to compose and assimilate herself. 'My dear I am so happy to have you here with me. Since Captain Bates suggested the idea, I have thought of little else—a delightful young person to bear me company—so much more amusing than poor old Matilda Tartt, who has been my companion this past year. Such a sour, humourless woman— eminently respectable of course, the perfect chaperone and her French unexceptionable. She would insist upon speaking it, too, even though everyone in

Switzerland spoke English! Ah! Poor Matilda. I should not abuse her. I took her into my employ just after my husband passed away. Of course, I was all at sixes and sevens then, quite unequal to making important decisions.'

'My sincere condolences, ma'am,' Jane murmured.

Mrs Sealy sighed. 'Thank you. The poor Admiral— how I miss him! We were married such a short time. He was much older than I, of course. People thought the difference in our ages quite scandalous! But he was determined and a woman who can't walk—be she ever so witty and pretty—cannot expect lovers to be flocking to her door. And, naturally, there is no question of children; *that* would be an insuperable obstacle to most *young* men. But the Admiral did not care. He had a child already, you see—his late wife had provided him with that, if with little else. He was kind and generous, quite deaf to the idea that my incapacity was any impediment whatsoever. Ah!' with another sigh, 'I had not expected to love him as much as I did, or to miss him so much when he died.'

'My papa died just a year ago,' Jane said. 'Mama felt his loss very keenly at first but I think having us girls with her was a reason to remain optimistic and now she feels able to face the future with every prospect of happiness.'

'I am extremely glad for her,' Mrs Sealy said. 'I must say that I feel more sanguine now than I have done for some time. My accident, you know,' she cast a glance at her incapacitated limbs, 'was a severe blow at the time. I was a very young girl when it occurred—a carriage accident—I was thrown out of a curricle and crushed and have never walked since.'

'How terrible,' Jane exclaimed. 'You must have suffered a great deal.'

'In spirits, yes, but not physical pain. One has no feeling at all below the waist. The spine is damaged to such a degree, you see. But one has grown accustomed to it now. No, I have had causes for unhappiness since Bertram died but this,' she indicated her fixed situation on the chaise, 'is not one of them. And now,' with a bright, resolute smile, '*you* are come and I am determined to be cheerful. The season here at Brighton is well underway. I shall pay your subscriptions to the Assemblies and the coffee houses and the circulating libraries and we will go out and about, see and be seen and enjoy ourselves a great deal.'

Jane put down her teacup. 'This is not at all what I had expected, Mrs Sealy. I fear that I … I have been so little in the world and I … I may not have suitable attire.'

'Dear Jane, do not distress yourself on any account,' Mrs Sealy cried. 'Dresses can be made up! They *shall* be made up. There is an excellent dressmaker here in Brighton and a very good milliner too. I shall be delighted to give you any little hints pertaining to etiquette, not that I imagine for one second that you shall require any.' Mrs Sealy leaned forward and pressed Jane's hand very warmly. 'You have had a very long day and are no doubt fatigued. I have arranged for the fire to be lit in your room and a light supper served there for you. While we have been conversing Mrs Mallard has been drawing you a bath—or, rather, Lottie and Ironside have been doing so, since Mrs Mallard rarely sullies her hands with any menial task. In the meantime, if you will allow me, I shall write a note to your mama assuring her that you are comfortable and begging her to do me the honour of calling on us tomorrow morning. She stays with the Fairfaxes does she not? Ironside will deliver the note immediately.'

'She will be glad to know I am so comfortably settled, ma'am,' Jane replied, feeling, suddenly, quite overwhelmed with tiredness. 'She asked me to send her a note but if you will be so very good …'

Mrs Sealy was already ringing the bell. 'Ironside,' she said when the burly footman entered the room, 'please to bring my writing desk. I would have you deliver a note to Mrs Bates at Mr Fairfax's residence in East Street. You know it?'

Ironside nodded assent as he lifted a sloped lap-desk from a side table and brought it to his mistress.

'While I write a few lines, please inform Mrs Mallard that Miss Bates is to be shown to her room,' Mrs Sealy said as she deftly prepared paper and ink. 'In the morning we will discuss things in more detail, Jane, but for now I think you had better retire—poor thing! Your eyelids are drooping and you can scarce stay awake!'

Chapter 5

East Street

Brighton

Dear Mr Knightley

It is very late. The house has but just settled for the night and I was only half an hour ago shown to my room. I am extremely fatigued but will not miss the opportunity of the coachman's return to Donwell tomorrow to send you a letter.

Firstly, I must thank you once again for your kindness in providing the coach. Your coachman Mr Burkett has been all consideration and helpfulness. I do hope he gets back to Donwell without mishap.

He brought us safely to Brighton and we arrived in the early evening. Jane was left at Mrs Sealy's door. I have heard from Mrs Sealy, a most elegant and reassuring note, to say that Jane is well and happily settled and that I shall see them both in the morning. What a comfort and a relief to know that my youngest is in safe hands!

I am sorry to have to recount that I arrived in East Street to a scene of some disorder and alarm. Indeed, to tell the truth, the household was in uproar; Lady Cecily ill, Mr Fairfax from home and no preparations made for my arrival. The housekeeper, Mrs Brigham, in a manner most agitated, declared herself quite ignorant of any expected houseguest. You can imagine my consternation! This unwelcome and disturbing information was imparted with a brusqueness amounting to rudeness. She complained that the house was ill-managed! I forbore to suggest that if the house was poorly supervised, she need look no further than her own failings to know why. A housekeeper who cannot make good any little deficiencies or inexperience of her mistress—or master—is no housekeeper at all, but I do not recommend you broach this topic with your Mrs Lemming; she will not be happy to know you have fathomed her secret!

I learned from a tearful parlourmaid that the house was in a state of trepidation attendant on an alarming deterioration in Lady Cecily's health. The master was expected back this hour gone. One footman had been sent out to find him, the other to fetch a doctor; neither had returned. From above I could hear the most pitiful cries. My heart broke for poor Lady Cecily, who is with child. The sounds of distress from above were met by noise of riot and argument from below stairs, and in order to secure supper for the coachman I descended to see what had occurred to occasion such commotion.

The kitchen was in as much disarray as it was possible to conceive, the congealed remnants of dinner still abundantly present on the table, plates and dishes stacked anyhow, dirty pans strewn over the cooking range. The cook lolled before the fire with her feet on a stool and from that easy position harangued the kitchen maid and a starved looking pot-boy. Her opinion was far from flattering. She saw no very rosy future for either, predicting the girl would finish as a drab on the street and the boy find a quick termination to his life at the end of a rope. Naturally I intervened. Both the unfortunate recipients of her displeasure were in tears, the boy howling quite as loudly as the girl. The cook's liturgy was fuelled by a decanter of wine at her elbow from which she frequently paused to partake with a liberality that—I quickly recognised—would render her quite useless for the rest of the day. Therefore, I dismissed her to her quarters. The woman voiced no argument, making unsteadily for the door at the rear of the kitchen, ricocheting off the dresser and tangling with a chair leg as she went. I supervised the boiling of water and the washing of the dinner dishes myself, making for myself two steadfast friends in the little kitchen servants as I did so. They have been abominably treated and I shall tell Mr

Fairfax so. You can be sure I also ensured the coachman got his supper.

In the morning I will speak to Mr Fairfax about his entire household. I am afraid the cook's inebriation, purloining of household supplies, the parlous state of the kitchen and the filthy condition of the two kitchen servants add up to no very small indictment. However, I was afterwards to learn that the establishment's poor governance is by no means confined to the kitchen.

Presently I went upstairs, presuming to take with me a cup of ginger tea and some arrowroot which I know to be efficacious in cases such as Lady Cecily's. I found that poor girl in a swoon on a chaise in her bedroom, her chamber strewn with clothes and soiled linen, the bed stripped but not remade. There was no fire, the shutters remained open. All was muddle and confusion where there ought to have been order and calm but at least her cries of distress had subsided. Lady Cecily herself was extremely pale, her skin clammy, beads of moisture clung to her forehead. Of her lady's maid there was no sign at all and by that time Mrs Brigham was also conspicuous by her absence. Thankfully the parlour maid I had spoken to before was able to assist me and between us we got Lady Cecily into some clean nightclothes, made the bed and helped her into it where I managed to encourage her to drink the tea I had made.

The poor lady was really very ill, feverish, mistaking me for her mama and unknowing where she was. I was quite afraid for her. Afterwards I learned that although eating scarcely a crumb all day she had still been to the medicinal baths in the morning, a recital in the afternoon and had set out to the Assembly before being taken ill and brought home.

Mr Fairfax came home as I tended to his wife. I like him enormously, he is a large man, very energetic and decided, and obviously very attached indeed to his wife. He was distressed almost to tears by her condition. Only the support and calm reassurance of his brother kept him tranquil. Mr Angus Fairfax is nothing like his brother, slender and reticent where he is burly and forthcoming. He has red hair and that milk-pale complexion that so often accompanies the ginger cast. He wears eyeglasses which make his eyes—pale blue and very intense— even more penetrating. He is apprenticed to a physician and in that role, in addition to his being a concerned brother, took careful note of all I had to tell him about Lady Cecily's condition. He listened with equal attention to the maid's account. I liked that about him very much.

I retired from the room while Mr Angus made examination of Lady Cecily. I had no place there now that those more qualified *and far more entitled had gathered. On my way downstairs I encountered Mrs Brigham with a portly, bewigged gentleman I assume to be the doctor. His breathing was much laboured, his visage empurpled as he struggled with the easy ascent of the long, shallow staircase. If his management of his own health is anything to go by, Lady Cecily would do well to place herself in her brother-in-law's hands, but of course I forbore to voice this notion. He paused at the turn in the stair to mop his brow and neck with a large handkerchief, none too clean, and I took the opportunity of informing Mrs Brigham of all I had done in her absence.*

As I got to the bottom of the stairs, I encountered a thin, dishevelled young woman whose hastily tied shawl revealed the uniform of a lady's maid. Taking her to be the one who had so signally deserted her post, I wanted very badly to take her to task but restrained myself, feeling that I had already meddled more than was polite in Mr Fairfax's household.

Dear Mr Knightley, I would not have you think for one moment that the Fairfaxes are neglectful of me as a guest. They are very young, barely home from their honeymoon tour and not yet settled into routines of household management. The servants here were hired by the landlord's agent; it is to him we must make application for their dismissal. I am engaged to go tomorrow with Mr Fairfax to make representation to that effect. Lady Cecily will be confined to her chamber for the next several days. Naturally I will do all I can to smooth things for her.

At long last the parlour maid—who is called Lucy but known in the house as Janet due to an initial error by Mrs Brigham which has never been corrected—showed me to a very pleasant chamber on the second floor, with a view over the promenade ground called the Steyne. If I stand on tiptoe and lean over the sil,l I can even see the sea! I have had tea and some supper and will ensure this letter gets into the pocket of your coachman before he departs in the morning.

I take the liberty of enclosing one also—shorter, I would not alarm her—to my Hetty. May I ask your indulgence to watch for her return from the archdeaconry and see it safe into her hands?

In the meantime, I close with the affectionate presumption that I may call myself

Your very dear Marie.

Chapter 6

'Mrs Bates, I cannot thank my father's friend Knightley sufficiently for sending you to us,' Mr Fairfax declared as he drained his bowl of tea. 'You have been a ministering angel to Cecily. She quite depends upon you now, you know, and as far as the household is concerned—you have worked wonders.'

Mrs Bates had been in Brighton some five or six days and in that short time had—with characteristic discretion and admirable circumspection— revolutionised the management of the Fairfax household. It had taken her no very long interval to ascertain that Lady Cecily was too indisposed as well as constitutionally un-adapted to the supervision of domestic affairs. This being so it had taken but a very small hint to Mrs Brigham that it was useless to wait for direction—any that came from the mistress would be confused, ambiguous and likely impracticable—but that, providing she felt herself sufficiently able, it would be a kindness to her mistress to take over absolute control of domiciliary concerns. Such a gauntlet having been thrown down, with so clever and unexceptionable a reason for accepting it, Mrs Brigham had risen to the task, substantially improving the atmosphere both above and below stairs. From that moment the two women had established a cautious entente. Mrs Bates was careful to do nothing that would impinge on Mrs Brigham's authority, nor to step beyond the bounds of propriety for a guest. At the same time, she firmly established beyond any possibility of doubt that the parlour maid's name was Lucy—was not Janet, had never been Janet and that she could not henceforth even out of habit, convenience or a lazy forgetfulness be known by that name.

At Mrs Bates' recommendation—vigorously endorsed by Mr Fairfax—the cook and Lady Cecily's neglectful maid had been summarily dismissed by the house agent who had engaged them. The proposition had been mooted—nobody knew quite by whom—that the vacancies thereby created should be filled by staff from Woodley Court, the Fairfax's country seat; it would augment their comfort to a significant degree. Their butler, for instance, would better manage the intractable menservants and it would be reassuring for

Lady Cecily to regain the services of her own familiar, eminently capable maid. To this idea—wherever it originated—Mr Fairfax had readily acquiesced, avid as he was to do anything that would materially add to his wife's wellbeing. He had summoned them post-haste and included in his directive, for good measure, the cook, whose ministrations would substantially add to his own.

The arrival of these functionaries at the house in East Street had brought perfect regulation and much relief to the lady and gentleman in occupation. Under the martial authority of the butler, the footmen had been dressed down and spruced up and had become as attentive and alacritous as Mr Fairfax could desire. Lady Cecily's linen had been laundered and mended, her pillows thoroughly plumped, her bath was just the temperature it ought to be. Meals arrived on time in the dining room, of a type and in quantities calculated to tempt the lady's delicate palate and to satisfy the gentleman's more voracious one.

Under Marie's personal supervision the two little kitchen servants had received a thorough bathing, a set of clean clothes and a succession of nourishing meals which improved their welfare as well as their appearance to some significant degree.

'I have been delighted to make the occasional small suggestion,' Mrs Bates replied, pouring her host more tea. 'As for Lady Cecily, it is an honour to me to know her, and a pleasure to assist her in any way I can. She is between the ages of my two daughters, you know. I look on her in quite the same way. Her own mother is abroad, I believe?'

'Yes indeed, and Cecily feels her absence most strongly. I have been invited to go sailing by more fellows than I can count but Cecily will not hear of it; she fears I will abscond! It is nonsense, of course, but for her sake I have declined.'

'You are quite wise to indulge her in this, I think, for the time being at least. I shall go up and see her after breakfast. I am hopeful that she might have managed to eat a little today. Her appetite returns, I believe, since we have persuaded her to take the air in the garden for a period each day.'

'By God! There's a garden? I had no idea.'

'You have been too busy enjoying the wider delights of the town. Yes, a very pretty walled garden—quite sheltered. We have found a shady spot beneath a sycamore tree. Lady Cecily and I spent almost a full hour there yesterday. I have known several ladies suffer her complaint. Ginger tea—or raspberry leaf, if it can be got—and arrowroot are my invariable recommendations, along with fresh air. The air of the sick room can become stagnant and being confined in one room depresses the spirits. But this condition is not of long duration, Mr Fairfax. Have no fear. By next month you will see a marked improvement in her health.'

'I see a marked improvement already,' Mr Fairfax cried. 'Dr Quake is a quack—I have sent him packing. Dr Tinniswood will be sent for from London if the need arises; it seems he is the up-and-coming man. In the meantime, we have you. My brother Angus says you have a more complete understanding of medicinal herbs than he does. That is a quite a compliment, madam, from a man who has his nose in a botany book morning, noon and night.'

'Mr Angus is a very promising young physician,' Marie replied, quietly. 'His manner is so gentle. I am sure that when he sets up his own practice, he will have patients flocking to him.'

'Let me help you to some more of this excellent kedgeree, Mrs Bates,' said Mr Fairfax, reaching for the salver. 'No? Oh well, I will have another helping. Reggie Cumberland and I are to watch the cricket this afternoon and that always makes me hungry. Oh! On the subject of Angus, I am sure he will be besieged by patients he is too good natured to charge for their cures. He attended a fisherman yesterday who had got a hook through his hand. I don't suppose he received a penny for his treatments. I wish he would spend more time in society. If he wooed a wealthy wife he could heal everyone for nothing, so far as I am concerned. Does your daughter visit you today? She is a very fine girl, I must say.'

'You are very kind sir. Jane visits when she can; Mrs Sealy often rests before dinner. But Jane has no dowry; let me make that perfectly plain. Personally, I am not convinced that wealth is essential to a successful marriage. I married a poor curate. We had little, but we were happy.'

'I grant you equality of mind and a likeness of temper is just as important. I would have Angus marry for love, as I did. I would have him fall in love with an heiress; that is all! There are plenty of them here. Ah!' Mr Fairfax threw his cutlery down on his plate. 'That was very good. Speaking of heiresses, Cecily's friend Louisa Churchill will call today. She has been in town a day or so but I have put her off her visit. She is a lively girl and rather stubborn. I do not want her persuading Cecily she is ready to go out.'

'Oh,' said Mrs Bates, 'I am acquainted with Miss Churchill. That is, we met her very briefly on our way here. She is a charming young woman but, as you say, very determined. Have no fear. I have no intention of going out today. I will stay and bear Lady Cecily company and, if her friend seems intent on undoing all our good work, I will intervene. Does Mrs Churchill accompany Miss Churchill?'

Mr Fairfax shuddered, 'Not if I can prevent it. That woman would sour milk. My poor friend Charles Churchill—what *has* he done? Eustacia Fishwick was nobody, you know—of inferior rank and virtually no education. But she was ambitious and set her sights on Charles. Before he knew it he was an engaged man, and too honourable to give back word.'

'I fear I was so unfortunate as to provoke Mrs Churchill's displeasure when we met at the inn,' Marie admitted. 'She will not wish to meet me again. If she calls, I had better not be present.'

'By no means! I pray you will not abandon Cecily to her spleen.'

Mrs Bates laughed. 'Very well, I will risk Mrs Churchill's anger and remain at my post.'

'You are all goodness,' said Mr Fairfax, standing up. 'I beg you will excuse me. I have business at the coffee house in half an hour and then a delegation is to meet with the quartermaster from the barracks. It seems more militia are due and there is talk of enlarging the encampment on the Steyne. It is not to be borne; there will be no room to play cricket!'

Lady Cecily was rather later getting up that day and it happened that Louisa Churchill arrived as she and Mrs Bates were making their way to the garden.

'Oh, I will join you,' Miss Churchill declared after the ladies had greeted one another. 'I am determined to be out of doors as much as possible. The air in Yorkshire is fresh but so damp. Here there is no trace of moisture even though September is half gone. I believe, in Brighton, the summer goes on quite until Christmas.'

'I do not think that is likely,' Lady Cecily demurred. 'Look how the leaves are already turning. There is quite a golden carpet around our little seat, is there not, Mrs Bates?'

'But the sun shines through the canopy and there is no hint of breeze,' Mrs Bates said. 'It is quite warm. I have no fear of you catching a chill, my dear.' She placed a cushion on the seat and draped a quilt across its back. 'Let Lady Cecily take this place, if you please,' she said, as Miss Churchill made a move towards the seat she had prepared, 'she needs the extra care, you know. You and I will be quite comfortable at either side.'

Miss Churchill manufactured an expression of astonishment. 'You intend to join Cecily and me, then? Cecily, I had quite anticipated a confidential little chat.'

'Mrs Bates has been all kindness,' Lady Cecily said dreamily, her eyes closed and her face tilted to the sun. 'I do not know how I should have managed without her. I like having her close by.'

'I do declare, Mrs Bates,' Miss Churchill said with a shake of her ringlets, 'you have established yourself very intimately here. I doubt Cecily's mother has more licence. You are quite a surrogate.'

'I am a mother, even if not Lady Cecily's,' Mrs Bates remarked, 'but do not fear I shall interrupt. I have a book here, you see, and will be quite engrossed in it while you converse.'

'Of course, I met your daughter Jane at the inn,' Miss Churchill said, just that moment recalling Jane although, at the time of their meeting, she had determined that the two should be intimate and life-long friends. 'I liked her enormously. I have yet to encounter her in Brighton, though.' She turned to Lady Cecily. 'I have been *so* delightfully occupied, Cecily. We spent the first day going round to pay our subscriptions. I have joined *everything,* even the archery club although I do not practice the sport—have never so much as picked up a bow! Isn't that amusing? I wished to attend the Assembly on our first evening but Eustacia wouldn't allow it. She said it showed unseemly eagerness. She retired early and I tried to persuade Charles to take me after she had gone to bed, but he refused. I think I am losing my hold on my brother. Since his marriage it has slipped little by little away. Did you find the same with your brother?'

'I never had any hold on Francis,' Lady Cecily murmured. 'He always does exactly what he wants with no regard to my wishes. He is not married yet but I do not anticipate a wife will make any difference to him.'

'I would tame him,' Miss Churchill said stoutly, 'if I had a mind. Thankfully though, my thoughts run in a different direction.'

'Louisa! Do you have a beau?' Lady Cecily asked, roused from her reverie.

'Well …' Miss Churchill said, coyly. She cast a glance across the seat but Mrs Bates' eyes remained fixed on the page before her. 'There was a gentleman visiting Yorkshire … But there is no engagement. Nothing has been fixed.'

'I suspicion nothing *will* be fixed if you show your interest by running five hundred miles away to Brighton,' Lady Cecily said.

Miss Churchill smiled. 'Perhaps he intends to visit

Brighton …'

' …and you have come to lie in wait! I see your strategy. The poor man is all but caught and skinned and trussed, then. Does Charles approve?'

'Charles has no inkling. Eustacia knows. She does *not* approve but that shall make no difference to me. I do not need her permission and I flatter myself that although Charles grows less malleable, in *this* I shall have my way.'

'I have no doubt of it either, then. Shall I send for tea?'

'Not on my account. I have been at the coffee house these past two hours and am quite surfeited with liquid refreshment. I expect Eustacia any moment. She has been calling on the Pelhams and the Macartneys, establishing what she calls 'connexion.' And *she* chides *me* for unseemly eagerness! She said she would call in here for me afterwards.'

'She will not find the Pelhams or the Macartneys at home,' Lady Cecily sighed. 'No one ever is at home here. Everyone is out from morning till night. It is exhausting.'

'*You* are at home, Cecily. I wish you could come out with me this very moment. Mr Abergavenny has invited me aboard his sailing yacht. I am sure he would be delighted to include you in the party.'

Lady Cecily gave a shiver and turned a sickly hue.

'I think it is time we went inside,' Mrs Bates said firmly, closing her book. 'Miss Churchill, you may wish to wait for Mrs Churchill in the drawing room. Lady Cecily must have her rest.'

Mrs Bates took Lady Cecily's arm and began to escort her towards the house, but they were met by Mrs Brigham to announce the arrival of Mrs Churchill. 'She is in the drawing room, ma'am,' said Mrs Brigham stiffly. 'She declined to be escorted to the garden, refused refreshment and says her carriage is waiting.'

'Oh, I shall have to see her,' Lady Cecily groaned, 'just for a few moments. We had better go back inside.'

They found Mrs Churchill in the drawing room, surreptitiously examining some silver candlesticks. 'Lady Cecily,' she said, with a thin, artificial smile, 'I am so very distressed to hear that you are unwell. I do so hope it is nothing serious. Oh,' seeing Mrs Bates for the first time, 'you are the person who was so very anxious to recommend yourself to us at the inn. I had not expected to encounter you here.'

'My recollection of our encounter there is rather different,' said Marie. 'It must have slipped your mind that I specifically mentioned that I had been so fortunate as to have been invited to stay here,' Mrs Bates replied smoothly. 'I hope you are well, Mrs Churchill? Are you recovered from your journey?'

'But barely. Thus far I have found Brighton's claims to healthful benefits quite without foundation. Lady Cecily's indisposition inclines me to think Brighton a most unwholesome place.'

'Lady Cecily's indisposition is attendant on her happy expectation,' Miss Churchill said, with delighted venom.

Mrs Churchill paled and for a moment it was hard to tell if she or Lady Cecily was the greener. A tear glinted in her eye but she said in a voice which was hard and bitter, 'Indeed? My hearty congratulations, my dear. Louisa, we must take our leave. The horses have been waiting this quarter of an hour. Charles has gone to engage bathing women for us for the morrow and we must procure costumes from somewhere.'

When they had gone Mrs Bates said, 'Let me escort you to your chamber, Lady Cecily. I fear the company has tired you. Tell me, have Mr and Mrs Churchill been long married?'

'They married before we did, I do not recall the date,' Lady Cecily replied with a yawn.

'They have no children I believe?'

'No, they have not. Louisa let drop a hint that it is a source of chagrin between them.'

'Yes,' said Mrs Bates, 'I gathered as much.'

Chapter 7

From the first morning of her waking in her little apartment on the second floor of the house on North Street, and drawing back the curtains to see the shining vista of the sea, Jane had seemed to fairly fly over Brighton on winged feet. The town, her situation with Mrs Sealy and Mrs Sealy herself were all Jane had hoped and more. The days passed in a succession of enchanting experiences, each one bringing something fresh or remarkable.

She was no sooner up than she was out, at liberty for the morning while Mrs Sealy bathed at the medicinal spa. She explored the streets—more or less deserted at that hour, a wonderland of colour and novelty. She walked around the Steyne, admiring the Dragoons as they paraded there. The beach was her particular delight; the sight of the fishermen as they drew up their boats and landed their catch was a daily source of interest. She walked along the cliff path to marvel at the bathing machines which stood at the furthermost eastern end of the beach. The ladies making their precarious, shrieking way down the narrow cliff steps to bathe made her laugh. The men were bullish, launching themselves into the waves, splashing and choking themselves with spume. She liked to untie the strings of her bonnet and let the sea breeze tangle her hair, to feel it catch at the hem of her gown and tug on her shawl. She stared across the waves with such intensity that her eyes watered, trying to make out the coast of France.

Then she would return to North Street, ravenously hungry for breakfast and full of the kind of news which Mrs Sealy liked to hear; which pieces were to be performed at the afternoon concert, what play was to be shown at the theatre; new hats in the milliner's window; new tenants at a lodging house.

'The Churchills *are* in town,' she announced one morning when she had been about a fortnight in Brighton. 'I wonder that I have not seen Miss Churchill at the Assembly or on the Steyne, but then there are so many opportunities for amusement here. I suppose it is *more* surprising that two people *should* happen across one another than that they should not. Indeed, she may well have been at the Assembly without my seeing her—such a crowd as they attract. I estimated over four hundred the night before last. I saw Miss Churchill and her sister-in-law at the bathing machines. How they squealed! Mrs Churchill had to be carried bodily into the waves—it took two bathing women to subdue her.'

'I am not acquainted with the Churchills. Their seat is in Yorkshire, I believe. The Duke of Marlborough I *have* met, though but once. The Churchills are a distant relation?'

'Mrs Churchill would have you believe the distance is not so very great,' Jane said with a smile. 'If I may venture to offer an opinion, I do not recommend you pursue the connexion. She was cold and very haughty to my mama when she discovered we were related to the very lowliest branch of the Bates family.'

'I know her sort, then, and am duly warned,' Mrs Sealy replied, 'I cannot abide sycophants. Ah! Here is the morning post. Thank you Ironside.'

'Good morning Mr Ironside,' said Jane brightly, 'a very fine morning is it not? I think I saw you on your way to the post office this morning. If it would be in the least degree helpful to you, I could undertake that task. I pass the post office every morning on my walk so it would be no trouble.'

Ironside bowed but made no reply. He rearranged the breakfast dishes and then left the room.

'Oh dear,' sighed Jane. 'I do not think Mr Ironside likes me. It is awkward, since we are out together so often. I would like to establish some kind of accord.'

Ironside made up, with his strength and bulk, what Mrs Sealy lacked. He was her constant attendant when away from home and carried her from room to room when she was within doors. He presented a stalwart, silent, unblinking figure, hovering discreetly beyond the periphery of the polite company but always within sight of Mrs Sealy lest she indicate to him that she required his aid. He pressed himself into shop corners while the ladies perused the goods on display from seats which were instantly produced by the assiduous proprietor. He stood in readiness hour after hour by the carriage, lifting Mrs Sealy with no apparent effort in and out of it, carrying her to a seat at the concert, coffee house or ball and then melting back into the shadows leaving Jane to arrange Mrs Sealy's skirts and limbs on a folding footstool which was brought everywhere with them. Should rain threaten he would appear with an umbrella and hold it over her while the rain drenched his hair and clothes. If it turned chilly, he would produce a shawl, if sunny, a parasol. At night he carried her up the stairs of her house and into her chamber where a maid provided for her personal care. He spoke rarely, smiled less. Jane's attempts at cordiality had been met with a stony, blank stare.

'Jane, dear, it is not for you to notice Ironside, any more than you would notice my legs or my back—*that*, essentially, is what Ironside is,' Mrs Sealy replied. 'He provides the strength and the mobility that I lack. Whatever attention is drawn to him places my disability in a glaring spotlight—just what I wish to avoid. And it is not Ironside's business to like you,' she went on. 'It is not for the servants to harbour partiality, only to serve you. Ironside *will* do that, though, for my sake, should you ever require it. He is very loyal. He has proved *that* to me in circumstances,' she gave a little shudder, 'that I prefer not to recall.'

'Yes, ma'am,' Jane said, much chastened. Then, to change the subject, 'I think we shall have a fine afternoon for our engagement at the tea garden. May I pass you the butter?'

'Thank you. Captain Bates is most anxious to make your acquaintance. He is a very old and trusted friend of mine. I have sent a message to your mama, asking her to join us. It is unnatural and painful for families to become estranged.'

Jane sighed. 'I do not know if the other Bates brothers have remained in regular communication but, if so, my papa was excluded. I may have cousins. It is very curious to think I have relatives who are strangers to me.'

'Relatives can be very strange in and of themselves,' Mrs Sealy said cryptically. 'Here is a letter for you. It is very thick. Who can be writing you such volumes?'

Jane took her letter and glanced at the handwriting. 'It is from my sister Hetty. No doubt she regales me with a moment-by-moment account of her time at the archdeaconry. She was bridesmaid to her friend Hermia Winwood. I will save it, and read it later, if I may. It must be time for us to dress.'

'Indeed, it is. I will send Hardy to you, my dear. Your hair looks as though you have had a flock of gulls caught up in it!'

It was Mrs Sealy's invariable routine to return from the

baths, breakfast and then retire to dress and have her hair made ready for the remainder of the day. Jane, eager to fit in with her employer's habits, had adopted the same custom. The brief separation from Mrs Sealy, like the period in the early morning and another, while that lady rested before dinner, provided time for privacy and respite. Otherwise, they were always in each other's company and while Jane found Mrs Sealy very agreeable and lively—by no means a troublesome task-master—some time for solitary contemplation was also most welcome.

On this day as on most others, their hair dressed and clothes smart, Ironside settled Mrs Sealy into the carriage, Jane took her place and they set off into the town. The speed of their travel and the variety of things there were to see and do left Jane breathless even after so many days. Jane had been introduced to the Master of Ceremonies, her name duly registered and her presence in Brighton officially recognised; no door was closed to her. They went in a whirl; from seamstress to milliner, from bookshop to gallery. Sometimes they patronised coffee houses or visited the circulating library. They might view exhibitions or hear concerts. She had seen plays and watched sports. Mrs Sealy moved not perhaps in the very premier sphere of Brighton society but only a tier or so below it, and into this rank, as her companion Jane was graciously absorbed. Of course, Jane was not a girl to presume. She might be treated as an equal but she knew she was not one. She did not speak unless spoken to. She made Mrs Sealy's comfort and enjoyment her first duty; passing tea, settling shawls, running errands. At the Assembly she stood behind Mrs Sealy's chair but she held no dance card and when invited to the set, gently declined although, beneath her skirts, her feet were restless.

On this particular afternoon they made their way to the Steyne, a grassy sward abutting the gardens of East Street on its western periphery and the sea on its southern. The Steyne formed the centre of Brighton activity; the libraries were situated there, sports and games played, carriages driven and horses ridden. It also did service as the parade ground for the Dragoons and numerous battalions of militia who were stationed in Brighton against invasion from France. The multitudes of Brighton society promenaded on the

Steyne, seeing and being seen; it was the liveliest, the most exciting and fashionable of Brighton's attractions. Games offered diversion. Acrobats and jugglers entertained, passing round their hats for pennies afterwards. Menageries with exotic birds, monkeys and performing animals vied for attention. Occasionally Mrs Sealy would submit to being wheeled in her bath chair, Ironside at the handles to propel her over the short turf while Jane walked alongside and drew Mrs Sealy's attention to the things which would amuse her. But Mrs Sealy disliked the spectacle she felt she presented in her bath chair and today chose to settle herself on the terrace at Mrs Widget's library where Brighton society could come to her, which it did abundantly, as though she were a bright, exotic flower and they the helpless bees.

'Good day to you, Mrs Hart. May I present my friend Miss Jane Bates? Miss Bates, this is Mrs Hart. How is dear Lucinda? I am happy to hear it. Do give her my kind regards. Jane, dear, would you be so good as to adjust my wrap? Thank you. I see we are to have a string quartet. How very delightful. Mr Strachan! What a pleasure it is to see you! I do not know if you are acquainted with my friend Miss Jane Bates. Miss Bates, this is Mr Strachan—a very old friend. You seem quite recovered from the gout sir—you found the sea bathing efficacious? I thank you, no. We will take no refreshment at present. We go this afternoon to the Rookery—there is a tea garden, you know, and in the evening, I believe there are fireworks. Jane has never seen them. We are to be the guests of Captain Bates. Yes indeed, Miss Bates' close relation. Good day to you sir. Who is that man over there? He seems to have very ill control of his horse. A very spirited creature indeed! If he is not careful, he will be galloped over the cliff. Ah! There is his groom. I wish men would not try horses which are too strong for them. Oh!' with sudden coldness, as though a dark cloud had obscured the sun, 'good day, Arthur. I was not aware you were in town.'

Mrs Sealy addressed an extremely tall, very broad-shouldered young man with a heavy brow beneath a beetling cliff of forehead and a thick mop of unruly hair. His frockcoat was finely cut, his stock tied very tight and high, a froth of lace fell from his cuff. Altogether he cut a handsome—even brilliant—figure but it was a brutal, rather frightening beauty. Jane did not think she had ever seen such a toweringly large man; his physical presence was quite oppressive—he threw their table into shadow—and the expression on his face by no means denoted a benign character. His face was hard, his eye proud and cold. Since Mrs Sealy did not offer her hand, he lifted it from her lap and bowed over it, placing a kiss on a particularly large and brilliant stone on her finger. 'I wished to surprise you, Mama. I hope you *are* pleasantly surprised.'

'I am astonished, indeed,' said Mrs Sealy, retrieving her hand. 'I thought it understood between us that you would be on the continent for many months.'

Ironside—himself a fine physical specimen but not on the scale of the newcomer—had positioned himself behind a pillar which supported the overhanging canopy. At the appearance of the gentleman, he had stepped out of the pillar's shadow and given Mrs Sealy a questioning look. She shook her head slightly and the manservant withdrew, but not entirely. He remained behind the pillar and maintained a careful watch. The young man—Arthur—saw Ironside's gesture quite clearly—Jane followed his glance—but went on as though oblivious, 'It was my fixed intention to remain abroad, but it cannot be done without funds. Who is this charming young lady, Mama? Won't you introduce me?'

'This is my companion, Miss Bates,' Mrs Sealy said reluctantly. 'Miss Bates, this is the Admiral's son by his first wife, Arthur Sealy.'

'Good day to you Miss Bates. I am charmed to make your acquaintance. Do you attend the Assembly this evening? I would be honoured to engage you for the first dances.'

'Miss Bates does not dance,' Mrs Sealy said quickly.

'She certainly ought to, then,' Mr Sealy drawled, 'she should not deprive a fellow of such a partner. I overheard you telling that gentleman that you are going to the Rookery. I think I will join you. It is a delightful afternoon for a stroll in the gardens is it not Mama? Oh, but I forget,' with a cruel, mirthless laugh, '*you* can not stroll.'

'I am afraid that won't be possible,' Mrs Sealy replied. 'We are going as guests …'

'Of Captain Bates. Yes, I heard. An excellent man and

an old acquaintance. He will not mind my joining you.'

'*I* will mind,' Mrs Sealy said, 'we have particular family reasons for meeting Captain Bates this afternoon and your presence would frustrate them. Arthur, I pray you would leave us now. If you wish to call in the morning you may do so.'

'Family reasons?' Mr Sealy cried. 'Since I am family, I can think of no better reason for me to do myself the pleasure of joining your party. It will be a duty, indeed, if 'family' is at the crux of it. What do you plan to do behind my back, I wonder?'

Mrs Sealy summoned patience from a cache which was all but dry. 'Not *our* family, Arthur. Miss Bates' family. You could make no contribution whatsoever.'

'I think I will be the judge of that, Mama,' the young man said with an unpleasant smirk. 'Come, let me carry you to your carriage—I see it waiting there, and that cur with it.' He bent and made as though to scoop the defenceless Mrs Sealy up in his arms.

Jane leapt from her chair, gasping at the man's audacity. She reached out, fully ready to fight for possession of Mrs Sealy, if necessary, quite determined that he would not touch her, much less lift her from her seat. 'Sir, I pray you will step away,' she said. 'You impose yourself.'

Ironside materialised at her side and interposed himself between the young man and his mistress but it was a move calculated to exacerbate, rather than to defuse, the situation.

'You will not man-handle me, you dog,' Arthur Sealy spat out, shouldering the manservant so that he staggered and almost overturned a cabinet of confectioneries.

'Gentlemen,' said a soft-voiced man whom no one had remarked before but who had been hovering on the terrace for some moments awaiting an opportunity to approach Mrs Sealy's table. He had red hair, a thin but perfectly proportioned face and wore wire spectacles. He was tall but slender, dwarfed by the bulk of both Arthur Sealy and Ironside, not a man to be supposed could match either in a fight. 'The cricket match is to begin presently,' he remarked mildly. 'See how the spectators are gathering?' He threw his arm out to indicate a team of liveried servants arranging chairs on the grass and an assemblage of the great and the good of Brighton strolling quite within sight and probably within earshot of the fracas which had been about to occur on the terrace. 'There is the Duke of Cumberland and Mr Pelham. The Macartneys—father and son—and Mr Poole. Is that Lord Montesquieu? I can't quite make out … My eyes, you know, are not keen … Can *you* see?'

Almost imperceptibly the man edged Arthur Sealy away from his stepmother and Miss Bates. Under guise of interesting him in the august company gathering to watch the cricket he also no doubt brought forcefully to the young man's mind that a display of fisticuffs with such an audience would sink his reputation so low it would probably be beyond retrieval. With Mr Sealy's attention distracted Ironside soon had Mrs Sealy in her carriage. Jane gathered her mistress' things and quickly followed. They were almost ready to depart when the red-haired stranger stepped up to say, 'A thousand pardons, madam. I am sent with a message from Mrs Bates. She regrets she is unable to join you this afternoon. My sister-in-law, Lady Cecily, is not well enough be left. She asks you to convey her apologies to Captain Bates.'

'You must do me the honour of knowing your name,

sir. You have performed a heroic service,' Mrs Sealy cried, grasping his hand. Her voice, full of gratitude, also betrayed that tears were near. She had been badly shaken by the encounter with Arthur Sealy.

'It was nothing at all,' he said, 'I felt compelled to intervene.' He looked at Jane. His eyes, behind their glass lenses, were intensely blue. He gave her a penetrating, searching look. 'Such courage,' he said. 'Let me commend you, Madam. *You* would have taken him on single handed. I doubt you needed me at all.'

Mrs Sealy's coachman had taken up the reins. The horses were restless, ready to be off.

'Your name, sir?' Mrs Sealy repeated.

'Oh,' said the young man, stepping down from the carriage. 'I am Angus Fairfax.'

The incident on the library terrace had unsettled Mrs Sealy more than perhaps she cared to reveal to her young protégée. She was silent as they rode towards the Rookery, appearing to take pleasure in the countryside. But her hands trembled in her lap and she could not still them. Jane saw her distress and respected her silence. She kept her counsel but her mind roved over the afternoon's events. That Arthur Sealy was a tyrant there was no doubt. She pitied Mrs Sealy from the bottom of her heart, to be so vulnerable, unable to get up and walk away from such a man! Ironside's stalwart, hefty presence now made perfect sense—he was much more than just a footman, he was a guardian and had been called upon, she suspected, more than once to champion Mrs Sealy against her overbearing stepson.

From his place behind them in the phaeton, Ironside seemed unusually restless, shifting in his seat and continually adjusting some fixing just behind them. Usually so reticent, immobile to the point of invisibility, it was almost as though he wished to reassure them that he was there.

Angus Fairfax's words also stayed with Jane. He had been right—she *would* have come to blows with Arthur Sealy if it had come to it. She could not abide a bully. Mr Fairfax's look had struck her very powerfully; there had been a light—an intense light—in his eyes which amounted almost to recognition. But she had never seen him before, of that she was quite certain.

Presently, Mrs Sealy took a deep breath. 'I must apologise my dear,' she said. 'The scene you were forced to witness was quite disgusting. I had hoped to spare you any interference from Arthur. As I think you gathered, he is supposed to be in Europe for a tour of a long—an indefinite—duration. I paid him to stay away. He came to me in Lucerne, penniless, his money spent and debts amounting to a king's ransom in every place he had been. The truth is he did not approve of his father marrying me and did all in his power to dissuade the Admiral from doing so. When the marriage went ahead he determined to ruin us. That has been his fixed intention ever since, and if he carries on this way he will succeed.'

'I am very sorry, ma'am,' Jane said sincerely. '*How*

sharper than a serpent's tooth it is, to have a thankless child.'

'Thankless indeed. I gave over quite half of the Admiral's legacy immediately. Arthur had as much as I, but his is squandered away.'

'Is there no clause in law which can protect you from him?'

Mrs Sealy shook her head. 'I do not know. It would break the Admiral's heart to know there was such animosity between us. I thank the good Lord *he* knows nothing of my agony.'

'And what will you do, when he comes in the morning?'

'Which he will surely do. See? Already you can discern his conniving intentions. He believes himself so subtle, so very clever but in fact he is utterly transparent. I suppose I will arrange funds. It is the only way to be rid of him, even if it is only temporary.'

'Ma'am, if you will take my advice, you will not. Giving him money will only make him return. Tell him you have put your capital beyond reach; that you could not access it even if you chose to do so. If he knows it is quite hopeless, that no threat can move you, he will desist.'

'Do you think so, Jane? Oh, but to oppose him …'
Mrs Sealy cringed at the idea. 'You do not know how
violent he can get.'

'He may threaten violence, but he will do none. It is
the way of all bullies. Do you have no man of business
you can consult?'

'Perhaps. Indeed, there may be one near at hand. Well,
my dear, I will think on it. But here we are at the tea
gardens. We will speak of this no more today.'

The phaeton turned between a set of ornate gates,
down a gravel sweep and drew up alongside a
colonnaded portico, the entrance to an elaborate,
elegant stone pavilion. Within, a vast tiled hall led to a
number of smaller chambers—private rooms for
dining, card-playing or tea. A broad, sweeping stone
stair rose to the balustraded landing of an upper floor.
The strains of some beautiful, ethereal music drifted
from the lofty ceiling.

Ironside carried Mrs Sealy through the hall, passing
urns of exuberant flowers and tumbling foliage,
marble statuary and burbling fountains, stepping at last
onto a rear terrace where the afternoon sun shone

onto tiered walks, neatly clipped shrubberies, lawns and arbours. Parties of ladies and gentlemen strolled amongst the topiary and in the shady pathways. Games of chance and skill invited the daring to spend their shillings and try their luck. Here and there creeper-swathed gazebos housed tables where refreshments were being served. Servants scurried to and fro with trays.

'Mrs Sealy?' They were approached by a manservant. 'Captain Bates has reserved a dining room, ma'am. Please to follow me.'

He took them along a narrow terrace and through some French doors into a modestly sized room where a sofa stood before a small fire. A table laid for dinner took up the central space. After the brightness of the day, it took their eyes a little time to adjust to the gloom.

A voice issued from a shadowed corner. It was of such an arrestingly peculiar quality that Jane, in the act of seating herself beside her mistress on the sofa, almost leapt off it again. The voice was low, rasping, almost gasping, accompanied by stertorous breathing denoting a chest much congested. 'I do not know about you, ma'am,' the voice croaked, 'but I find that being unable to move of one's own volition makes one very vulnerable to the cold, so I always insist upon a fire.'

There was a rasp, a creek, a squeak of wheels and Captain Bates propelled himself from behind an inner door.

Captain Bates had, as a relatively young man, had the misfortune of sustaining an injury whilst serving in His Majesty's navy. The injury had not been serious in and of itself but its treatment had been shockingly mismanaged so that at first a foot and then a good portion of the entire leg had had to be sacrificed. The trauma of this ordeal had been considerable, naturally, and its consequences severe to a man as active and as ambitious as Captain Bates—a young man, as he had then been, with all his hopes before him, very desirous of serving with distinction and of accruing to himself positive notoriety, plaudits and acclaim. *This* had all been taken from him. He had been forced to retire, maimed and incapacitated, to live the life of an invalid. He faced confinement to a wheeled chair or the indignity of being carried wherever he wished to go.

He was denied the sporting pursuits enjoyed by other gentlemen; romantic and matrimonial attachments likewise seemed beyond his reach. He had been required to live—in short—without the natural pride of a man who can stand upon his own two feet.

He had settled in Brighton with a view to conquering his disablement through sea-bathing and rigorous physical therapy. But no amount of saline submersion or pummelling by a masseur could re-grow his missing leg, and he had lost the will to continue. There had grown in him a deep-seated resentment against whatever power had prevailed to deny him what other men took for granted, a resentment which had eaten away at what small quantity of pride and courage which remained to him. The only remedy he found which offered any relief was to treat and cosset himself; he indulged in fine linens, richly ornamented waistcoats and superior tailoring. His shoes (right footed only) were made of the softest leather and adorned by showy buckles and intricate embroidery. He collected curios both rare and expensive: ancient coins, oriental porcelain, Turkey rugs and lavish silks. These treasures delighted and soothed him but food became his most precious panacea. It would be wrong to imply that he became a glutton—he did not eat for eating's sake—but a gourmand he certainly became, delighting in rich dishes and expensive cuts, sauces laced with cream and brandy, exquisite confectionary and all that was choice, rare and exceptional. To indulge himself thus took away to some extent the bitter sting of umbrage. Of course, as the years had gone by, such extravagance had taken its toll—he had become fat. An excess of rich fare and a deficiency of exercise can never result in excellent health and the captain's remedy for unhappiness served rather to exacerbate the difficulties of his situation than to alleviate them. Nevertheless, his expanding figure—and it had expanded exponentially—had not negated his considerable charm; he had a certain handsomeness of feature and an elegant manner which made him popular; he was a person of note in Brighton, which pleased his vanity if it did not add to the happiness of his banker. To tell the truth he lived far beyond his means; his lifestyle stretched his pension as well as his waistline. Both, by the time of Jane's encounter with him, were beginning to give quite serious cause for alarm. But his appetite was insatiable; he could not deny himself what he still felt, in some inner, needy core, he was owed.

Jane had never seen so rotund or so resplendent a man as her uncle, Captain Jeremy Bates. He was the size of at least two men in girth. His flesh was barely contained by his clothing, bulging between his coat buttons and straining the seams of his breeches, but the coat and breeches were of superior cloth, richly ornamented with embroidery and gold braid. His chins stacked atop his stock—immaculately white and very neatly tied—and pressed upwards, encompassing his jowls, so that it was impossible to tell where one ended and the others began. His eyes were large and very dark yet still—for a man in his fifties—rather handsome under heavy brows. He wore his own hair, powdered and abundantly curled and tied back with a dark ribbon. The whole of his person was contained in an over-sized bath chair. A sash or shawl—undoubtedly silk, of oriental origin and very fine—draped across his lap and over the place where his missing limb should have been. He was immensely impressive, almost gorgeous, but also appallingly large.

Mrs Sealy, who was already acquainted with Captain

Bates and had therefore become accustomed to his voluminous figure, replied naturally to his observation. 'A fire is always pleasant, and although we have been enjoying unseasonably warm days, the evenings do grow cooler.' At the same time, she managed to convey to Jane, through speaking looks and a warm press of the hand, that she had meant to prepare her for her uncle's appearance, had fully intended to drop a hint which would have made the encounter less shocking, but the episode with Arthur Sealy had driven the objective from her mind.

'And so you are my young niece,' Captain Bates rasped, reaching a swollen hand out to Jane. 'You have no look of my brother Frederick, so far as I can recall him.'

Jane suffered her uncle to take her hand. 'I believe I have my mother's looks, uncle,' she replied. My sister Henrietta favours Papa more.'

'Your mother has not accompanied you?' the captain said, through a productive cough. 'I pray she harbours no grudge for I assure you my intentions are of the most cordial and brotherly kind.'

'By no means, sir,' Jane exclaimed. 'Mama is the very

last person in the world to do such a thing! She fully intended to come, but her hostess is unwell and she felt it her duty to remain behind. She sends her sincere apologies, indeed she does. She sent a messenger to convey them most particularly.' Speaking these words brought that messenger powerfully back to Jane's remembrance. She found the image thus conjured helped to temper the one so abundantly present before her.

'I have ordered dinner,' said Captain Bates, 'but it will not be here for half an hour yet. You will take a glass of port, I hope.'

Even with the partially open French doors the room was stifling and very hot. He seemed to occupy all the space and breathe all the air. Jane felt the colour begin to drain from her face. 'I wonder if you might excuse me,' she said faintly. 'The gardens look so very pleasant and,' she grasped her reticule and felt the folded wedge of Hetty's letter within it, 'speaking of Hetty reminds me that I have a letter from her which I have not perused.'

'Of course,' Mrs Sealy said quickly, 'go and enjoy the pleasure grounds, Jane. Some air will do you good.'

She turned to Captain Bates. 'I am sorry to say that my miscreant step-son has made an appearance. We had an unpleasant encounter at Mrs Widget's library which I fear Jane found rather unsettling. And, as it happens, I have a matter of business to discuss with you, if you would be so kind as to do me the honour of your attention for half an hour. You are such an old and trusted friend.'

Captain Bates quite quivered with pleasure. 'An honour, ma'am,' he burbled.

Jane stepped out onto the terrace and then across a broad swathe of smooth lawn towards an opening in a high hedge, hoping to find a quiet arbour where she could recover her equilibrium and read Hetty's missive. The path took her through to a series of shaded walks separated by tall trellis thickly entwined with climbing shrubs, espaliered fruit and ivy. The walks were bordered by beds of perennial flowers and fragrant herbs, deliciously pleasing on the eye and soothing to the spirits. Every so often along the walk there was a secluded seat and, finding one unoccupied, Jane sat down. The heat of the day had by this time passed and a pleasant, cooling breeze offered unspeakable refreshment. Jane gave herself up to it for some moments before reaching for her reticule and Hetty's letter. But familiar voices, coming from the other side of the fencing at her back, stayed her hand.

'I do not know why you have brought us here, Louisa,' carped a shrewish voice, unmistakably Mrs Churchill's. 'Charles very much wanted to watch the cricket, you know.'

'I can watch cricket at any time,' a low, reasonable voice replied. 'I have heard this venue spoken of very highly and indeed the gardens are quite lovely.'

'That fellow made great trouble about our dining,' Mrs Churchill complained.

'We ought to have sent ahead and reserved a room,' Louisa said. 'By the time you had finally made up your mind to it, it was too late.'

'We can dine a little later than usual,' Mr Churchill remarked. 'It is no matter. An hour or so spent in these grounds is no hardship.'

'But we must be finished in time for the fireworks,' Louisa said, with some agitation, 'otherwise there is no point in us having come at all. I am quite wild to see them, Charles. You will not linger at table?'

'Oh no, of course, we will gobble down our food like pigs at the trough. *Your* constitution will suffer no evil from it,' Mrs Churchill said bitterly, '*mine* will plague me until the small hours of tomorrow. We should have made arrangements to come another day; *that* would have been by far a better plan. But no. Louisa *would* have us come today. No other day would suit.'

'My dear Eustacia, you know we have engagements every other day this week. Tomorrow you are to attend the debate with Mrs Pelham and the following day Charles and I are to sail with Mr Abergavenny. We are to go to Hove on Monday—or is it Tuesday? I forget, but certainly we are not at liberty for many days after this and, you know, this fine spell of weather is not guaranteed to last. Imagine coming here in the pouring rain! Nothing could be a more miserable prospect.'

There was silence for a while—Louisa having gained her point—and Jane hoped that the Churchills had moved along their side of the dividing lattice so that she would cease to be in the embarrassing position of eavesdropping on their discussion. If they did not move, she was resolved to call out, and alert them to her presence. She could not move herself; the pathway was gravel and her footsteps, be they ever so light, would have been overheard. There would have been something ignominious about being caught in the act of creeping away.

But it seemed that the Churchills remained on the other side of the vegetation. Presently Mr Churchill said, 'What is that plant, there? It is very pretty, is it not, Eustacia my dear? Do we not have something like it in the border at home? But I believe ours is pink. It could be of the genus …' he went on for some time naming plant varieties, comparing habit and form. Jane was just about to announce her presence when Mr Churchill was interrupted by a voice which turned her blood to ice. It came at first from some little distance along the pathway occupied by the Churchills but a rapid tread on the gravel denoted its owner moving at haste towards them.

'Mr Churchill, I do declare,' cried Arthur Sealy (for it was he), 'forgive me for intruding. I could not pass the end of the walk without coming to offer you my hand, once I had recognised you. We met in Avignon last year. Arthur Sealy, you recall. Mrs Churchill, what a very great pleasure it is to see you again ma'am.'

'Mr Sealy, indeed, how do you do, sir?' Mr Churchill's voice betrayed no very great pleasure in resurrecting this acquaintance.

'Mr Sealy,' exclaimed Mrs Churchill, her voice suddenly fawning, 'what a very fortunate happenstance. Is the Chevalier with you? He was a most gentlemanlike man, I found, quite charming. He was so kind as to invite us to his chateau but unfortunately we were unable to give ourselves the honour of a visit.'

'Lamentably no, he was injured in a … gentlemen's disagreement. He recuperates in the Alps. It is hoped that in time he will regain partial sight in at least one eye.'

'Mr Sealy,' interjected Mr Churchill, 'what brings you to Brighton?'

'Family business, it will soon be concluded, a trifling matter. I expect to be abroad again before many days. Venice, I find, is very agreeable at this time of year. Who is this delightful young lady, Churchill? Won't you introduce me?'

'This is my sister, Miss Louisa Churchill.'

'Good day to you Miss Churchill. I am charmed to make your acquaintance. Do you attend the Assembly this evening? I would be honoured to engage you for the first dances.'

Jane was at once amused and appalled by Arthur Sealy's triteness; he had used the exact same words to her earlier in the day.

'I would be delighted on another occasion,' said Miss Churchill, 'but this evening we remain here.'

'You dine here?' asked Mr Sealy. 'You are most fortunate. I was engaged to dine with some fellows but they seem to have altered their arrangements without telling me. Dashed inconsiderate. I find myself rather at a loose end.'

'Oh, but you must join us, Mr Sealy,' Mrs Churchill said, 'you would be most welcome, would he not, Charles?'

Charles Churchill made a sound which might have been taken as an assent but nobody could have believed him pleased with the arrangement. 'There is a full hour to wait until we can be accommodated.

Perhaps you will not wish to wait so long.'

'I am very happy to fall in with your arrangements, sir,' said Mr Sealy. 'Have you seen the water gardens yet? They are magnificent. Let me urge you to see them, since we have time. Miss Churchill, will you do me the honour of taking my arm? It is but a short walk, this way.'

Thankfully their steps took them away from Jane. Their voices soon faded and she found she had been holding her breath, so awkward, so unpleasant had the whole episode been.

A quiet tread alerted her to Ironside, approaching along the path. 'Dinner is served, ma'am,' he said, in the lowest possible voice. He stepped back and held out an arm to indicate the most direct route.

'Thank you, Mr Ironside,' said Jane, suddenly glad of his solid presence. 'I would not alarm Mrs Sealy, but I will mention to *you* that Mr Arthur Sealy is here. He must have followed us.'

Ironside nodded gravely but made no reply.

Chapter 9

Jane returned to the pavilion to find dinner ready and the other diners seated at table. Mrs Sealy seemed more sanguine after her conversation with Captain Bates. Jane assumed she had found the captain's advice beneficial.

The captain had ordered a lavish banquet; the table was so laden with platters and dishes that a side table had to be brought forward to accommodate the overspill. He partook of all the dishes with utmost enjoyment and liberality, encouraging the servants to put large quantities of everything on his plate. Jane was astonished at his capacity although naturally she made no remark. As he ate, he discussed the fare, remarking on its seasoning, texture and flavour, its gastronomic origin, speculating on the receipt and comparing it with similar dishes he had sampled. Food, clearly, was his chief delight and predominant interest. In between tasting and assessing he regaled them with anecdotes of his travels; tours of wine regions, olive groves and markets. He spoke with great erudition, eager to entertain the ladies and put them at their ease. But Jane ate sparingly, the malevolent presence of Mr Sealy quashing what appetite she had. Ironside stood sentinel in the shadow beyond their room.

Course followed course as the day beyond the French doors waned and evening came on. Torches were lit around the gardens. Somewhere, an orchestra began to play.

'I regret your mama's absence,' the captain said, diverting at last from his culinary narrative. 'I hope you will tell her from me that I very much hope we *will* meet, when she has liberty from her hostess, before she returns to Surrey. There are matters of mutual interest which we must discuss.'

'Sir?' Jane could not imagine what business the captain and her mama might have in common.

'I rather suspect that our brothers have been underhand in the arrangement of our family affairs,' the captain elucidated with a new note in his voice, almost a whine. 'I know *I* have seen no penny from our father's estate. Are you aware of any benefit your father may have accrued?'

'I can state categorically that he received nothing, sir,'

Jane said. 'However, I do not think he expected to. He saw the education he received in lieu of a legacy. I believe there was something from his mama, but it ceased when Papa died.'

'Yes, she left him the interest on half her capital. But where is that capital now, I wonder. Brother Edgar has manipulated things to his own good, I doubt not,' the captain grumbled. 'He lives exceedingly well, for a common lawyer.'

'Jane was speculating about the wider family,' Mrs Sealy said. 'Do either of your brothers have children?'

'Bertie has a daughter—I am sorry to say she is sickly; she has an Italian name I cannot pronounce. Edgar has a multitude of progeny, mainly boys. The oldest will inherit Hazelwoods in due course, I surmise, for of course the estate is entailed. *That* puffs Edgar up a great deal, as you can imagine. Anyone would think *him* the second son! I believe your mama and I should exert ourselves. Together we might uncover whatever devious machinations Edgar and Bertie have employed to deprive us of our rightful inheritance. I am certain that our father would not have left his other sons un-provided for.'

'Girls are overlooked entirely in these matters,' Jane observed. 'They but rarely receive any consideration where there is a Will in question. They have only their education and their wits to rely upon. I am thankful to Papa that he gave me the first, at least.'

'Young ladies have beauty, which goes a long way,' Mrs Sealy said.

'*Some* ladies have beauty,' Captain Bates qualified, turning his eyes towards Mrs Sealy in a look manifestly intended to convey a compliment.

Mrs Sealy gave a self-deprecating smile, 'It is all some ladies do have,' she said.

'It is all some ladies need,' the captain remarked, with considerably gallantry—marooned as he was in his bath chair, his chest, paunch and shoulders so swathed in capacious linen napkins that he rather resembled a pudding trussed up and ready to be steamed. Mrs Sealy looked down at her plate. Jane sipped her wine. From somewhere outside there was a ripple of applause before the orchestra struck up a new melody. 'I hope I can tempt you to some of this side dish,' the captain went on, pointing at one of the salvers and motioning the servant to remove the lid. 'It has just the sufficient quantity of butter—chefs so often scrimp on that condiment, don't you find?' The captain resumed both his favoured topic of discourse and his preferred occupation until all the dishes were empty.

At last, the table was cleared and, the room being somewhat warm, it was agreed to adjourn to the terrace to take the evening air and await the fireworks. Ironside transferred Mrs Sealy to a chaise he had made ready for her. Two manservants manoeuvred Captain Bates' chair through the French doors and onto the veranda. The Rookery by this time was quite teeming with people; those who had dined had emerged, like the captain's party, to enjoy the evening entertainments. Others had travelled from Brighton. Parties of ladies and gentlemen strolled about the grounds. A man on stilts in bright, striped pantaloons juggled batons and a gypsy woman performed summersaults and cartwheels. Courting couples melted into the seclusion of groves and bowers where a waist may be encircled and lips kissed without observation. Inside the pavilion there was the noise of high jinks from the ballroom on the first floor, gentlemen carousing and the high-pitched shriek of women. Altogether Jane felt that the Rookery might be a less than respectable venue for a young lady such as herself. The night air, the flaming torches, the dissipation of the company made it seem a dangerous, distasteful place. She determined to stay close to Mrs Sealy. Even the captain, she felt, could offer some protection, some shade of respectability. *She* had not come to indulge in intemperance; *she* had no nefarious assignation in view.

They had settled themselves at their appointed spot when the Churchill party emerged from within. Arthur Sealy was with them, a towering figure impossible to mistake, even in the half-light cast by the guttering candles. They had dined less gastronomically and more speedily than the captain's guests, so although they had started later, they finished at more or less the same time.

Miss Churchill saw Jane and hurried over to where she sat. 'Miss Bates!' she exclaimed, 'how glad I am to see you again. I have been looking out for you daily in Brighton. Have you not been in society at all? Do not tell me that the old woman whom you serve has denied you all liberty and pleasure?'

Jane blushed. 'By no means Miss Churchill. I believe I have had more liberty and pleasure than I ever enjoyed in my life before.' She turned to Mrs Sealy. 'May I introduce you to my patroness, Mrs Sealy? Mrs Sealy, this is Miss Churchill of Enscombe in Yorkshire.'

Miss Churchill turned to look at the comparatively young and undeniably beautiful lady seated next to Jane with her skirts prettily arranged on a stool. 'Mrs Sealy!' she exclaimed, and then, clapping her hand to her forehead. 'Of course! I *knew* when we were introduced earlier that I had heard the name Sealy before! How very obtuse of me! Ma'am, we have had the pleasure of your son's company at dinner. He is just yonder, with my brother and sister-in-law. Do let me alert him to your presence.'

'Do not think of it,' Mrs Sealy replied. 'I would not break up your party on any account. I saw my stepson earlier today and I believe he intends calling tomorrow. We will say all that needs to be said then.'

'But surely you would like to present him to …' Miss Churchill turned to Captain Bates and was scarcely sufficiently mistress of herself to suppress a response

which was half a shriek of surprise and half a shudder
of utter revulsion, ' … your companion,' she managed
to gasp out, swallowing hard.

'I pray you do not, Miss Churchill,' Jane urged. She
took Louisa's arm and guided her a few steps away.
'There is animosity between the parties, Miss
Churchill. I make no accusation as to guilt or blame, it
is none of my business, but I do know that bringing
Mr Sealy before his stepmother will distress *her* very
much and will inevitably lead to great unpleasantness.'

'But Miss Bates,' Louisa Churchill hissed, quite as
emphatic as Jane had been, 'you *must* assist me with
him. He clings like a limpet. I cannot shake him off
and I have *reason*—such a pressing reason—to slip
away from my brother for just half an hour. I have
arranged … I am engaged to meet … oh, but it is a
terrible secret. If you only knew the labour I have had
to get my brother to Brighton, and then *here* to the
Rookery on *this* evening, all for the sake of the next
half an hour. I *beg* of you Miss Bates—Jane—I implore
you to do me this service.'

Jane shook her head. 'I am very sorry Miss Churchill. I
would do you any service within my power but I

cannot do this. It would be a betrayal of Mrs Sealy and, to own the truth, on my own account I would not like to find myself alone with Mr Sealy. I am unable to aid you in your scheme.'

'Oh Miss Bates,' Miss Churchill looked as though she would weep. She pressed a lace handkerchief to her eyes. 'If I am not at the place we arranged he will think I am false. I would give my life not to disappoint him.'

'I am very sorry,' Jane repeated.

Seeing that tears would not move Jane, Miss Churchill ceased to affect them. 'Well,' she said, looking down the terrace where her brother, sister-in-law and Mr Sealy seemed engaged in conversation with a party of others, 'if you will not help me, I shall just slip away. I am not observed and the crowd will soon hide me from view. If you are asked, perhaps you will say that I saw some acquaintance and went in the direction of the fountain to speak to them. It will be only half an untruth, since I *will* see acquaintance and my direction takes me by the fountain. Do at least that much for me, Miss Bates, and I will be your friend until my dying day.'

Without waiting for an answer, or for Jane to dissuade

her from such a rash and improper act—which she would surely have attempted—Miss Churchill stepped from the terrace and melted into the crowd on the twilit lawn.

Jane re-joined Mrs Sealy and the captain. 'I have spared you, at least for the time being,' she whispered. 'Surely, if he sees us, he would not make mischief here?'

Mrs Sealy took Jane's hand, gave a rueful smile and murmured only, 'The 'old woman you serve' thanks you most heartily.'

Suddenly there was a loud boom, the crowd gasped, a few ladies screamed, and the sky came alive with showers of coloured sparks and shooting arrows of light. Every face turned upwards to watch the display. Jane was captivated—she had never imagined that the natural beauty of the firmament could be improved upon. Bright points of light whooshed into the sky and then exploded into a million shards, showering down like luminescent rain. The noise was deafening. Every so often she looked over towards the fountain but could see no sign of Louisa Churchill. That her brother had not missed her was very curious but he remained in company with Mr Sealy and a small group of others oblivious to her absence. Jane hoped she would not be called upon to make any explanation.

She turned her attention to the fireworks once more. A particularly brilliant cascade of bright streaks lit up the whole crowd, picking out the ladies' jewels, the gentlemen's buttons. An officer's gold braid and richly embroidered gold lapels shone with particular brightness, his red coat and white breeches standing him apart from the evening dress of the other gentlemen. Unlike the rest of the crowd, he did not observe the sky. His eyes roved across the gathered company. Jane gasped. She knew him! It was Lieutenant Weston! She rose from her seat, raised her hand, the sight of him reviving in her memory all that had passed between them the previous Christmas. He had danced with her, walked with her, told her of exotic places and daring exploits. He had braved a blizzard to escort her to dinner, and scooped her up in his arms to carry her over snow drifts. He had looked at her—oh!—with such intensity in his soft, grey eye, had smiled down on her with such warmth. He had told her that she was beautiful, quick, spirited and intelligent, that she was a girl in a thousand. He had clasped her to his breast and kissed her hand and told her—not in words but in every other language it was possible for a man to use—that he loved her. She was on the point of calling out—not that he would have heard her, the gasps of the crowd and the pop and fizz of the fireworks would have drowned out her voice— but the throng moved just then and he was lost to her view.

Jane sank back down to her seat.

'Jane, my dear, are you quite well?' Mrs Sealy asked. 'You have gone pale.'

'I have just seen a very old friend,' Jane replied unsteadily. 'I did not think to see him here. I thought him very far away.'

'Perhaps you mistook?'

'No, indeed, it was him. I would know him anywhere.'

Lieutenant Weston was in Brighton!

The fireworks came to an end and there was a general surge for the pavilion. Look as she might, amongst the crowd, along the terrace, around the fountain or the gazebos, Jane could see no trace of Lieutenant

Weston.

'I think it is time we called our carriage round,' Mrs Sealy said. 'It has been a most pleasant occasion, Captain Bates, I do thank you for your hospitality,' she paused, '*and* your advice.'

'You are most welcome to both, Mrs Sealy,' the captain gargled. 'I wonder if you might indulge me with five minutes private conversation with my niece?'

'Of course. Ironside will take me to the carriage and come back for you, Jane dear. I would not have you negotiate the passage alone. It sounds to me as though some of the revellers within have taken too much wine. I fear you will be exposed to debauchery.'

Mrs Sealy made her farewells and Ironside carried her along the terrace. They passed Louisa Churchill coming from the other direction. Her face was a radiant smile of happiness. She brushed past Jane and joined her brother's party unremarked.

'My dear,' Captain Bates said, 'I wanted to enquire as to your satisfaction with the situation I have procured for you. Are you quite settled? Quite comfortable?'

'Oh yes, Uncle, indeed, I am most grateful to you. Mrs

Sealy is delightful; very kind and easy to serve.'

'I am glad of it, my dear. I wanted to do you good, to give you the opportunity of advancement. As much benefit as you are to Mrs Sealy, my chief object, you know, was to serve you, for my brother's sake, and your mama's.'

'I am conscious of your kind intention, sir.'

'Good. Very good. While Mrs Sealy and I have been friends for many years I find a warmer regard grows between us every time we meet. She turns to me now for financial counsel. She seeks my wisdom in handling that malefactor Arthur Sealy. I am her first resource. I posit the idea that already she begins to consider me in a passionate light. I will own to you that, although an unlooked-for development, I find it is not an unpleasant one. I am by no means confirmed in bachelorhood. She has married an older man before and found happiness by it, why not again? And,' with a chortle which caused a wave of undulation and tremor to agitate the entire barrel of his body, '*some* would say ours is a match made in heaven! Who better for one incapacitated person to marry, than another?'

'I … I cannot say,' said Jane, quite truthfully, for she

was speechless.

Captain Bates reached out a puffy hand and rested it on Jane's. 'So, my dear, in return for the good I have done you, perhaps you would be so good as to speak a word in my favour, if you get the opportunity? To suggest, perhaps, how easily friendship can bloom into love, and what a natural development that would be? She is very beautiful, quite the most beautiful creature in Brighton. To possess such a one would be,' with a sigh which set his flesh a-quiver, 'exquisite. I collect beautiful things, you know. Mrs Sealy must bring you to my villa. I have cabinets full of curios which you will delight to look over, I am sure. Perhaps I may find a little gift for you. ' He gave her a significant look. There was no doubt what kind of transaction he had in mind—a reward, should Jane promote his suit.

'Thank you, Uncle,' Jane stammered out.

'Miss Bates.' Ironside was beside her.

'Good night uncle,' she said.

The press of people within the pavilion was quite overpowering. Ironside went before her to clear a way but the jostle of bodies made progress almost impossible. The air was thick with the smell of wine and heated bodies. At one point there was a surge; breaking glass and the shout of angry voices made some crane forward to witness the fracas, others to veer away. Jane was separated from Ironside and felt a fist of panic rise in her chest. A man with a red face and foul breath barged into her. A woman behind began to swoon. Then she saw his hand, the braiding on his coat sleeve identifying it as his, thrust between two persons. She grasped it and he pulled her through.

'Forgive the liberty ma'am,' he said, sweeping her into his arms. 'Make way,' he cried in a voice which carried unsuspected authority, 'make way for this lady.'

The crowd fell back, and they made their escape.

Chapter 10

High Street

Highbury

Dear Jane

*I am home at last after my stay with the Winwoods at the
Archdeaconry. The fortnight initially suggested for my visit was
extended to three weeks. Quite a holiday for me, who has never
been from Highbury before! I must say it was strange to be away
and even stranger to come back and find no Mother at the door
to greet me and your belongings gone from the bedroom. I have
spread out my stockings ever so thin but they still only occupy
half the drawer. You may wonder why the Winwoods allowed
me to stay so long after my time and indeed I did ponder it
myself since, after Hermia's departure I had no particular friend
at the Archdeaconry apart from the smallest Miss Winwoods, of
whom more anon. After the nuptials of Hermia and Mr Paling
Miss Bland was to have returned to Lambeth and I to
Highbury but she was so reluctant to do so—the associations of
her old home were so strong, and the unfamiliarity of the new
also weighed heavy—that Reverend Winwood (I ought to call
him Archdeacon Winwood now but I continually forget to do so,*

and did forget to do so while I was with them, much to Mrs Winwood's chagrin) and Mrs Winwood were persuaded to allow her to remain, and since you and Mama were from home and the Winwoods knew I would be returning to an empty house, they permitted me to stay also.

I have much to write to you, a vast deal of news to impart. I am sure you will wish to know the minutiae of the wedding—the frills, the flowers, the garlands and ribbons—and all that took up every waking hour of our lives for the weeks beforehand, not only Hermia and all her sisters, Miss Bland and me but several florists, an army of seamstresses and a French pâtissier who took up residence in the kitchen—to the annoyance of the cook—to bake and construct the cake. Mrs Winwood directed the whole with more precision and authority than a general and woe betide anyone who forgot the smallest flounce. Poor Cordelia was often the recipient of a severe dressing down which was a great pity and quite unfair as she had enough to bear with Sophia repeatedly sticking pins into her. I must admit that there were times when I myself was the object of Mrs Winwood's censure for forgetting a detail of the seating plan or getting my ribbons in a tangle. There was so much we were expected to remember and you know my memory is not reliable. I could not recall if the bridesmaids were to wear white or purple ribbon, carry posies or baskets or who was to precede whom in the procession to the church. In the end it was thought best that I betake myself to the nurseries to entertain the youngest Miss Winwoods, and there I had a happy and, I like to think, a productive time of it, rearranging the furniture in their dolls' house and serving tea to a constant stream of guests including the entirety of the animals on Noah's ark and a broom mischievously purporting to be the Venerable Bishop Bland.

The day itself went off very well and I think that none of the guests took the least note of the decorated pews, garlanded sconces or beribboned door handles, all of which had seemed indispensable to the success of the wedding only the day before. Hermia's dress was very beautiful, with plentiful satin and a long train which I only managed to drop once and trip up on a very few times. I felt my own costume to be perfectly suitable and I shall call on Miss Grace tomorrow to let her know that, in spite of Sophia's assertion, I think the lady who referred to 'a ladder-back chair wearing a curtain' could not possibly have meant me. Hermia and Mr Paling said their vows quietly but with great sincerity. Reverend Winwood—the Archdeacon— was visibly distressed but that may have been because, at the last possible minute, his brother-in-law the Venerable Bishop Bland insisted upon stepping in to conduct the service.

I returned to Highbury yesterday, the Winwoods' coach bringing me all the way. Martha was very pleased indeed to see me, once she had woken up, got over her surprise and removed herself from Mama's chair before the fire in the parlour. She was anxious to show me the results of her industry while we have been away—the china she has washed, the polished sideboard, the shine on the brasses, the beaten rugs. I praised her very highly and said I was sure Mama would be pleased, but in truth I could see little difference myself. Home is the same comfortable place as before. Perhaps I ought not to mention this, since you will not come here again, or only very rarely. However, I have written it now and even if I cross it through you will make it out. I think these little rooms feel like home to me now quite as much as the vicarage did in former times, although I believe I will never trust that treacherous step at the turn in the passageway.

This morning I was up early and out and about to greet our friends old and new. Mrs Cole greeted me quite like an old friend even though she is comparatively new. She is a worthy woman, quite genteel and elegantly spoke; to speak to her you get no hint that her husband is in trade. She kindly invited me into her house to ask my opinion on the improvements she has made there. I do not know what Mrs Snell would make of the new wallpapers and fresh-glazed windows. I said they were extra-ordinary and quite astonishing, which seemed to satisfy Mrs Cole. She says she intends a new addition at the rear of the house to create a larger space for entertaining. I think any opportunity for neighbours to mingle is a very good thing and commended the scheme very highly. There is a tear in my pelisse *which I fear I will not be able to mend to any degree of usefulness. You know I am no seamstress anyway but this tear is particularly jagged. I think Mama may decide it needs a patch if she can find any material to suit. To that end I did call into Fords. Mr Obadiah Ford is engaged! I never was so surprised in my life! He is to marry a Miss Wix from Kingston. I never heard of her and told Mrs Ford so, but she said that my not knowing the young lady did not mean she was not a highly respectable person and also an excellent milliner. I could only agree, although as to the excellence of her millinery, I think the proof of the pudding will be in the eating. I saw some most unusual and unwieldy hats at Hermia's wedding. One lady's was so abundantly and exuberantly feathered I thought she wore an ostrich on her head. We have received a vast quantity of pears from Donwell orchard. Our neighbours are so very good to us, are they not? Martha thinks to make perry.*

General Bramhall continues with the improvements at Randalls. I wonder he thought to purchase the place, so dissatisfied as he seems to be with every aspect of it. The builders continue their works but of the new owner himself there is no sign.

The new apothecary's practice flourishes. I wonder what made me think of him? I saw a stream of patients visiting his rooms and he is out and about on horseback at all hours attending patients. Mr Woodhouse will be pleased. His new property—Mr Woodhouse's new property, the apothecary does not have a new property, so far as I know—is built up to the windowsills—a vast place it is going to be! Mr and Mrs Woodhouse will be a very valuable addition to Highbury society. I do not mean to denigrate the apothecary—his name escapes me just now—I am sure he will also be a great asset. These days I try hard not to foresee disaster and alarm in every occurrence but I must confess it is a comfort to know that, should the worst happen, we have a man at hand with medical knowledge. To be sure an apothecary is not a physician nor yet a surgeon—that is, I think they are different but I am not certain how—but he has skills of healing. Work at the Abbey Mill goes on apace. Great lifting and shifting of machinery and timber, a confusion of pulleys and ropes, teams of cart horses straining as the old workings are removed and the new installed. Mr Knightley supervises, consulting his plans and directing the men, and also works alongside them. I declare he works as hard as many men half his age! He passed Mama's letter to me when I went down this morning and required me to send her his particular regards. George has gone back to school, apparently most dismayed that the work was not completed before he was obliged to go.

Martha says we shall have a pie for dinner. You can say what you like about her custards but her pastry is not to be improved upon anywhere; even the exclusive pâtissier at the Archdeaconry could not equal her, in my estimation. I called upon Mrs Goddard at the new school. She too has wrought many wonderful improvements and has several little girls as boarders already. It was quite lovely to see them in their pinafores, their hair all braided and neat, playing on the lawns together. I am sure Mrs Bittern's heart would be warmed by the knowledge that her old home is so happy a haven.

Mrs Hopley and Mrs Cropley are at odds! I am sure I will make no sense of it to you for I have had the story from both ladies and still am unable to fathom what has happened. As clear as I am able to relate, it seems there was confusion at the post office and a letter for one was mistakenly given to the other, opened and read before the error properly perceived. The letter was from the sister of either Mrs Hopley or Mrs Cropley and made reference to some remarks of a derogatory nature made to her by the one about the other. This is an awkward as well as a surprising state of affairs as the two have always been—or have seemed to be—fast friends very much attached to one another. I cannot for the life of me conceive how such an error came to be made at the post office but you can be sure I will direct this letter with extreme care and clarity to make sure no such misdirection occurs in Brighton.

Mrs Cropley's bunion is worse than ever, by the way. She thinks standing at her stall in the market will soon be beyond her.

I must not cross the page again or you will be able to make nothing out of my news. I have not asked about your situation but I pray you will write in detail when you can. Mrs Weston sends her regards to Mama. When I asked her she told me she has had news of her son but she did not say what. I hope he is well. Winters in Yorkshire can be very severe. I hope he has a good supply of thick socks.

Your affectionate sister

Hetty.

Chapter 11

The following morning Jane did not wake as early as usual; the emotional toll of the previous day had led to a troubled night. The tall spectre of Arthur Sealy had infiltrated her dreams in a strange conjunction with Lieutenant Weston, who remained a nebulous figure, perpetually out of reach. When she did at last open her eyes, she found it was to a day much more autumnal than those that had preceded it. Grey clouds hung over the town; the sea was all murk and dullness. Jane had, on that particular day, a reason for sadness, and her depressed spirits added to her lethargy. It was a full hour after her normal time when she descended the stair and prepared to go out. She had learned from the little maid who attended her that Mrs Sealy had also diverged from her customary routine and was to neglect the medicinal baths.

'She awaits Mr Arthur, miss,' the girl had said, her voice betraying the trepidation attendant on the visit, not just for Mrs Sealy, but for the entire household.

In the bright hallway Jane encountered Captain Bates,

just decanted from a sedan chair and into his own, and a dark-suited gentleman she supposed to be a man of law or business. Captain Bates greeted her with great cordiality, the other man with strait-laced decorum. She wished both gentlemen a good morning and went down the steps, turning left and walking along the pavement towards the corner of East Street, thankful to shake off the leaden atmosphere of Mrs Sealy's house, and to be far away from the scene of the difficult and distressing interview that would inevitably take place there. But she was not to escape entirely. Walking towards her along the same piece of road was Arthur Sealy. It was quite impossible to avoid him and Jane steeled herself for the meeting.

'Good morning, Miss Bates,' he said, making his bow but still managing to loom over her, making her feel very small, 'I hope you enjoyed your evening at the Rookery?'

'Very much indeed, I thank you sir,' she replied, gathering her courage and looking him boldly in the eye. 'Did you?'

'Ah! You saw me there, did you? Yes, I had a delightful time in company with some old acquaintance.'

'The Churchills? Did they remain very late at the pavilion?'

Arthur Sealy sneered. 'No, Mrs Churchill developed a headache and was determined to go home. I would have escorted Miss Churchill—she was game to stay on—but her brother would have none of it.'

'*You* remained, however?' The bleariness of his eye and a decidedly unhealthy pallor intimated to Jane that he had stayed at the Rookery very late indeed.

'I certainly did. I have had but two hours sleep I believe, but a note awaited me at my lodgings summoning me here at this unconscionable hour and so here I am. What has the widow-woman got to say to me, do you know?'

'I cannot enlighten you. She does not consult me on matters of business.'

'Of course not. Louisa Churchill suggested as much. She raves enthusiastically about you, nonetheless; declares you remarkably beautiful and extremely clever.' Sealy paused a moment before adding contemptuously, in a tone intended to offend, 'She says it is just such a pity you are so poor.'

Jane bridled. 'I would rather be respectable than rich,' she said sharply, thinking of the licentious behaviour at the Rookery. She could quite imagine Arthur Sealy equalling or surpassing any of the gentlemen she had seen the night before in bawdy, dissolute behaviour.

'I hope to be both,' Arthur replied archly.

'Respectability is not a garment one can put on or take off at will,' Jane said.

'Like a hair shirt, you mean, or a chast … However, I will miss my hour with my nemesis if I am to continue this interesting debate, Miss Bates. I must wish you good day.' He bowed once more and walked on.

Jane continued on her way to the Steyne, fairly fizzing with indignation at Arthur Sealy's arrogance but wounded too. Had Louisa Churchill really been so scornful? She walked briskly for some half an hour, striding with energy across the cropped, grassy expanse, breathing the sea air deeply into her lungs until the fresh air, exercise and the freedom of the open space began to restore her spirits. Towards the eastern side of the ground, where the soldiers' encampment was situated, all was busyness as more tents were erected and an enclosure for horses marked out. Jane hailed a little drummer boy running by with hot rolls from the bakery for his sergeant. 'Do more militia come to join your ranks?' she asked, giving him a penny.

'Yes ma'am, the men of the Hampshires come tomorrow. There are scarce billets in the town sufficient for the officers and our camp here is to be enlarged to half its size again.

The Hampshires being Lieutenant Weston's regiment, Jane was more certain than ever that it was him she had seen the night before. As much as she had schooled herself to hear of him with calm and restraint, his presence in Brighton caused her great joy. To take up their attachment again where it had been so suddenly cut short was Jane's dearest wish; the only thing that could add to her happiness in her new situation and certainly news that brightened very considerably the melancholy of this particular day. It being autumn, it seemed likely to her that the regiment would remain encamped in Brighton the whole winter through and although she did not know what Mrs Sealy's plans for winter might be she very much hoped that there would be opportunities for her to spend time in Lieutenant Weston's company.

When Jane returned to the house on North Street all was quiet, the gentlemen had departed and Mrs Sealy reported to have taken to her bed with a severe migraine. Jane sat alone in the drawing room, turned the pages of a book and looked out at the street below. For the first time since coming to Brighton she felt lonely and homesick, very much in need of familiar faces and beloved voices. At last, she took up pen and paper and employed the time in a lengthy reply to Hetty's letter. The clock struck the hour as she laid down her pen.

'If Mrs Sealy has no need of me this afternoon I will go to East Street,' she told the housekeeper. 'I will be no more than an hour. Should I be required I pray you will send a message and I will return directly.'

The afternoon had turned cold; a stiff breeze blew carrying smatterings of rain with it. Jane pulled her shawl tightly around her shoulders as she ran the short distance to the Fairfax's house in East Street. Mrs Brigham admitted her and she was shown into a pleasant drawing room. Lady Cecily lay on an elegant

sofa in company with a lady Jane knew to be Mrs
Poole and a younger version unmistakably Mrs Poole's
daughter. Angus Fairfax sat beside Miss Poole but her
severe expression and unbending posture suggested
that his efforts at conversation had fallen on stony
ground. He looked very uncomfortable indeed, his
pale complexion flushed, his bearing tense, his hair
mussed and unruly as though he had been tearing at it
in an effort to think of some topic that would engage
the lady's interest. On Miss Bates' entrance to the
room he fairly sprang from his seat and almost
launched himself across the room in welcome.

'Miss Bates,' he cried, 'your mama has just but stepped
from the room. She will return presently.'

No one could describe Angus Fairfax as a handsome
man but he had such a look of eagerness and pleasure
just then that he did seem to Jane to be almost
attractive. His eyes, through the lenses of his
spectacles, were bright and warm, his smile was wide
and very engaging. She liked the redness of his hair,
and its untidiness. His clothing was sober if a little
worn and perhaps not of the very best quality, his
stock white but not very neatly tied. She could see

quite clearly in the pocket of his coat the outline of a book, a small volume he no doubt kept to hand in case of ten minutes' liberty for reading. This struck a decided note with Jane, who kept a book just like it and for precisely the same reason in her reticule.

Angus Fairfax's words seemed to conjure Mrs Bates into being. She walked at that instant through a doorway in the far corner of the room. 'Jane, dear,' she exclaimed, crossing to embrace her daughter.

The sight of her dear mama made Jane's throat constrict and brought tears to her eyes. Angus Fairfax stared, transfixed, as they trembled on her lashes, so moved by her emotion that it seemed likely that sympathetic tears would swell in his eyes too.

'Miss Bates,' Lady Cecily said, lifting a languid hand in greeting, 'I am happy to make your acquaintance at last. I fear I have been monopolising your mama. She came to Brighton to look after you and has spent her time looking after me.'

Jane curtseyed. 'You could have had no better nurse ma'am. I hope I find you much improved.'

'*Much* improved,' Lady Cecily smiled dreamily. 'So much so that we had ordered the carriage to take us out, but the breeze has been declared too strong—they think it will blow me quite away! And so, we have postponed our outing. Do you know Mrs Poole and Miss Poole? It is apparent that you know my brother-in-law, Angus Fairfax.'

'We … we have not been introduced,' Angus Fairfax said falteringly. 'But we have met.'

'How improper,' Lady Cecily murmured, 'one really ought to observe the proper etiquette, Angus.'

'The circumstances were unusual,' he demurred. 'There was no opportunity for formalities.' He flashed a conspiratorial smile at Jane.

'Mr Fairfax was a knight errant,' Jane said. 'He came to our rescue.'

'*Angus* did?' Lady Cecily exclaimed. 'Well. I never was more surprised in my life, were you, Anastasia?'

Anastasia Poole raised a quizzical eyebrow but if she felt astonishment, she disguised it admirably.

Mrs Poole, a very stiff and forbidding lady, squinted through her pince-nez. 'You are Mrs Sealy's companion? Yes, we were introduced. How is that poor soul? I hear the Admiral's son is back on English soil and already causing difficulties.'

Jane felt she would be betraying confidences if she discussed her mistress' business in general company. She restricted herself to confirming that Mr Sealy was in Brighton. 'Mrs Sealy has a migraine this afternoon,' she said, 'so I took the opportunity to call on Mama. I hope I do not intrude. I have but a letter to deliver, and some messages from our relative, Captain Bates.' She turned to her mother. 'Mama, I can call another time.'

'On no account,' Lady Cecily crooned. 'Mrs Bates, take your daughter into the small sitting room and when you return, we shall have some refreshment. Mrs Poole, I hope I can persuade you to remain? Anastasia, you are not rushing off on some other engagement? Everyone in Brighton does always seem to be in a hurry to get from one thing to another. Douglas is scarcely at home but he is off, out again. Angus is just as bad but his engagements are of a professional nature. I declare Dr Bushell does no work himself. Angus sees all his patients. He was out almost all night with a fisherman's daughter.'

'You make me sound quite dissipated,' Angus Fairfax

said, laughing, but with an anxious light in his eye. 'I would not have these ladies think me degenerate. The young lady was but five years old and had a high fever.'

Miss Poole shrank, slightly, at the distasteful image, but not in such a manner as to suggest an iota of sympathy. Mrs Poole drew herself into greater rigidity and inhaled through her nostrils. Fishermen's daughters were of no interest to her, feverish or otherwise. But both acknowledged themselves at liberty and, thus released, Marie took Jane into a smaller room where they sat together on a sofa. Jane passed on Captain Bates' messages.

'He is a most extra-ordinary figure,' Jane said, 'corpulent to a degree that I would not have believed possible. He bears a heavy grudge against his brothers. I distrust him, Mama, and I fear for Mrs Sealy. *She* relies upon his advice and wisdom and considers him a trusted friend. I do not share her opinion; he has his own interests at heart.'

'I shall take no part in his schemes,' Mrs Bates said. 'Your papa had no expectations from the estate and I think, if he is truthful with himself, Captain Bates will acknowledge that his naval commission was his inheritance; his being invalided does not negate it. It is what most second or subsequent sons receive—the means to make their own fortune.'

'I suggested as much to Captain Bates. Papa considered his education a valuable gift. But the Captain wishes to investigate the matter of his mother's capital.'

'I wish him good fortune,' Marie said. 'I want no part in it. Now, show me Hetty's letter.'

They read over Hetty's letter together and Jane showed her reply.

'I will write some lines to Hetty myself this evening,' Marie said, 'but now she is home, and I have satisfied myself that you are quite happy with Mrs Sealy, I think I must soon follow both our letters home. You *are* quite happy, Jane?'

'*Quite* happy, Mama. Mrs Sealy is all generosity and my duties are light. But there was another reason I wished to see you today,' Jane said, lifting her hand and touching the black lace at her mother's throat. 'It is a year since we lost Papa. You did not think I would forget?'

Marie sighed. 'No, of course, I knew you would not, and I have spent a great deal of time this morning at prayer. I give thanks for him. I believe he is at peace.'

'And so do I. I would give everything for five minutes more in his company, but it cannot be so and it does no good to spend time lamenting what we cannot change.'

'Dear Jane,' said Marie, embracing her daughter. 'How like him you are—I do not mean in looks; that has fallen to Hetty's lot—but your character is his; steady, kind, courageous. And you have his pragmatism. He was very proud of you, you know.'

'Yes Mama. And he would think as I do about your engagement to Mr Knightley. That it is good—very good—and that you should marry and be happy.'

Marie nodded, too full of feeling for words.

'Tomorrow you will put this aside,' Jane said, touching the mourning lace again.

'Yes.'

'There is something else I must tell you,' Jane said in a small voice, scarce able to keep the blush from her cheek. 'Lieutenant Weston is in Brighton.'

'James Weston? Well, that is happy news on this melancholy day! I am much cheered by his proximity. His mother intimated he would be many months in Yorkshire.'

'He *has* been many months there. He has been many months away, at any rate. Where he has been is irrelevant so long as he was not in Highbury.'

Marie looked at her daughter closely. 'You have missed him?'

She nodded. 'I had hopes … I *have* hopes … I expected my feelings to fade but I find … I find they have not.'

'I understand. We will say no more. But if you see him do please ask him to call on me here. I should very much like to see him.'

'His regiment arrives tomorrow. I believe he travelled in advance to make the arrangements. But I saw him at the Rookery; he must have some time for leisure, therefore I am certain he will be at liberty to call on you before you return home.'

Presently they joined the others in the drawing room where a footman proffered a silver salver and the butler served Madeira.

'The cook has sent up a tray of canapés,' Lady Cecily said. 'They smell quite appetising. I believe I will eat one—see how I am improved?'

'In all conscience, you have eaten enough arrowroot to last anyone a lifetime,' Mrs Bates said with a smile, 'it is no wonder that other fare begins to appeal.'

'I wonder what the food is like in Madras,' Lady Cecily mused. 'Douglas has been asked to consider accompanying Lord Macartney there as special attaché. Lord Macartney is to be the new governor of the East India Company, you know.'

'Indeed,' Mrs Poole replied. 'Well, that is a very great honour.'

Angus Fairfax had returned to his labours with Miss Poole. His hands toyed restlessly with one another as he spoke. 'The weather has been clement,' he observed desperately.

'Yes,' she replied in a wooden tone.

He waited for her to elucidate, but she remained tight-lipped.

'You have driven out a great deal, I conjecture?' he

tried, after a few moments.

'We have.'

Another pause.

'There are many places of interest in the environs I suppose?' he asked with a note of frantic enquiry.

'Indeed.'

Mrs Poole commenced a long account of the difficulties she had encountered in securing the correct type of feathers for a new hat. Miss Poole stared fixedly at a point on the turkey rug; she had heard this story before, knew its origin, its narrative and its outcome.

Angus Fairfax abandoned his attempts to draw her into conversation and took Jane into the bay window. 'I am so happy to see … to have this opportunity, I mean, of conversing with you,' he said, but a little tremor, a slight hesitancy in his voice suggested some trepidation also. His eye did not quite meet hers. 'I wished to enquire if that gentleman has continued to cause you annoyance.'

'Not me, but his step-mother is in no little quandary about him. They met this morning. Of course, I do not know what passed between them, but I have not known Mrs Sealy to suffer with a migraine before.'

'She might try valerian. It can be efficacious. I would suggest Oleum Succini also. It is not so much the tincture itself as the rubbing on the spine and neck that can relieve the symptoms. If Mrs Sealy has had a taxing morning it is likely tightness in the neck and shoulders that is causing the headache.'

'I will tell Hardy, her maid.'

'Which physician attends Mrs Sealy?'

'I do not know. While I have been with her, she has not consulted one.'

'I hope it is not Quake. He will drain her dry of blood and may even attempt blistering. I would not recommend that on any account.'

Jane nodded. She remarked that while Mr Fairfax spoke of medical matters his hesitancy of speech left him entirely. The light of shyness she had discerned in his eye had likewise disappeared. 'I have not seen you very much in society, Mr Fairfax. I conjecture you prefer your own company. You favour quiet and contemplation. And reading.' She cast a significant glance at his coat pocket.

He smiled ruefully. 'You have found me out, Miss
Bates. I do not have that easiness that my brother has,
and hardly any facility for small talk. My brother urges
me to dance, to drive out, to loiter in coffee houses
and waste away the afternoons at the circulating
library. But the talk there is all trifling and
inconsequential—not at all to my taste. And he forgets
that quite apart from my personal incapacity for empty
pleasantries, the apprenticeship he was so kind as to
buy for me must be earned out. I am not at liberty,
Miss Bates.'

'And when will you have completed your indenture?'

'Very soon—next month indeed.'

'And what is your intention? Shall you open your own
practice?'

'To wait on the worried—well, the gouty, the
dyspeptic and the liverish? Their cure is in their own
hands! No. I would work where I can do real good.'
He lowered his voice. 'I have low tastes, Miss Bates. I
prefer to serve the poor. I would rather tend a feverish
fisherman's daughter or a scalded kitchen maid than
any number of fine ladies and gentlemen who fancy

themselves ill when they require nothing but a regime of regular exercise and a plain diet. But,' with a sigh, 'there is no money in that.'

'I commend you for your altruism, Mr Fairfax. I hope you will forgive me if I speak out of ignorance, but surely it is not only the poor who suffer genuine illness. Everywhere in Brighton I see well-to-do ladies and gentlemen enduring real ailments.'

Mr Fairfax looked contrite. 'That is true of course, Miss Bates, and you do right to correct me. Certainly, there are those whose indispositions are serious and incapacitating. They have my compassion and shall have my prescription too, if they will take it.'

'And pay for it. The rich will pay for the poor. It is a happy compromise.'

'Would that it were so simple. But health—or, more accurately, illness—is a fashion these days. People fancy themselves ill when they do not enjoy perfect good health. But perfect good health is a fallacy. Was there ever a day when you felt wholly and entirely well? Is there not always a slight ache, a scratch, a knock, a bruise? Is not the stomach quite often unsettled? Do we not regularly find a little redness on the skin? Toothache, headache, a stiffness in a joint? These things are normal! The body is a wonderful entity, self-healing in the vast majority of cases.'

'*We are fearfully and wonderfully made*,' Jane quoted.

'Indeed we are! But I am afraid my profession panders to the quest for an ideal of healthiness. Quack cures and faddish treatments abound for the least rash or sniffle. Tinctures that are no more than coloured water are sold at extortionate profit to those who have no need of any medicine at all! There are so-called treatments that are not only without any benefit whatsoever but which it is a cruelty to inflict. Well,' Mr Fairfax concluded, 'I will not offer them. I fear that is not likely to make me a popular physician.' He paused, somewhat astonished by his own outburst. 'Forgive me, Miss Bates. I have become heated in my enthusiasm for my subject.'

'Please do not apologise, sir. I found your opinion most interesting, and your passion is refreshing. It is rare to converse on a matter with real feeling.' She cast a glance over her shoulder and dropped her voice, 'I find your conversation much more interesting than the latest fashion for millinery and the quantity of trimming that is quite proper for a lady's gown.'

Angus Fairfax gave her a genuine, open unaffected smile. 'Indeed. Will you take some more Madeira Miss Bates?'

'No thank you. I must return to North Street very soon. I have already been away more than the hour I promised. But you cannot be ministering to the sick all the time. What do you do for leisure?'

Mr Fairfax looked coy, 'In point of fact I am often in the library, but not where I can be seen. The upper galleries have books that are unsuitable for general reading. Mrs Widget in particular has a number of excellent and very well annotated books on botany. Nature produces her own medicine, you know Miss Bates.'

'I have often heard my mama say so, sir.' She held out her hand. 'I hope we will meet again Mr Fairfax.'

'It is my fervent wish,' he replied. 'For your company I believe I could endure society.' He looked across the room, 'I may even learn to love haberdashery.'

Jane withdrew her hand and went to say her farewells to Lady Cecily.

'Your mama says she must soon return to Surrey,' Lady Cecily said. 'I hope you will add your voice to mine. We must dissuade her, indeed we must. We need her here, do we not? I declare *I* cannot spare her.'

Indeed, Lady Cecily did look quite distressed at the thought; a slight pallor, a little trembling of the hands and the lip.

Angus Fairfax crossed the room to stand behind her sofa. 'Your own mama will return very soon, Cecily,' he said soothingly. 'In the meantime, Douglas and I are here to take care of you. And I dare say Miss Bates will call in when she can. She is the next best thing to Mrs Bates herself, I am sure. You will not be alone.'

Chapter 12

A week passed and Mrs Bates remained in East Street; Lady Cecily's claims, when added to her own desire to remain at least until she could secure an interview with Lieutenant Weston, presenting inducements sufficient to Mrs Bates to delay her departure. But a deterioration in the weather meant that she could not put off her journey above another fortnight. Hetty being in Highbury by herself was a strong enough incentive to her return, and, now that her mourning year was over, she was eager to let her engagement to Mr Knightley be known. She missed *him* a great deal, she found. Christmas could not come soon enough.

Whatever arrangements Mrs Sealy had made with her stepson, he did not confront them again in public, but neither did he leave Brighton. Jane saw him at the Assemblies, dancing with a succession of young ladies but most frequently with Miss Churchill. He stood head and shoulders above most of the other gentlemen—it was impossible not to see him—and although Jane resolutely kept her eyes away from him, she could not prevent some inner sensor from being aware of him in the room. Sometimes she felt that he watched her; she had a prickling sensation, a non-specific but quite definite sense that she was the object of somebody's scrutiny. When this perception overcame her she steeled herself not to look around, kept her eyes on the generality of the room or bent to murmur something to Mrs Sealy.

Miss Churchill was as cordial as ever; their conversation in the twilight of the Rookery might never have occurred. Jane found it difficult to believe that Arthur Sealy had reported Louisa Churchill truthfully—she saw no trace of condescension or pity in her manner. But the differences in their situations meant intimacy was impossible; as elegantly dressed as Jane might be—she possessed as many new gowns now as she had owned in the whole of her life before—and as socially accepted as Mrs Sealy's protégée, she had not the rank or the prospects of Miss Churchill who sought out the society of Miss Poole, Miss Abergavenny and the Honourable Lady Alicia Punnet.

Mrs Sealy seemed to Jane somewhat subdued. She laughed less and their outings lacked the carefree exuberance they had enjoyed in the beginning. Captain Bates was a frequent visitor to the house. Jane was not privy to their discussions but she gathered there was a difference of opinion between them as to how Arthur Sealy ought to be handled. She could understand how awkward this might be for her patroness—to ask advice but then find she could not quite agree with it. On the other hand, she hoped that the variance would disabuse the captain of the notion that Mrs Sealy harboured amorous feelings towards him; perhaps their friendship would cool. But she saw no hint of reserve between them when they met in town—which they frequently did. The captain and Mrs Sealy often found themselves drinking coffee together, seated side by side at concerts or partnered at cards. He exerted himself in her company, was charming and full of compliments. Mrs Sealy received all his blandishments with polite discouragement but he was by no wit deterred. For her own part Jane declined to be drawn by him into any further discussion about the wider Bates family, sent her mama's respectful regards but said it was unlikely she would be at liberty to meet him. There was nothing base about his character or his manners; he was greeted with eagerness by acquaintance, his company sought out, his conversation encouraged. No one seemed to particularly remark his extraordinary figure—Brighton was full of those recovering from injury or suffering illness. Bath chairs, crutches, limps and hobbles were commonplace, likewise a look in the eye that denoted inner turmoil, angst or a wounded heart. Though manifestly unable to partake in dancing both Captain Bates and Mrs Sealy were regular attendees at the Assembly, taking pleasure in the music, the company and even deriving vicarious delight in the energy of the set. There were many like them, who attended but did not dance. For such as these the Assembly offered cards, billiards and coffee rooms where conversation and debate were as lively—sometimes livelier—than the dance. Captain Bates was quite a conversationalist, energetic and erudite to a degree Jane would not have suspected. But she found that, for all his easy manner, she distrusted him and she distanced herself from him. It was easy to do so—Jane held herself at a distance from all the company; she knew her place. She stood behind Mrs Sealy who generally sat with the older ladies and chaperones at one end of the vast ballroom, ready to adjust a shawl or to summon a servant.

Occasionally she was sent with a message, begging some lady or gentleman to give Mrs Sealy the great pleasure of a few moments' conversation. When the time came, she would go ahead into the supper room to secure seats while Mrs Sealy was borne through the throng in the capable arms of Ironside. When not required she would allow her eyes to drink in the splendour of the ballroom; the beauty of the ladies, their gowns and jewels; the elegance of the gentlemen, some in evening clothes, others in uniform. Those in uniform attracted her eye especially and the ballroom was increasingly thronged with their number now that the Hampshires had joined the Dragoons and other regiments in the town. She was avid to see Lieutenant Weston once more.

Then, one evening, she saw him. Indeed, she almost ran into him. *En route* from the supper room on some errand for Mrs Sealy, she bumped into him in a passageway that connected with the ballroom.

'Lieutenant Weston,' she cried, her face betraying her enormous pleasure.

'Miss Bates!' His wide smile told her that his joy equalled hers, but he diffidently indicated his epaulettes and insignia. 'They have seen fit to promote me, you see. I am Captain Weston, now. But that is of no consequence. My mother informed me that you were come to Brighton. I believe your mother is here too. I did not expect to meet you at the Assembly, however. Do you have an evening's furlough?'

The passageway just there was quite narrow. Ladies and gentlemen came and went in and out of the supper room and a constant stream of waiters bearing trays pushed past them.

'Let us move to a quieter locale,' Captain Weston suggested, taking Jane's arm and guiding her into an antechamber. 'We can talk more easily here.'

'It is true that when I came to Brighton I expected to be much indoors,' Jane said, her voice suddenly seeming very loud in the comparative quiet of the room, 'very retired, restricted to reading and tucking in blankets. But my employer is a relatively young lady, incapacitated but very sociable. She is in the supper room now, quite the most animated and popular lady in the room. We have been regularly at the Assembly, and in other places. The Rookery, for example. I believe *you* went there last week.'

Captain Weston laughed a little awkwardly. 'I did indeed. That is, I looked in briefly. You saw me there?'

'I did. I glimpsed you fleetingly through the crowd. Were not the fireworks magnificent?'

'They were splendid. I am glad I saw them for I am told they were the last hurrah of the season. Brighton will get quieter from now on I believe. The London season begins and the fashionable ladies and gentlemen will transplant themselves there. You will remain, however?'

'I think so,' Jane nodded. 'That is, Mrs Sealy has intimated no other plans. She *may* decide to go abroad.'

'You will like that, Jane, will you not? I know how you long to travel.'

'Oh yes, of course. But it is for her to decide. And I hope, that is, it would not surprise me, if I were to be at Highbury again at Christmas.'

'At Christmas?'

'Oh yes,' Jane reminded herself that the plans of Mrs Bates and Mr Knightley were as yet strictly confidential. 'Last Christmas was so very wonderful, was it not? The snow, in particular, was …' she faltered, blushing, the memory of her walk with the captain very vivid in her mind, 'I recall it with great pleasure,' she concluded.

'I also,' Captain Weston said warmly. 'I would very much like to pay my respects to your mama. Where does she reside?'

Jane told him the address. 'She hopes to see you too. I do not know how much longer she will remain in Brighton.'

In the ballroom the orchestra struck up a new tune.

'I fear you must excuse me, Miss Bates,' Captain Weston said. 'I believe I am engaged for this dance. I must find my partner.' He took her hand and pressed it. 'I shall call on your mama. I very much hope that we will meet again.'

'It is my fervent wish also Captain Weston.'

A bustle at the doorway alerted them to a lady. She had entered unnoticed by either and must have overheard the last sentences of their dialogue. 'Captain Weston,' she said sharply. 'I am not accustomed to coming in search of my dance partners.'

'Miss Churchill,' Captain Weston said, dropping Jane's hand. 'Forgive me. I was just on the point of coming to find you.'

'Miss Bates,' said Louisa Churchill, 'how delightful it must be to encounter a friend from home. I am sure you and Captain Weston are very old friends indeed. Otherwise, it would have been rather scandalous of you to have been closeted in here with him unchaperoned.'

'Indeed, our families are intimately acquainted,' Jane cried, shocked and dismayed by Louisa's high-handed attitude, 'there is no whiff of impropriety.'

'None whatsoever, Miss Churchill,' said the captain smoothly, threading Miss Churchill's arm through his in a manner that Jane thought was authoritative but alarmingly familiar. They proceeded through the doorway. Jane heard Miss Churchill hiss, 'What were you doing with *her* James, when *I* have been waiting all evening for you?'

'How utterly charming you look this evening Miss Churchill,' was the captain's only reply.

Jane sank onto a chair to ponder the import of this exchange but was almost immediately disturbed by

Arthur Sealy.

'Excuse me,' he said, bowing. 'Did I not see Miss Churchill step into this room?'

'You did,' Jane affirmed, 'she has gone to join the set with her partner.'

'Oh.' Arthur Sealy looked disconcerted. 'I thought she was engaged to me for this dance.'

'It seems not. Perhaps the next?'

'Perhaps.'

Rather than quitting the room, Mr Sealy stepped further into it. 'But now that I have the opportunity of a private conversation with you, I will just hint that I am extremely unhappy about the involvement of your uncle in my stepmother's affairs. It seems to me that you and he are in league to deprive me of my inheritance.'

Jane stood up. 'I refute any such accusation,' she said stoutly, squaring her shoulders and looking him boldly in the eye. 'I pray you will let me pass.' She took a step or two toward the door but Arthur Sealy blocked her path.

'Not until I am certain that you understand me,' he

said. His great height seemed to fill the room. He stepped closer and, in spite of her courageous demeanour and brave face, Jane felt herself retreat. 'I have plans in train that require capital,' he said, 'capital that is rightfully mine in any case. I will not permit anyone to meddle, either your bloated bladder of an uncle or a chit of a girl like you.'

'Sir, you are unmannerly to accost me in this way,' Jane asserted, struggling to keep a note of panic from her voice. 'It is ungentlemanly of you. We are alone here. I am unchaperoned. You risk my reputation and your own honour, indeed you do. Mrs Sealy awaits me. When I am missed, she will send her man.'

'Ironside?' Arthur Sealy almost shouted. 'I have bested *him* before and could do so again.' He took hold of Jane's elbow and squeezed it until she felt the bones grate.

'You are hurting me, Mr Sealy,' Jane cried. 'I protest in the strongest terms!'

'Stop squirming then,' Arthur said, using the other hand to encircle Jane's throat. 'Spare me a kiss in token of our understanding and you will be quite at liberty.'

Jane turned her face as far away as she could. 'I will *not*,' she spat, but she was choking and must soon pass out.

'Unhand that lady,' said a quiet voice from the doorway.

Arthur Sealy spun round, releasing Jane's throat but retaining his grip on her arm. 'I will do no such thing at *your* behest,' he shouted, when he saw who stood there. 'Who will make me? You? I could snap you in half with this one arm. Leave us alone. This lady and I have business.'

'You are probably right,' said Angus Fairfax reasonably, '*I* would be no match for you. My brother, however …' He stepped into the room to make space for another gentleman whom Jane had never seen before. Douglas Fairfax was not as tall as Arthur Sealy but he was a great deal broader, more heavily built and very thickly muscled.

He carried a horsewhip in his hand. 'I will have not the least hesitation in using this,' he said, flourishing it menacingly, 'although I would rather follow the example of Jack Broughton and beat you with my fists.'

Ironside stepped into the room. 'I would be honoured to second you, sir, if I may be so bold.'

'Ha!' Arthur Sealy blustered. 'Three to one? Hardly London rules.' He let go of Jane's arm, however.

Angus Fairfax held out his arm and Jane ran into the shelter of it. 'Are you hurt,' he asked quietly into the soft hair above her ear.

'My arm, a little,' Jane admitted, 'but I am determined that he shall not make me cry.'

'Sir, will you give me satisfaction?' Douglas Fairfax roared.

'I will be duped by no conspiracy,' Sealy sneered. 'You,' he pointed at Jane, 'have connived this. It is a parcel with my suspicion. You will not get the better of me, by God.' He shouldered his way past Douglas Fairfax and Ironside and was gone.

Jane felt herself pressed into a chair and a glass of some strong spirit held to her lips. Some moments passed but she was unable to say if it was but a few or a great many. In the distance the noise of the orchestra and the exuberance of the dance continued unabated. In this it seemed that time stood still. 'I should return to Mrs Sealy,' she murmured at last, 'I will be missed.'

'Mrs Sealy is well cared for,' Douglas Fairfax told her. Her maid has been sent for. I need you to accompany me, when you are able.'

Jane turned in confusion. 'You came in search of me?'

'I came to remove a fish bone from someone's throat,' Angus Fairfax said. 'It was but by chance that I encountered Douglas. *He* came for you. There is news and your mama needs you by her.'

'News? From Highbury?'

'Indirectly,' said Douglas Fairfax. 'If you are ready, Miss Bates, I beg you will take my arm.'

The short journey to East Street was accomplished in silence. Both brothers were grim-faced. They mounted the steps to the front door, which was opened immediately by Mrs Brigham.

'Lady Cecily and Mrs Bates are in the drawing room sir,' she said.

The Fairfax's house was quite different at night. Candles burned in every sconce and from candelabra on side tables and pedestals, but the gloom seemed to press in from the high ceilings and corners. The servants were all in bed, a sole footman stood in attendance at the bottom of the stairs. The drawing room was well lit and a cheerful fire burned in the grate but the atmosphere had none of its usual easiness. Lady Cecily wore a long dressing gown. Her hair was loose. She had either been in bed or on the point of retiring. Mrs Bates was dressed but very pale; dark shadows hollowed her eyes. She clasped her hands tightly on her lap. At Jane's arrival she rose and rushed to embrace her.

'Mama, what has occurred?' Jane gasped.

'I know not. Mr Fairfax has received a letter the contents of which in some way concern us. Oh! Jane I am so frightened. He came in such a hurry—he still held the deck of cards he had been dealing, such was his haste—and he held a letter. Lady Cecily feared it was news about her mama—that she had drowned or come to other harm. But it touches *us*. He would tell me nothing until you could be brought. It has taken him an hour to locate you. I have been—oh Jane—I have been in a state of utter terror. And now you come with Mr Angus. What does it all mean?'

'I do not know Mama.'

'Please to sit down,' Douglas Fairfax said.

His brother poured brandy into glasses and handed them round.

'The letter is from my father. The man wrote there on another matter entirely and happened to mention … They must have had some business … but that is of no moment …'

'Douglas,' Angus said, taking his brother's arm and guiding him towards a chair. 'I fear you are making little sense.'

'Is it Hetty?' Mrs Bates said, though her voice was little more than a whisper. She found her mouth was parched. Jane clutched her mother's hand. Angus Fairfax moved from his brother's side to stand behind them lest either should swoon.

'Madam,' Mr Fairfax said, 'I have news from my father. News he received from …'

Mrs Bates swallowed. 'Highbury?' she croaked.

'From Donwell Abbey. It concerns your friend—and my father's friend—Mr Knightley. There has been a terrible accident. He is …'

'Dead?' Marie's lips formed the words, but this time

no sound at all issued from them.

'I fear, I very much fear … This letter has spent two days on its way. The letter my father received perhaps lay on his desk a while before he read it. The news may be days old.'

'It cannot be more than a week old,' Jane said, practically. 'Hetty made no mention of an accident when she wrote last week. And surely, if anything so serious had occurred, she would have written immediately?'

'She does not *know,*' Mrs Bates whispered, 'she does not know the particular reason why this should be of such moment to me.'

'No, Mama, of course.'

Mrs Bates said no more, but stared before her, Jane's hand still tightly held in hers. She refused more brandy. Her eyes blinked, but no tears came.

Lady Cecily wept, although the news did not affect her.

'The coach.' Mr Fairfax said, glad to have delivered the news at last and ready now to replace words with action. 'You shall have the coach to take you home. It shall be readied immediately and you shall be on your way in an hour.'

'Wake the cook,' Lady Cecily roused herself to say, with uncharacteristic practicality. 'Tell her to prepare food for the journey. Franklin shall see to your packing.'

'Mrs Bates, I beg the honour of accompanying you,' Angus Fairfax said. 'You cannot make this journey alone and it may be, when we get there, that Mr Knightley's condition is not so very bad. I may be able to help.'

Douglas Fairfax perused in his mind the contents of the letter in his pocket. A frayed rope, a heavy piece of machinery dropped, crushed limbs, concussion … It sounded very bad indeed, but he forbore to contradict his brother. 'An excellent notion, Angus,' he said.

'Yes,' Mrs Bates murmured presently. 'Yes. I must go home.'

Chapter 13

Angus Fairfax returned from Highbury not many days after he had departed for it, his arrival there too late to do more than witness Mr Knightley's passing. He called on Jane to deliver messages from her mama and as much detail as he thought wholesome. Mr Knightley had been beyond any kind of aid but had not suffered unduly at the end. He had known Mrs Bates when she knelt by his side, and smiled at her as she cradled John on her lap. Theirs had been the last faces to gladden his eyes before they clouded, darkened and closed.

'Poor George,' Jane lamented, 'was he not brought from school?'

'He was summoned, but did not arrive in time. He is quite the little gentleman, is he not? He did not cry where anyone could see him, but went immediately to visit the miller's apprentice who had also been injured in the accident.'

'That is just like George. And William Larkins is his particular friend. Will *he* recover?'

'He will now,' Angus said grimly. 'Mr Perry has much understanding of human nature but his belief in the power of a poultice is overly sanguine. The leg had a compound fracture! No poultice known to man or nature can heal a fracture, you know. I had to re-set it. Had I not done so it would certainly have required amputation. William was very brave.'

'And you left Mama …'

'In the good hands of your sister. Your mama intimated to me—very discreetly—the nature of her association with Mr Knightley. But we agreed it would do no good to broadcast it. Highbury mourns together—to all intents and purposes they are equally bereft. Mr Paling is returned from his honeymoon. Like a good shepherd, he comforts his flock.'

'It is just like Mama,' Jane said, 'she would not wish to be the object of anyone's pity, or to take to herself a greater share of sympathy. George and John should receive all.'

'They will do, of that I am certain.'

Jane allowed her tears to fall. 'Poor Mama,' she said. 'Her heart is broken for the second time. How will she bear it?'

Angus Fairfax reached out a tentative hand. It was cool, soft and very gentle. 'I will not deceive you,' he said in a voice that was all tenderness. 'She is laid very low by this tragic development, the more so perhaps because she cannot share the true nature and depth of her grief. But people do not die of broken hearts, Jane. She will recover, she will carry on.'

Presently he said, 'I very much enjoyed seeing Highbury, the places you must have played as a child, your church and the vicarage, your former home.'

'It is very pretty, isn't it?' Jane replied, wiping her eyes.

'Your family is thought of very highly. I went into Fords to buy a boot lace. Mrs Ford sang *your* praises for a quarter of an hour.'

'Oh, if you bought anything at Fords you will be welcomed in Highbury for the rest of your life,' Jane said with an attempt at levity.

'I certainly hope so.'

Three weeks had passed since that conversation and now a late October shower beaded the windowpanes of Mrs Sealy's house in North Street.

'I think I will not venture out this afternoon, Jane,'

Mrs Sealy said. 'My bath this morning and my meeting with Mr Shawcross has tired me more than usual.'

That work was on-going to resolve Mrs Sealy's difficulties with her stepson was evidenced by the frequent visits of Mr Shawcross—the sober suited gentleman—and the captain. Sometimes there were documents to be read over and signed. Jane had been called to add her name as witness on more than one occasion. Of the substance of the arrangements Jane had no knowledge but she knew the captain had his reservations about them—he called for consideration and urged caution, raised quibbles and caveats, but eventually signed the papers where indicated. Towards the end of that morning's business he had issued the promised invitation to his villa, to look over his collection. He had done so with a significant glance at Jane, bringing to her remembrance his mention of a gift, which had made her shrink with revulsion. It was this appointment to which Mrs Sealy now felt herself unequal.

'Yes Mrs Sealy,' said Jane, quite relieved to be spared the visit, 'I will write a note to the captain to inform him.'

'But if *your* captain—Captain Weston—wishes to escort you to the library, he has my permission,' Mrs Sealy went on. 'I like him very much. An unaffected gentleman, kind and agreeable.' She sighed. 'I wish Arthur would take a leaf out of his book.'

'Thank you, Mrs Sealy. But I expect he will be engaged with the Churchills. With Miss Churchill at least; she seems to require a great deal of his time.'

The ladies from North Street had happened upon Captain Weston and the Churchills several times, sometimes separately but more often together. Mrs Sealy had been charmed by the captain and by Miss Churchill also. Mrs Churchill she did not like at all, finding her cold and proud.

'I think,' she had confessed, following their happening to meet at the play, 'my liking for the captain stems from my desire to spite Mrs Churchill. Of course, I like him on his own account but *she* so obviously disapproves the connection that *I* am determined to like him just to defy her. Her lip is so permanently curled in contempt at him I fear it will need surgery to return to its proper shape!'

Arthur Sealy was another frequent companion of the

Churchills; he appeared to have attached himself to their party from the moment of their meeting at the Rookery. His presence made encountering the Churchills more awkward. While the rest of the party exchanged greetings he tended to fix on a point on a far rooftop and consider it with lofty abstraction until they could part. Jane was glad there was no need to engage with him—the very sight of him made her blood run cold. She was only surprised that Louisa Churchill tolerated him. She even broached the topic to Miss Churchill, thinking to warn her of Mr Sealy's potential for evil, the violence of his behaviour at the Assembly still very raw in her memory.

But Louisa had replied gaily, 'Oh yes! He is a sulky curmudgeon is he not? Eustacia likes him enormously—they are kindred spirits! But it amuses me to tease him.'

'I think you told me Louisa Churchill and Captain Weston became acquainted in Yorkshire?' remarked Mrs Sealy now, turning from the rain-splashed window. 'What a strange happenstance that the Churchills should remove to Brighton not two weeks before the transfer of his entire regiment here.'

'I am beginning to think it not such a happenstance,' Jane said sadly. 'I believe Miss Churchill engineered it all.'

It was undeniable that Miss Churchill considered Captain Weston in some way her own particular property. It had been him, Jane was convinced, whom she had been meeting at the Rookery and thus, on the evidence of her own words on that night, it had been on *his* account that she had carried her brother and sister-in-law the length of the country to Brighton. She monopolised him at the Assembly, cantered with him across the Steyne in the early mornings and went out into the Sussex countryside with him beside her in the curricle, absent, according to the Brighton rumourmongers, sometimes for many hours.

On his side Jane discerned no partiality. When asked he declared Louisa Churchill a spirited girl, very determined on her pleasures and hard to deny once she had set her mind on something, all of which Jane knew to be too true. He laughed away any suggestion that there was more to their association than a friendly acquaintance and pointed at the rumoured engagement between Miss Churchill and Mr Arthur

Sealy.

Inwardly Jane recoiled. Even if it removed Miss Churchill as a rival for James Weston's affections, she would not wish her connected to such a man as Arthur Sealy. Successive applications of arnica had reduced the bruising from her elbow but the joint was still very sore and the memory of the encounter pained her even more. Jane forbore to express her thoughts on this subject to Captain Weston however, musing only, 'I wonder that *he* does not object to your seeing so much of Miss Churchill if they *are* engaged.'

Captain Weston shrugged. 'Sealy is out late carousing and so stays in bed until the day is half done. He is not awake when Louisa Churchill wishes to go riding. In the evenings he would rather stand at the gaming tables than dance. Someone must partner her and it occasionally falls to my lot. There is very bad blood between him and your friend Douglas Fairfax, by the way. They almost came to blows again the other evening over a game of billiards.'

'I pray he comes to harbour no grudge against *you*,' Jane replied. 'I feel Mr Fairfax is well able to take care of himself …'

'And I am not?' Captain Weston laughed. 'Well, there is no denying Sealy is an intimidating figure. But do not worry, Jane, it will not come to that. Sealy has no reason to be envious of me.'

Jane believed him. A more determinedly tenacious girl than Louisa Churchill she had yet to meet. *She* was quite capable of manipulating everyone into her way of thinking and would certainly not stop at deceit if it meant getting her own way. But Captain Weston was the last man in the world to dissemble; she believed him incapable of a lie. Since her mama's return to Highbury Jane had enjoyed a half an hour's private talk with him on two or three occasions and it had seemed to her quite as though their relationship carried on seamlessly from the previous winter. They were as easy in one another's company, as interested in the same subjects. He held, for her, the same attraction, not only in his looks—which were pleasing—but in character and in his fund of interesting anecdotes. She never tired of hearing of his travels abroad and could listen to them hour by hour. For his part he seemed as pleased with her as previously; as eager for her company. Her status as a lady's companion was as immaterial to him as it had been when she had been a poor parson's daughter. He treated her as though she was quite on equal footing with the Honourable Lady Alicia Punnet or the Viscountess of Romford, lately arrived in Brighton for the treatment of spasmodic hysteria.

'Take my arm, Jane,' he had said to her on one occasion. 'I swear I grow three foot in stature when you do.'

Jane had felt as though she would melt into a puddle.

Mrs Sealy broke into Jane's reverie by saying with a heavy sigh, 'Oh, it has been pleasant at Brighton since you came, Jane. In sending you, the captain has proved himself a steadfast friend. I can count my present contentment from that moment. The sharpest pangs of grief at the Admiral's loss are behind me. Even Arthur, I hope, will not trouble me for much longer if, as I understand, he is to be married to Miss Churchill. I would not wish him on her but she seems to me to be the kind of girl who makes up her own mind. Perhaps she feels she can manage him. If I do not have mobility, I have relatively good health and plentiful acquaintance. We must count our blessings, mustn't we?'

'I pray your contentment will be of long duration Mrs Sealy,' Jane said earnestly.

'I will be content,' the lady replied with a shadow of a frown, 'but things may not continue just as they are.'

'How so?'

'Oh!' Mrs Sealy shook off her melancholy. 'The season is almost over. It always makes me a little sad. Already I see houses being closed up, carriages departing. Did you not think the ballroom much less crowded last evening? There were many more gentlemen—and most of those officers—than ladies. I almost felt ashamed that you did not stand up. It is not often that we see men sitting out dances.' She turned to look at Jane. '*Do* you dance?'

'I dearly love to dance,' Jane admitted.

'Then why have you not?'

'It did not seem … appropriate, or kind to do so.'

'Because I could not? I would not have minded.'

'It was not my place. I attend the balls to serve you, not to enjoy myself. That is not to say I do not enjoy myself by serving you. I *do,* very much.'

'I am glad of it.' Mrs Sealy turned back to the window, adding in a low voice, 'but things must change.'

'Change can be very pleasant,' Jane observed, determined to cheer Mrs Sealy if she could. 'Variety adds zest to life. We have been busy, out and about in society these last weeks. In contrast we will have a quiet and very enjoyable winter. When the weather is clement we will go out and take the air, with no crowds to contend with, no difficulties about finding the most advantageous spot for sketching. I have yet to see the white cliffs—how dramatic they will be, with the spume of the winter tide at their foot! When it is too stormy to go out we will remain here to read and enjoy the comfort of the fire. Perhaps we will have company—those who, like us, are permanent residents in Brighton—for tea and cards. Even for dinner. In Highbury that is how the winter passes, in the company of good friends and neighbours. Then, when spring comes and the visitors return and the Assemblies re-open their doors we will be refreshed and ready to throw ourselves into the season.'

'Perhaps,' Mrs Sealy murmured, but doubtfully.

There was silence between them for a little while. Jane

had half promised to call on Lady Cecily if Mrs Sealy had no need of her, but something restrained her. She felt there was a matter on that lady's mind that troubled her.

'It is none of my business, of course,' Jane observed, 'but I wonder if the business over Mr Sealy troubles you.'

Mrs Sealy sighed. 'I will own to you Jane that it does. He expected the whole of his father's estate and instead has had to make do with only half while a young widow stands between him and the remainder. It could be many years before he comes into his full inheritance. Of course, it makes him bitter.'

'You have no sympathy for him, surely,' Jane cried. 'In my opinion you have treated Arthur Sealy with far more generosity than he deserves.'

'I do see his predicament, Jane. I feel myself a cuckoo in his nest.'

'If he marries Miss Churchill, he will have no need of funds from you. Miss Churchill will be very comfortably provided for.'

'It appears Mr Churchill is disinclined to hand his

sister over to a man without a shilling.'

Jane frowned. 'I am surprised. I had not imagined Mr Churchill to make quibble over money. I presumed he would give Louisa's hand to any man she chose, if she loved him and he was convinced she would be the happier by it.'

Mrs Sealy considered. 'Perhaps he is *not* convinced and makes this difficulty in order to hamper the engagement.'

'I think Mr Churchill does whatever his wife tells him, on the whole.'

'Oh? So you surmise this application comes really from her hand? Ah! If I had realised, I might not have … but what's done is done,' sighed Mrs Sealy.

Chapter 14

'I wish we could go to London,' Eustacia Churchill said. 'It is November—the season there will be at its height. I am sure we have quite exhausted the diversions of Brighton. What say you, Mr Sealy?'

Arthur Sealy stood before the grate in the Churchill's house in North Street, his coattails parted to feel the benefit of the fire. 'I hope I have made my sentiments clear, madam. Where Miss Churchill goes, I will follow. Unfortunately, my wretched stepmother continues to make difficulties over finances. Until they are got through, I dare not remove myself. There is no knowing what she may do if she feels my eye is not staring fixedly at her.'

'Is she really as devious as that? To defraud you of your rightful inheritance would be a shocking crime.' Mrs Churchill poured tea and stirred it. 'At my urging Charles has written to her requesting clarification. You know that you have *my* endorsement, for what it is worth. You are worth ten of … other so-called gentlemen who have dared to look as high as Louisa's hand.'

'Only ten?' Arthur Sealy drew himself to his full height before stooping to take the tea she proffered him.

'Exactly. You make my case for me. *You* have unexceptionable pedigree, excellent education and irreproachable manners. It is only the matter of funds …'

'Funds will be forthcoming. I have said all I can to convince Mr Churchill of it, but the widow prevaricates. It is the very last hurdle that must be got over before my engagement to Louisa can be announced and, in all conscience, it is a comparatively small one.'

'*Very* small,' Mrs Churchill agreed, 'trifling, indeed. But Charles *will* have things tied down to a nicety. In point of fact though, Mr Sealy, I believe there is one more obstacle to be got over. Louisa has not yet absolutely given you her hand.'

Arthur Sealy caught sight of his reflection in a mirror and admired himself thoroughly whilst pretending to be absorbed in smoothing a stray hair over his forehead. 'That too is a triviality,' he said smugly. 'In truth, until step mama has come to the point, I have felt it wrong to urge my case with as much forcefulness as I wish. It seems dishonourable until I know I have Mr Churchill's complete sanction, which must come after Mrs Sealy lets her intentions be known.'

'It is precisely that honourable restraint that makes me esteem you so highly, Mr Sealy. For myself, I am convinced that you are the perfect husband for Louisa.' Mrs Churchill paused. A shadow of malevolence crossed her face. 'She is headstrong, you know. In my opinion she has had far too much of her own way. *You* are not a man to indulge her, I think.'

'Certainly not.' Arthur Sealy put his cup down. 'No one wants a spoilt, wilful wife. I will bring her …'

'To heel?' Mrs Churchill interrupted, with vindictive relish.

'Round to my way of thinking, I was going to say,' Mr Sealy demurred, with a cold, self-satisfied smile

Voices in the hallway without announced the return of Mr and Miss Churchill. They came into the room flushed with exercise, their clothes be-smattered with mud.

'Oh, we have had a simply splendid day, have we not Charles,' cried Louisa, falling on the plate of muffins. 'I am so glad you have not eaten all of these, Eustacia. I could not have borne to wait five minutes for some fresh ones to be sent up. I am famished.'

'Louisa, you eat like a farmer's daughter,' Mrs Churchill scolded. 'Here. Take a plate and a napkin, for heaven's sake.'

Louisa settled herself with more decorum on a low stool.

'Good afternoon Miss Churchill,' Mr Sealy said. 'I trust you enjoyed the hunt. Did you find a fox?'

'*Two* foxes, both in the same copse. One went to ground but the hounds got the trail of the other. Charles and some of the others took the higher ground. I took another route, leaping two fences and a stream and rather annoying a farmer when we crossed his ploughed field.'

'You did not give chase alone, Louisa?' Mrs Churchill said.

'Of course not. I was well chaperoned. Lord Macartney, Mr Fairfax and Captain Weston were all with me. They said to a man that they had never seen a woman ride with such daring. Pour me some tea, if you please Eustacia. Charles, you had better ring for more muffins if you want any. I have eaten all of these.'

Mr Churchill rang the bell. 'Have you been here long, Mr Sealy? Did you call on a matter of business?'

Sealy shook his head. 'I called by arrangement with Miss Churchill. I was to drive her to Chalybeate this afternoon. I fear she forgot our engagement.'

'It was not quite definitely agreed,' Louisa replied with a little simper, 'I believe I said I *might* accompany you, if the weather was fine.'

'And the weather *was* fine,' Mr Sealy said coldly. 'I really did expect you to honour your agreement.'

Louisa shook her curls, which were becomingly tousled. 'I preferred to go hunting,' she said airily.

'Upon my word, Louisa,' Mr Churchill chided, 'if I had known you had made arrangements to accompany Mr Sealy I would not have agreed to your going hunting.'

'I had not absolutely made arrangements …'

'Mr Sealy believed you had,' Mrs Churchill said. 'He

has been waiting this hour and a half.'

'Did *you* not wish to accompany him, Eustacia?' Louisa enquired artlessly.

'*I* was not invited. If I had accepted such an invitation nothing on earth would have prevented me from fulfilling my obligation. It is disrespectful, Louisa. Frankly, it is insolent.'

Louisa put her plate down and rose to her feet. 'I do most humbly beg your pardon Mr Sealy,' she said with specious contrition. 'I misunderstood the nature of our discussions the other day. I thought them tentative and speculative. I will not do so again.'

Arthur Sealy looked down on her with a haughty expression. 'You have much ground to make up, Miss Churchill. Nothing will assuage my disappointment of today other than that you sit next to me at Lord Cumberland's dinner and dance with no other partner afterwards.'

Louisa curtseyed. 'Very well, Mr Sealy,' she said.

The maid answered Mr Churchill's summons and brought with her a letter on a silver tray. 'Delivered by hand this afternoon, sir,' she said.

'A letter?' Mrs Churchill cried. 'Why was I not informed? In Mr Churchill's absence *I* can attend to any correspondence, girl. You should have brought it in here. What is it, Charles? Let me see it?'

Mr Churchill perused the lines quickly and handed his wife the paper. 'Your step-mother requests an interview,' he said to Arthur Sealy. 'I am to call on her tomorrow.'

'*We* are to call on her,' Mrs Churchill corrected him. 'I shall not allow you to attend alone. There is no knowing what she might attempt to get past you.'

'I doubt not that there is a similar missive at my lodgings,' Arthur Sealy said. 'Surely she would not attempt to make negotiations with you behind my back?'

'From what you tell me that is precisely what she may attempt,' Mrs Churchill put in. 'You should certainly be present. Do you have a lawyer?'

Sealy waved an imperious hand. 'I need none. If I have not the wit to speak for myself in this matter I deserve to be bamboozled by that scheming woman.'

'I cannot see how this pertains to us at all,' Miss

Churchill declared. 'It is between Mr Sealy and his step-mother.'

'It may relate very nearly to us—that is to say, to *you*—Louisa dear, if you choose.' Mr Churchill said. 'Mr Sealy has made his intentions very clear.'

'Nevertheless,' Miss Churchill said, suddenly very serious, 'I advise Mr Sealy to deal with his step-mother on his own account.'

Arthur Sealy stepped across the rug to where she had retreated in the bay window and took her hand. 'It is my fervent hope that *my* account will be *your* account before very long, Miss Churchill.'

Miss Churchill sighed. 'I know you have said so,' she demurred, 'but I have made no promise.'

Mr Sealy bent down so that his mouth was close to her ear. 'But you shall do,' he whispered, gripping her hand very hard.

'Mr Sealy,' Miss Churchill began, attempting to remove her hand from his.

He turned her hand over with a roughness that went beyond the playful. 'Look at this,' he said with artificial joviality, 'your hand is caked with dirt from the hunt.

Let me clean it for you.' He produced a handkerchief from his pocket and wiped assiduously at her palm.

The following morning an interview took place between Louisa Churchill and her brother. She had managed to secure him alone—Mrs Churchill being engaged by the Viscountess Macartney to consult on an important question of braid trimming—and was determined to take advantage of his freedom from his wife's interference.

'Charles I am happy to have this opportunity to speak to you alone,' Miss Churchill began.

Mr Churchill put aside the newspaper he had been reading and gave her his attention. 'Indeed, Louisa?'

'Yes. I wish to speak to you on a matter close to my heart. It concerns my marriage.'

Charles Churchill leaned back in his seat. 'You have accepted Arthur Sealy then?'

Louisa shook her head. 'No, I have not. I do not wish to marry Arthur Sealy.'

'There is no requirement that you should do so, Louisa. There is no pressing need that you should marry anyone, if you do not wish.'

'But I *do* wish to marry, Charles. I wish to marry very much. It is only that Arthur Sealy is not the man I have set my heart on.'

Mr Churchill nodded sagely, and picked up his teacup. He almost wished his wife was present. She was much better at managing Louisa's whims than he. 'And who is that lucky fellow?'

'Captain James Weston. You know how taken I was with him when we were introduced at the hunt ball at Enscombe and I subsequently found myself frequently in his company …'

'I am fully cognisant of the progress of your acquaintance with Captain Weston, Louisa. I have observed it with some concern, and so has Eustacia. I realise now our sudden and urgent removal to Brighton was not wholly unrelated to the transfer of his regiment here.'

'A happy coincidence,' Louisa said with a coy smile.

Mr Churchill sighed. 'And he has asked for your hand?'

'Oh no. He is too respectful, too conscious of the great disparity in our situations. He would not presume … unless he was encouraged. If *you* told him, dear Charles, that my happiness being your chief object you have no objections to the match …'

'But I *do* have objections, Louisa. Captain Weston is a most amiable gentleman. Honourable, I have no doubt. An excellent officer—everything that is respectable and worthy. But Louisa, he has no family. You can look higher—much higher. His people are in trade—successfully perhaps—but in trade. He has neither birth nor fortune.'

'And neither did Eustacia, come to that. As to fortune, his family is better situated than you might think; better, I think, than Eustacia's. But he has other qualities that I esteem more highly. I love him, Charles. I want to be his wife and, in short, I am determined to have him.'

'And I am determined that you shall not,' said Mrs Churchill from the doorway. 'Charles, I can hardly express my disappointment that you have allowed yourself to be drawn into this conversation without my being present. And how dare you stand by and allow my parents to be impugned, categorised with quarrymen and lumber-traders, which I believe is the trade of the Westons. *My* father is the cousin of a baronet.'

'A distant cousin,' Louisa murmured. She had been pacing the room, energised by her attempts to bring her brother round to her way of thinking but she sat down heavily now. Mrs Churchill's arrival had put an end to her hopes; she knew she would not prevail with her brother now.

'As to *your* determination, lady,' Mrs Churchill went on, moving further into the room. 'Mr Sealy is determined to have *you*. He has left me in no doubt of his decided inclination or his resolve.'

'Mr Sealy has a bad reputation,' Louisa said. 'He is not gentle. He keeps bad company.'

'And no wonder, when you leave him to cool his heels for weeks on end,' Mrs Churchill exclaimed. 'You have been remiss in your handling of him, Louisa. When he is married, away from Brighton and established in your own property you will see any little wayward tendencies utterly eliminated. *I* already have him eating out of my hand, as gentle as a lamb.'

'*You* marry him then,' Louisa retorted.

'Now you are being ridiculous. Mr Sealy is an unexceptionable gentleman, very well connected, with what I understand to be a sizeable fortune and more to come.'

'You understand from *him*,' Louisa pouted.

'Nevertheless,' Mr Churchill said, moving across to where Louisa sat and kneeling down beside her. 'You do not have to marry Arthur Sealy. I place no compunction on you to go against your own inclinations. But you will cease to think of Captain Weston. You would have to have sunk very low indeed to consider such a match.'

'You would indeed!' Mrs Churchill crowed. '*I* would not sanction such a match unless he was the only man left in England who would take you. And I assume we are *very* far from that eventuality.'

Louisa remained silent, her eyes fixed ahead of her at the fire irons.

'Louisa?' Mr Churchill's voice was gentle, infinitely kind. 'We *are* very far from it, aren't we? There is no … pressing necessity for a marriage, is there?'

'Oh!' Mrs Churchill shrieked. 'Well, if she has debased

herself not even the quarryman's son will take her. We will be lucky if the chimney sweep will so much as look at her.'

Louisa was silent for a long while. She met no eye in the room but continued to give the grate her unwavering attention. Her expression was not one of defeat nor one of defiance but rather of someone calculating at great speed, considering possibilities, rejecting some and accepting others.

'Louisa?' her brother repeated.

'No,' she said at last, her voice very low. 'Go and speak with Mrs Sealy. If you are satisfied by what she has to say I will consent to marry Arthur.' She turned to look her brother square in the eye. 'I place myself in your hands. I tell myself that whatever occurs you will have my best interests at heart, Charles. I will always be able to rely on you.'

'Naturally, my dear sister.'

'There now,' Mrs Churchill said, throwing up her hands. 'Sense at last.'

Miss Churchill rose from her seat and walked slowly towards the door. She stopped close to where her sister-in-law stood. 'I am resolved that in the future you will point to my engagement to Mr Sealy and know that it was *your* guidance and advice that brought me to it, Eustacia. Let that be a truth mutually acknowledged between us: *you* were the author of it and I bowed to *your* urging. Oh, Eustacia, I am determined that you shall have the everlasting satisfaction of it!'

'I suppose that is as close as I will get to thanks,' Mrs Churchill said when Louisa had left the room. 'Ah well, she has made the right choice at last. Now Charles you must put on your coat. We are due at Mrs Sealy's in half an hour.'

At the appointed time Mr and Mrs Churchill presented themselves at Mrs Sealy's door and were on the point of being admitted when, to their considerable surprise, they were joined by Miss Churchill.

'My future hangs on these discussions more than anyone else's. It is entirely appropriate that I be present.' she said as she breezed past them into Mrs Sealy's hallway. 'Since I am to be bartered over like a prize sow I might as well parade in the ring.'

'Louisa' Mrs Churchill cried, 'you shock me beyond

my ability to articulate—such a disgusting analogy.'

The housekeeper informed them that Mr Arthur waited in a small ground floor apartment and opened the door to show them in.

'I do declare,' said Mrs Churchill when she viewed the gathering within, 'we should have hired one of the rooms at the Ship Hotel. I was not aware that this was to be a public meeting.'

'*You* make an addition we had not expected madam, at any rate,' said Mr Shawcross from behind a large desk. 'Good morning Mr Churchill. Miss Churchill. I believe you know Captain Bates?'

Captain Bates, from the reservoir of his wheeled chair, said cheerfully, '*Woe unto them that seek deep to hide their counsel.*' He swivelled his eyes towards where Arthur Sealy lounged against a bookcase, 'Madam, the more people who witness a thing, the less chance for obfuscation later.'

'I hope you do not suggest that *we* would pervert proceedings,' Mrs Churchill retorted.

'I suggest nothing, ma'am,' the captain warbled. 'I merely speculate on the reason for your presence and seek to explain my own. *I* am here to provide witness, nothing more.'

'Well, I did not think you were here to provide ornament,' Mrs Churchill muttered.

'You are a meddler, sir,' Arthur Sealy said, savagely.

'Oh! Mr Arthur,' the captain chuckled good-naturedly. 'How you do divert me. But,' more seriously, 'since you mention it I do undertake to protect your step-mother. Who else has she? She is at the mercy of every rogue and charlatan.'

'You are in no position to bandy words, sir,' Arthur Sealy spluttered.

'Alas,' the captain smiled, blandly, 'words are all I *can* bandy.'

Mr Sealy seemed surprised and not altogether well pleased to see Miss Churchill but drew a chair forward for her. 'Since you are here, you had better be seated,' he said, pressing her into it.

'Gentlemen,' Mr Churchill said, shaking hands with all present, as affable as always. 'Let us be business-like. We do not know that there will be the least controversy.'

'You do not know Mrs Sealy, I think,' Mr Sealy observed darkly.

'Sir,' said Mr Shawcross, 'you would do well to kerb your spleen until Mrs Sealy has outlined her proposal.'

'Very well. I can just as well give vent to it afterwards,' said Arthur with a shrug. He folded his arms across his chest and purported to give minute attention to an area of gilded cornice above the fireplace.

Mrs Churchill remained by the door, unseated. 'You might do *me* the courtesy Mr Sealy offers Louisa, Charles,' she said sourly, 'before glad-handing the rest of the company.'

Mr Churchill showed his wife to a seat but she declined it, selected another, declared it too draughty and had at last taken a third when the door opened again and Ironside carried Mrs Sealy into their midst. It was as though she brought a small tornado with her. Everyone—excepting the captain—rose, lifted by some invisible current of energy. Mr Shawcross was drawn from behind the desk. Arthur Sealy crossed the room towards the fireplace but had scarcely reached it before abruptly changing direction. He circled, pacing restlessly as though in a vortex, his agitation belying his outward calm. Louisa Churchill fluttered helplessly on an eddy of fuss and kerfuffle, now in the bay window, now by the bookcase. Mr Churchill anchored himself to the captain's chair in order to manoeuvre it into a less inconvenient position, a task that proved impossible until Mr Shawcross gave his aid. Mrs Churchill was washed in a tide of movement into a corner where she almost dislodged a bust from a pedestal. Furniture was shifted, supernumerary tables removed, a fire-screen brought in. Mrs Sealy was at last arranged to her satisfaction and Jane, who had entered in Mrs Sealy's wake carrying a small footstool, disposed her skirts decoratively over this last addendum. When the commotion calmed Mrs Churchill discovered she had been relegated to the window seat, almost behind the curtain. Miss Churchill was next to Mrs Sealy, Mr Shawcross back behind the desk. Arthur Sealy and Charles Churchill stood either side of a Chinese lacquered cabinet. The captain basked where he had been placed which was, in point of fact rather too close to the fire. Jane retreated to the door but Mrs Sealy's, 'Wait. Jane dear, I would have you remain,' halted her retreat. She stayed beside Ironside who took up his habitual position by the door.

Arthur Sealy looked loftily over the assembly. He had wished for a private interview with his stepmother at which he could impress his wishes upon her very forcefully. It was imperative that he squeeze more funds from the widow—his gambling debts were mounting and he knew he would not secure Miss Churchill's fortune without a substantial sum to show in return. But the presence of the Churchills tied his hands; he dared not alienate them by a display of vitriol. But he worried that only vitriol would serve him to get what he so desperately needed. It mattered to him that Louisa—now she was here—should see him very much master of the situation; it would not suit his purposes to allow her to believe he could be cowed to any degree. He mulled these things over to himself as Mrs Sealy fussed and prevaricated and found himself very desirous of smashing his fist into something either very soft and vulnerable—the captain's bloated face would suit the purpose—or something brittle and fragile. He eyed the trinkets in the cabinet with a venomous eye.

'Mrs Churchill,' said Mrs Sealy, acknowledging that

lady with the faintest inclination of the head, 'I had no inkling that I would have the great honour of your company today. You are so much in demand by the first tier of Brighton society I had hardly dared to hope to be the recipient of such great condescension.'

'A family matter such as this,' Mrs Churchill crowed from her seat at the far extremity of the room, 'is of such peculiar importance that nothing less than the whole family is required to undertake its management. *Our* family feeling is very strong. It is perhaps something you have not experienced.'

Mrs Sealy made no reply but turned instead to Louisa. 'My dear,' she said affectionately, taking Louisa's hand. 'How delighted I am to see you.' The warmth of her smile and the demonstrative press of her hand undid Miss Churchill's brazen facade. A glazed eye and a slight tremble in her lip declared the delicate balance of her emotions. 'I want you to know, my dear,' Mrs Sealy went on in a confidential tone, 'whatever transpires you may always come to me if you find yourself in any kind of need.' Her gaze slid across the rug and rested on Arthur's boot. Her meaning, to Louisa, was very clear.

'I can conceive of no circumstances in which Louisa will need to come to *you*,' Mrs Churchill chimed. 'She has recourse to her own family.'

'Ironside,' Mrs Sealy said, 'please shut the window. I hear noises from the street. It is most disconcerting.'

Ironside crossed to the window but found the sashes firmly closed. He adjusted a clasp however and lowered a shade by a fraction of an inch.

Mrs Sealy turned her attention to her stepson. 'Arthur,' she said, holding out her hand, 'will you not bid me good day? I hope I find you very well.'

Reluctantly, Mr Sealy stepped forward and took the proffered hand. He bowed over it stiffly and resisted the urge to crush the delicate fingers in his grip. He said only, 'Tolerably well, thank you,' before retreating to his position beside the cabinet and adopting an expression of haughty boredom.

Mr Churchill came forward in his turn. 'Good morning,' he said with infinitely more warmth. 'I thank you most sincerely for responding to my note so promptly.'

'Its arrival was very timely,' Mrs Sealy acknowledged. 'I

have been putting matters in place this month or more past,' she said, 'since Arthur was so kind as to inform me of his return from the continent. It just so happens that the final details were settled yesterday.'

Finally, she smiled at Captain Bates. 'Good morning Captain,' she said, 'how very well you look this morning, your complexion quite flushed with health. And is that a new waistcoat? I like it exceedingly.'

The captain fairly quivered with pleasure but made no reply.

The room settled. A clock ticked and then chimed the hour.

'Mr Shawcross,' Mrs Sealy said quietly. 'Perhaps you would begin.'

Mr Shawcross cleared his throat. When he spoke he addressed the whole room but his words pertained solely to Mr Sealy. 'Mrs Sealy calls you to witness that she has made a new Will. She invites you to peruse it if you wish. There is but one beneficiary, with the exception of some small bequests to family retainers. That beneficiary is the son of the late Admiral Sealy. Miss Jane Bates and I witnessed her signature yesterday.'

'A Bates family conspiracy,' Arthur Sealy drawled, inspecting his nails. 'I expected as much.'

'Mr Sealy, I think you should wait until Mr Shawcross has finished,' Miss Churchill said quietly. 'There may be more to hear.'

'Indeed, there is,' Mrs Sealy murmured.

'Well then,' Mr Sealy said sulkily. 'Let us hear it.'

Later that afternoon, Mr and Mrs Charles Churchill took the air on the Steyne. The space was deserted now, the games and diversions having been cleared away. The weather was stormy but no rain fell. They walked with difficulty, buffeted by a strong wind from the ocean, Mrs Churchill's bonnet threatening continual defection. On the bathing beach the machines were empty, lined up and stored for the winter, the horses and bathing women gone to other work. In contrast the soldiers' encampment was busy; orders were barked and men marched. The blacksmith's anvil rang out a steady clang, clang, clang like a knell of doom.

Mr Churchill indicated the activity in the camp. 'In spring they will sail to the Americas,' he said, his voice struggling to make itself heard above the wind. 'The war there goes very ill for us, I am told. The enemy uses under hand tactics—night raids and ambushes. They do not fight by the rules. The government prepares to re-supply Cornwallis as soon as the winter storms subside.'

'I hope Captain Weston will be amongst those on board the fleet,' Mrs Churchill said. 'The greater distance that can be got between him and Louisa, the better.'

Mr Churchill patted her hand. 'I think she has seen sense, there, Eustacia. I believe we will be troubled no more by that young man. A pity, though. I rather liked him.'

The tables and chairs that had been outside Mrs Widget's circulating library all season were stacked away. The library remained open, however, and the Churchills made their way towards it. Above them gulls circled and keened on the rain-laden wind.

'I hope we can remove ourselves to London now,' Mrs Churchill said. 'I am heartily sick of Brighton.'

'I suppose we can, now. I consider Mrs Sealy has been more than generous,' said Mr Churchill. 'I was not aware that she had already settled half of her husband's legacy on Arthur—to add a further quarter is handsome of her. My assessment is that he has received £15,000 in all. He cannot in all conscience plead poverty *now*. Indeed, I would have thought £10,000 quite sufficient for any gentleman to live on very comfortably. I rather wonder he felt the need to press her for more.'

'I think it is the very least she could have done,' sneered his wife. 'Any decent woman would have handed the whole of the fortune over the moment the admiral had breathed his last. They had been married but a year. Really, she had no claim to it.'

'How then would she have supported herself my dear? I fear you are a little uncharitable to Mrs Sealy.'

'How did she support herself before ensnaring him? She must have money of her own.'

'I hope she has, Eustacia, for I surmise her establishment will have to be condensed after this. She cannot possibly continue in the same style on half the income.'

'I doubt not she has that revolting captain in her sights,' Mrs Churchill said with a decided shudder. 'A disgusting toad of a man! He will be her next victim.'

'I thought him quite genial.'

'You are no judge of character, Charles. If not for me you would not have entertained Mr Sealy as a suitor for Louisa's hand. It was *my* discernment that saw his potential. You were all for sending him packing.'

'I do not know that my fears were entirely unfounded,' Mr Churchill demurred. 'Mrs Sealy let slip one or two very decided hints I thought. She talked of wishing to deter Arthur from a course of which his father would not have approved, of wanting very much to see him live honourably and respectably—as though he has not been, heretofore. And then there was her suggestion that I do not absolutely release Louisa's fortune until such time as I see the marriage is a success. She must have reason for such reservations, don't you think?'

'Indeed, I do,' declared Mrs Churchill sharply. 'Her reason is that she is vindictive and devious. She seeks to excuse her own indefensible behaviour in stealing Arthur's fortune by impugning his good name. I have no doubt she married the admiral for pecuniary motives. She threw herself—a helpless cripple—onto his honour, knowing full well that she would outlive him by many years.'

They had reached the library. Mr Churchill took hold of the door but before opening it he said in a confidential but firm tone, 'It may be that she does not have good health, Eustacia. Her writing a Will is evidence of that. And while it is reassuring to see with our own eyes—as you insisted upon doing—that Arthur is her sole beneficiary, I would not by any means wish for her demise.' He cast a significant look behind them, where Louisa and Arthur Sealy walked arm in arm. 'If our families are to be allied, it is better that there be no animosity. I ask as a great favour to me that you try to overcome your dislike of Mrs Sealy.'

'Upon my word, Charles, I believe she has cast her spell on you,' Mrs Churchill replied. 'Now let us go inside. This wind is insupportable. We will have to send for the carriage to take us home.'

Although he would never own it, Arthur Sealy felt extremely relieved by the outcome of the morning's conference. His pecuniary difficulties could now be put at such a distance that they would cease to be of any material inconvenience and would be eradicated altogether once his marriage to Louisa Churchill took place. He was certain he could hold off his creditors until that day, which he was determined would be very soon indeed—by Christmas, or earlier. He had not the least fear that Charles Churchill would withhold an iota of Louisa's fortune, regardless of his stepmother's mischievous suggestion to that effect. Charles could not stand up to his own wife, let alone such a foe as Arthur would prove himself to be if crossed. Mrs Sealy's having left him—beyond any doubt, alteration or reverse—the remainder of his father's money in her Will was pleasing. If she lived frugally the capital could have doubled by the time she died but on the whole he would prefer her to die soon and leave less—*that* would make his triumph over her complete.

He drew Louisa's arm more securely through his. 'Miss Churchill,' he said very soberly, in a tone he intended to be stern and intimidating, 'It was quite wrong of you to attend this morning's theatricals. Your presence embarrassed me to some considerable degree.'

'How so?' Louisa queried.

'Because you ingratiate yourself with my step-mother. Indeed, it seemed as though you would take her part against me. It weakened my hand considerably. I could not have been seen to challenge her without insulting you.'

'I hoped my being there would soften her,' Louisa

pouted. 'Indeed, I believe it did, a little. Do you not think she has been generous?'

'Very generous, to allow me my own money,' Mr Sealy said. 'She has managed to embezzle only a quarter of it. I would have pressed her for more.'

'For more? You would have left her destitute?'

Mr Sealy snorted. 'She would not have been destitute. A woman always has the means to make a living.'

Louisa gasped. 'You would reduce her that far?'

'She is already so reduced, in my estimation. What she did before she will do again. But we will speak of her no more.'

'You have a very low opinion of women,' Louisa said, so quietly that the wind drowned out her words.

'What is that you say? I wish you would not mumble, Louisa.'

'I said I hope to raise your opinion of women,' she revised.

They had come to a low wall that separated the Steyne from the beach. A very few fishermen were at work on their boats. The waves crashed upon the shore, dragging and pushing the shingle restlessly to and fro.

Louisa pulled off her bonnet and allowed the wind to pull her curls from their restraints. The lace at her throat flapped and frothed, revealing a rapid pulse in her neck.

'In my opinion you are the ideal of womanhood, Miss Churchill,' Mr Sealy said, looking down at her with a mixture of complacent admiration and barely suppressed passion. He wanted very badly to grasp her hair and pull her towards him but he resisted the temptation, pointing instead at the men on the shore. 'I have been fishing with those men,' he said. 'From boyhood I was up before dawn and out on the sea with them before the earliest kitchen maid was astir. My father encouraged it—it was what he had done in his boyhood. But the fishing is tame, Louisa. The mackerel throw themselves onto the lures. They do not even require bait, so eager are they to be hooked and killed and gutted and eaten. It is no sport at all and, to me, the fish is tasteless. Off the coast of Spain, I went fishing with a different kind of crew. They sail far out to sea, to where the ocean is unfathomably deep. They fish with lines—their hooks are baited with whole fish. They hunt with guile, offering and then withdrawing the bait, bringing the prey closer and closer. And then they strike, and it is a battle of strength and endurance that can go on for hours. The fish they catch are leviathans, ten or fifteen feet in length. They fight with all their might against being conquered. Oh, Louisa, *that* fish is heavenly to consume, satisfying. A man can gorge himself and still want more.'

'You compare me to a fish?'

'I do.' He looked down on her, his face austere and very resolute, his jaw set, his eyes steely as fishhooks. 'I give you fair warning, Miss Churchill. I will lure you in. I will subdue you. You may fight as long and as hard as you wish but in the end, I will land you on my deck and then ...'

'And then?'

He bent over her so that his head obscured the iron sky, the spume of the waves, the uneasy beach. She held his gaze although it was penetrating and terrible.

'You know what.' He slipped his arm about her waist and pulled her roughly into his embrace. His kiss was very fierce, his breathing rapid, his arms like iron bars from which there was no escape. His hands caught at her hair, pulling it until tears seeped from the corners of Louisa's tightly closed eyes.

When he at last pulled away she touched a tentative hand to her bruised lips before summoning a reserve of spirit. 'I might refuse,' she said baldly.

Arthur Sealy laughed. 'For a while yes. I hope you do! That will make the victory so much sweeter. But you will submit at last. It is expected. To run around with me as you have—unchaperoned, heedless of both our reputations! Not to marry me would tarnish your character beyond recovery. You would be called a flirt. Indeed, you are already known to be wayward. Honourable Mamas look askance at you. I do not think they would sanction their sons to court you. If you jilt me, Louisa, I will make sure that no decent man ever looks at you again.' He held his hands out, indicating the broad stretch of beach, the Steyne behind, the shops and houses within easy view. '"Making love in broad daylight, she was as wild and eager for it as a bawd in a brothel." That is what they will say.'

Louisa blushed but held her head up high. 'I see the only way to thwart you is to acquiesce without a fight.

Do you wish to marry me?'

'Yes, I do.'

Miss Churchill shrugged. 'Then let it be so,' she said, turning and walking away.

Chapter 16

Some few days after the matter of Arthur Sealy's settlement had been concluded, Jane and Mrs Sealy sat at breakfast. If Jane had hoped to see an improvement in Mrs Sealy's spirits following the close of the business, she had been disappointed; something still troubled her mistress. The weather had turned wintery and unpleasant and they had been forced to remain much indoors. Even with fires in every room, thick wraps and hot soups, Mrs Sealy found the cold seeped into her limbs and exacerbated the aches and pangs that attended on her incapacity. In her own mind Jane felt sure that a removal abroad was on Mrs Sealy's mind. Except that it would separate her from Captain Weston, Jane felt no qualm about such a move, indeed, she longed for it, especially if it would alleviate her friend's suffering. She wondered if she should offer some reassurance on this point but felt it precipitate—she must not presume to form part of Mrs Sealy's scheme to quit Brighton. In any case, she did not wish to divert or delay her patroness from whatever it was on the tip of her tongue to say.

That she was on the point of saying something was very evident. Mrs Sealy was distracted, hesitant, on the cusp of a decision, an explanation, some momentous sentence, but holding back. Mrs Sealy kept taking a breath as though in preparation for speech, beginning several times, 'Jane, I …' but then breaking off again. She leafed through her post, crumbled toast upon her plate, peeled but did not eat an apple.

'Jane dear,' she began again, 'I wish to speak to you upon a matter …' but a knock at the door and the entrance of Ironside with a tray bearing a baker's box put an end to her discourse.

'Compliments of Captain Bates, ma'am,' Ironside said, with a wry eyebrow—who else would have sent such an offering?—placing the box on the table.

Mrs Sealy peered under the lid. 'Oh,' she said heavily, 'custard frangipanes. The captain must intend a visit. Well,' she pushed her plate away, 'I had better prepare myself.'

She rang the bell and Ironside returned. 'Please ask Mrs Mallard to have the fire in the downstairs sitting room lit, and coffee served, and these, I suppose,' she indicated the cakes. 'When you have dressed, Jane, please attend me downstairs. Bring some sewing or a book and ensconce yourself in the window seat. I do not think I can face the captain on my own and,' with a sigh and a sad smile, 'I may as well tell you *both* what is on my mind.'

Some half an hour saw the ladies in readiness and following the smart rap of the captain's cane on the door and the usual bustle and effort attendant on his arrival—straining, puffing liverymen, the squeak and complaint of his chair, the meticulous arrangement of his dress and the draping just so of the silk scarf across his stump—he was ushered into the room. His eyes were all for Mrs Sealy and he did not remark Jane in the recess of the window.

'My dear, *dear* Mrs Sealy,' he croaked, holding out his hand to her, 'I trust I find you well. Such unpleasantness as you have had to endure. But it is over now. He will be gone soon, to Yorkshire, I presume?' He gave a shudder that sent his jowls wobbling, 'Not a climate to suit *us,* I think? Anyway, far *far* from where he can trouble you.'

'Captain Bates,' said Mrs Sealy graciously, 'you are very kind. I must thank you most sincerely for your assistance in the matter. Yes, it is a relief to have it over with. I own it distressed me a great deal. I so wanted to do the *right* thing even if the right thing for him should have such deleterious consequences for *me.*'

'Oh,' the captain waved a dismissive hand, 'as to my assistance, it was nothing. I made no secret of the fact that I thought you too generous, my dear. So now you find that you are materially harmed by the transaction? Ah,' with a sad shake of the head, 'I feared as much, indeed I did.' The captain's chair had been positioned close to Mrs Sealy's so that she could serve the refreshments without assistance. He extended a fat hand, placed it on her arm and gave it a stroke, a gesture of sympathy but redolent also of a connoisseur assessing the quality of a precious artefact. Mrs Sealy moved her arm away and reached for the coffee pot.

'Ah!' Captain Bates' eager eye lit on the plate of fancy cakes, 'Have you partaken? The pâtissière has the lightest hand when it comes to almond essence and the custard is superb.'

Mrs Sealy offered the plate and the captain took a pastry, scrutinised it closely, sniffed it and finally popped it into his mouth. 'Mmm,' he said, through sugar and crème patisserie, rolling his eyes in a sort of ecstasy and holding his hands out as though in worship, 'you will not join me?'

Mrs Sealy shook her head and sipped her coffee. 'I have only just breakfasted.'

'That young man,' opined the captain when he had swallowed the cake and wiped his mouth and chins with a fine lawn handkerchief, 'has no notion of the kind of lady he has been blessed with as a step-mama. He needs flogging. His father would have done so, I think?'

Mrs Sealy smiled. 'If the admiral had been alive there would have been no dispute, no cause for bad behaviour and therefore no need for flogging. Arthur did not like the idea of his father marrying but he would have come round, I believe. Oh!' with a heavy sigh, 'in losing the admiral I also lost the possibility of a son. I *would* have treated Arthur as a son, you understand, knowing I would never be blessed with my own.'

'You *have* treated him as a son, dear lady. No natural mother could have done more than you have done, I assure you.'

'And then,' Mrs Sealy went on, 'Arthur reminds me of the admiral. Apart from the difference in their ages he is the facsimile of his father in looks. To see him, to have some regular intercourse with Arthur would have been a balm on my grief, I believe.'

'In looks,' the captain demurred, 'but not in character.' He ventured to put his hand again upon Mrs Sealy. 'I hope, that is, I wonder, if there are not others—that is to say, one other in particular—who might bare closer comparison to the late lamented admiral. In character, I mean. Is there not some gentleman of equal standing …' he faltered on his theme, realising, perhaps, his unfortunate choice of word, ' … that is to say, of comparable gentlemanlike qualities, of similar integrity, of equivalent *moral* stature that might venture to place himself in the admiral's stead in your affection?'

Mrs Sealy studied a flounce on the sleeve of her gown and did not reply.

Captain Bates rolled forward a little in his chair and brought his face closer to hers. 'There is *certainly* one,' he went on, 'who would replace him there if he could.'

'The admiral was a very fine man,' Mrs Sealy

murmured, 'so caring and capable, a protector, very strong and, for a lady such as I …'

'No one could understand as *I* do just what you mean,' Captain Bates said warmly. 'I, who have been the carer and the cared-for.' He looked down at his person partly in shame and despair but also with a kind of pride. 'My body is broken, as *yours* is, but I have the heart of ten men. My power to love is undiminished, the more so that I have not given my love to any other. It is as fresh and whole today as it would have been if I had met you forty years ago. Ah! That my body was as complete. Then I would show you what love could be!'

He sat back in his chair, exhausted by the strength of his feeling and the effort of his declaration. Mrs Sealy fiddled with the cups on the table at her side. Jane sat in the window seat with her breath held in, her novel unopened in her hand.

Presently Mrs Sealy turned to the captain with a bright smile. 'I doubt not your great capability for love,' she said, quite conversationally. 'Are you quite warm enough? I can ring for more coals. I confess I find this weather most disconcerting. English winter does not agree with me. I fear I must go abroad.'

'Oh!' the captain exclaimed, but with a quizzical contraction of the brows that indicated he had not expected this turn in the topic, 'precisely my intention. I am considering …' he narrowed one eye speculatively, 'Switzerland, perhaps?'

'Very pleasant,' Mrs Sealy said, noncommittally. 'Lucerne was delightful, last year.'

'Ah yes, Lucerne, to be sure. One longs to sample authentic Swiss chocolate. And the strudel, I am told, is nothing short of sublime. Do you have a lodging in mind?'

Mrs Sealy gave an affected start of surprise. 'Do *I* ..? But my dear Captain, I thought we were discussing *your* travel plans. *I* shall not return to Lucerne.'

The captain pressed his lips together in confusion, nonplussed by Mrs Sealy's statement. She took advantage of his hesitation to offer the cake once more. The captain took one and considered it again. 'The frangipane is really everything one could desire,' he mused. 'One ought not to have another but … well it is hard to resist. Do you remark the moistness of the crumb? Mmm. Exquisite. So,' he licked his fingers assiduously before going on, 'forgive me, ma'am, I am somewhat confused. Perhaps I have not made myself quite plain.'

'You have made yourself very plain Captain,' Mrs Sealy replied with a little note of shrillness in her voice, 'I can be in no doubt that you consider the frangipane very fine indeed. I think you will enjoy Switzerland very much—their desserts, you know, are …'

'Madam,' the captain interrupted with a little bark of laughter somewhere between bewilderment and astonishment, 'I fear I really must be expressing myself very ill indeed, or we are at cross purposes entirely. I wish to offer …'

'*My* plans,' Mrs Sealy said abruptly, 'are very much undecided at present. There are many considerations to weigh but one point upon which I have resigned myself is that I must quit this house. It simply cannot be afforded now and must be let next season. The income will be essential.' She gave the captain a very straight look. 'My capital is *much* reduced, you understand. I must retrench.' She turned her head slightly so as to encompass Jane in her next remark. 'Staff will have to be let go. It is all very distressing; to be quite frank with you Captain I am broken hearted about it.'

This, then, Jane realised, was the news that Mrs Sealy had been trying to convey. She—Jane—would not be going abroad, she would not even be able to stay in Brighton with Mrs Sealy, even in a smaller household. It was a bitter blow. She felt no resentment towards Mrs Sealy and only a little anger towards Arthur Sealy whose machinations had brought things to this pass. She leaned back against the window casement and gazed down to the street below. From where she sat North Street led east towards the Steyne where the dragoons were on parade. She could hear the blare of the bugle and the beat of the drums. Captain Weston came to her mind—not that he was ever very far from it—but he came more forcefully now. If he were to offer his hand Mrs Sealy's situation would be set at naught. It was not that Jane did not care about Mrs Sealy—she did care, very much—but it would not affect her. Her love for him and her future were bound more tightly; he *was* her future.

The captain put his head on one side, as astonished for his part as Jane was. The extent of Mrs Sealy's impoverishment was wholly unexpected. 'Are things as bad as that?' he asked.

Mrs Sealy nodded. 'Quite as bad. My choices are limited. I could take a lesser house here in Brighton, or I could go abroad where I can live more cheaply still.'

'*My* house …' the captain began, but half-heartedly.

'Oh yes,' Mrs Sealy said, deliberately misunderstanding him, 'houses in your locale are more affordable, being that short distance out of town but,' she indicated her lifeless limbs, 'the adaptations required, the narrow stairs. And then,' she shivered, pulling her shawl more closely around her shoulders, 'the cold …'

'To be sure,' the captain said, thoughtfully, 'the cold, and the expense … It is not what one had quite understood. And you do not think that *two* could keep each other … more comfortable?'

The clock on the mantel struck the hour. Mrs Sealy said, 'It has been such a comfort to talk these things over with you Captain Bates. I expect the masseuse at any moment. Thank you so much for your counsel. Jane! Please ring the bell for Captain Bates' conveyance.'

Jane emerged from the window seat and pulled the bell. She found she could not quite meet the captain's eye. His discomposure was plain to see.

'I have been quite lost in this novel,' Jane said, indicating her volume, even though it being closed gave the lie to her words. She showed it to Mrs Sealy. 'I do most heartily recommend it to you ma'am. The last hour has flown by and I have been oblivious to all else but these pages. Good morning to you, Captain. Thank you so much for your kindness.' She took up a confectionary and bit into it. 'Mmm. Delicious! Ah! Here are your attendants sir.'

When the captain had departed Jane took Mrs Sealy's hands in hers. 'I quite understand,' she said simply. 'You have been too generous to Arthur and now you must pay the cost. Do not concern yourself about me. Whatever happens I will treasure these months I have spent with you. Your kindness to me has been extraordinary and I will think of you with great fondness always.'

A tear slipped from Mrs Sealy's eye. 'Oh Jane,' she said, 'I have been dreading telling you. So much that is precious must be forfeited but some things are a sacrifice too far. Do you understand?'

Jane had but a vague comprehension of her meaning. 'The captain is genuinely fond of you, I believe,' she hazarded, 'but there was the slightest hint that money—though not his first object—was not quite his last. Regardless, if I must give an opinion, it is that to sacrifice yourself to *him* would be unthinkable. One can be poor *and* happy.'

'Yes Jane,' Mrs Sealy said earnestly. 'Poor *and* happy.'

Chapter 17

High Street

Highbury

Dear Jane,

I am sitting at the table in the parlour. Last week Martha placed a hot serving dish directly upon it and now there is a scorch that I fear will never be removed. Mama almost lost her temper with Martha—I have never seen her so angry although I suppose she has sometimes had cause. I am sure I have given her cause on many occasions! Mama is generally so mild and forgiving, though, is she not? It was quite out of character and I own to you it worried me considerably. Mama and Martha have tried a number of remedies on the scorch but to no avail. Mama became quite tearful at one juncture when I suggested a French polisher be got—more evidence that she is not herself. A French polisher cannot be afforded of course and it was very silly of me to propose it. The money you send augments our housekeeping and we are very grateful for it especially as there seems to have been some oversight at the bishop's office these past months and we have not been in receipt of our allowance. I told Mama she should make enquiries but she refuses. I tried placing a bowl on the spot, and then a vase of flowers, but the scorch is in such a position that does not lend itself naturally to that kind of ornamentation, so, for now, we have spread a cloth over the whole table as though we are perpetually in readiness for dinner. I have to explain to everyone who comes that they are not disturbing us, have not called at an inconvenient time and our dinner is not imminently to be served. Mama says it is not necessary but I see them glance at the cloth and draw their conclusion. I am particularly eager that we should have as many visitors as possible. They cheer Mama. She is never more jovial than when we have company although sometimes her spirits are depressed afterwards.

I think she misses you very much, Jane, and although I would not have you feel one whit guilty or remorseful on her account at your being in Brighton and not here, I feel you should know. I feel, at least, that I need to tell you. It relieves my mind even if it burdens yours. I am sorry, but there it is.

It is that cloth that we used at the vicarage, the one with daisies embroidered on it. I always liked it so it is a pleasure to me to have it here and to see it every day. Perhaps it will give you pleasure to think of it, and of us, here in Highbury.

Mr Sparks has come to Donwell. He is the cousin of Mr

Knightley who was to have inherited before the squire married and produced his own heir. Mr Sparks is a small, neat gentleman in his early thirties, very quick and quietly spoken. He reminds me of a sparrow, or perhaps a wren. It occurs to me that with the age disparity between him and the squire he must be a second cousin, or a cousin once or twice removed. Mr Knightley's immediate cousin would be closer in age, would he not? I must enquire next time I see him. His wife is a timid woman—like her husband in every way—clearly quite over-awed by Donwell and their new position there. She does not take to the role comfortably. Mrs Lemmings tells me she is frequently lost for hours, bewildered by the size of the house and the layout of the rooms. She is very kind to little John Knightley, however and John is her constant shadow. Mr Sparks refers to his position as temporary guardian—he does not at all presume to step into the squire's shoes, which I think very sensible of him. Who could? Abel Larkins guides him on matters of the estate—left to himself I do not know how Mr Sparks would manage as he has no experience of these things. I think by profession he is some kind of clerk. Grief in the village is still very keen. I notice Mr Knightley's grave has fresh flowers every week although nobody has owned to me who places them there. Mama has been repeatedly invited to Donwell Abbey but refuses to go. She has not even visited poor William Larkins. I think *this rather unfeeling of her; poor William. He is likely to walk with a limp for the rest of his life. How he will manage the ladders in the mill I do not know. However, I know I must rejoice that he will walk, and with his own two legs, for if your Dr Fairfax had not been here I am certain that one of them would have been lost. Mama walks a great deal but never in the direction of Donwell. She has taken to visiting Mrs Goddard at the school and the two are becoming intimate friends. I am glad of it but Mrs Goddard is a very young woman, much nearer to my age than to Mama's, and I had felt a friendship burgeoning between us which seems now to have cooled. But I do not begrudge Mama Mrs Goddard's company.*

We expect General Bramhall at Randalls daily. The scaffolding is down and gardeners have been attending to the grounds. Mrs Lemming tells me that a new housekeeper is come. I will call upon her when I have liberty, and encourage Mama to accompany me. I doubt not that the Bramhalls will consider themselves above the rest of Highbury society. Perhaps they will seek the acquaintance of the Claytons of Clayton Park. I presume them to be exactly the degree of persons that Mrs Winwood would have courted, had she still been here. Thankfully Hermia Paling is quite without social ambition. The Bramhalls must accept her as they find her.

There is a tiny cut in the hem of the cloth that you did with some scissors when you were very small. I recall it very vividly. Mama was angry then, too, but not with you. I had left the scissors out. She said it was a miracle you had not cut your fingers off with them. I have been inordinately careful of scissors ever since; I always replace them in my sewing box, or at least I always mean to do so but then find I have put them on the mantel or the dresser. Once I found a pair in my pocket. I have quite a horror of lost scissors but mine frequently do seem to be lost. I do not know how it comes to be so when I am quite determined always to put them away.

The feud between Mrs Hopley and Mrs Cropley shows no sign of abating. I called at the mill to see how William Larkins does but he has been removed from there to the Larkins' house so I was unable to ascertain. Everything at the mill is in devastation. Mr Hopley tries to make good the workings but his understanding of the new engines is vague—only Mr Knightley really understood them I think. The people at the forge are happy to lend aid but so much was damaged in the accident and I do not think anyone really has the heart for it. People go to the mill at Clayton for their flour now. Mrs Hopley told me of all this—her heart is heavy indeed. She is not sure if they will be able to remain. The difficulty with Mrs Cropley adds to her unhappiness. I could not say too much either in the way of sympathy or of blame as it is still unclear to me who has offended whom. I think the truth is that they have both now offended each other—words have been said that cannot be unsaid. What I have ascertained is that a jar of gooseberry preserve is at the heart of the disagreement. I know both ladies entered their gooseberry preserve into the village show and that Mrs Hopley won first prize. I am not surprised as her preserves are always exceedingly good. She is kind enough to send us jars from time to time. Gooseberry is not my favourite—I dislike the colour—but there is no gainsaying it for flavour. Mrs Hopley hinted to me that Mrs Cropley's preserve is too tart and she pulverises the fruit too much. She says it lacks texture. Perhaps that is what she told her sister. After visiting Mrs Hopley and gathering this much intelligence I made it my business to visit Mrs Cropley and brought the subject—with admirable subtlety—round to the subject of preserves. She was very warm on the subject, saying that Mrs Hopley makes her preserve with more sugar than necessary because it is the only way she can get it to set, Consequently it is more of a jelly than a preserve and ought to have been disqualified on that basis. Mrs Wiggins, the rector's wife at St Michael's in Kingston, was the judge at the village show. I will walk to Kingston at the first opportunity to canvas her opinion on the subject.

Mrs Cropley's bunion is somewhat improved. The unguent your Dr Fairfax recommended seems to have been very efficacious although she complains of the smell.

Mrs Cole and I are a good deal together. She says she has no patience for gooseberries in any form and only ever serves strawberry preserve, if she serves any at all. So far the promised addition to their property has not materialised but they hold very comfortable and informal musical suppers and I am frequently amongst the guests even though I have not a tuneful note in my body. Mrs Cole is passionately fond of music. To be sure there is not quite enough room for the grand pianoforte in the parlour and when she plays all of the gentlemen and some of the ladies are obliged to stand as there is not enough space for sufficient chairs. I am powerfully reminded of Mrs Winwood's musical soiree. What a fiasco! It is still spoken of in the village with great amusement, but of course not in Mrs Stokes' hearing. I learned that Simon Stokes has escaped transportation. He is at a gaol in the north doing hard labour. I doubt we will see him in Highbury again. So far Mrs Cole's musical evenings have not attained that height of drama or disaster and I can only say that I think it a very good thing.

I have just blotted the cloth with ink. Mama is out. I do not know what to do for the best. In my panic I threw a jug of water

on it but the water only spread the stain. I think I shall lay a
new cloth and ask Martha to wash this one. I know it is
deceitful of me not to own my clumsiness to Mama but her mood
at present is so unpredictable that I confess to you Jane I rather
quail at the prospect. Perhaps she will not notice the new cloth.
She cannot escape noticing the wet patch on the rug, though. I
will have to think of some way of explaining that.

 Hermia Winwood—or Paling, as she is now—seems
comfortably settled at the vicarage. I call on her often. She has
planted a new apple tree where the old one used to stand—the
one her mama so cruelly and heartlessly had felled. At my urging
Hermia intends reinstating also the climbing hydrangea on the
north wall. Mr Paling does very well. He is liked by all. He has
been frequently to call on Mama and she seems able to talk to
him with a frankness that must relieve her mind. She does not
speak much to me other than of everyday matters. I try to keep
up a cheerful line of chat to fill the silence—talking is no
hardship to me, you know. But sometimes Mama does not seem
to even hear me. I wonder if she is going a little deaf?

Mr Woodhouse's new property grows prodigious! I walk in that
direction most mornings and have got onto quite cordial terms
with the stone masons and carpenters. Mr Pole, the architect,
even asked my opinion yesterday, about the staircase which is to

lead to the gallery. 'Oh, Mr Pole,' I said, 'do not ask me for I know nothing about it. But for heaven's sake do not put in any unexpected stair at the turn. There is nothing so potentially injurious or more likely to cause a trip than a stair one had not expected, particularly where there is a shadow or a pool of gloom.' He seemed to be quite of my opinion and I am certain that Mr and Mrs Woodhouse will have no unforeseen hazards—no gloomy passageways or accidental steps—such as what I endure on a daily basis.

Miss Wix, who is to be Mrs Obadiah Ford, is come to Highbury. She lodges with Miss Grace the seamstress until the wedding, which is to be on Boxing Day. Mrs Ford tells me that she and Mr Ford will retire to a cottage. Apparently, Mr Ford is passionately fond of growing sweet peas and wishes to spend his retirement propagating them. Mr Obadiah and the new Mrs Ford will take over the business. Indeed, I already see her hand at work—a new window display with fresh ribbons and the season's latest gloves. But no hats, as yet. From the small amount of conversation I had with her after church she seems a serious, strait-laced young woman. For a milliner, her bonnet was very plain, hardly trimmed to any degree. I am sure she is an excellent young woman but she did not seem to me to be of a nature to much alleviate Mr Obadiah' spirits, which we know can be rather surly.

Christmas is almost upon us. I do not suppose we will be invited to Donwell this year. Mama and I will spend the day quietly here, and think of you with warm affection,

With which I also sign myself, dear Jane.

Hetty.

PS Mama noticed the cloth immediately. She is not very angry. She declares she never cared for it anyway.

Chapter 18

'I have had a letter from my sister Hetty,' Jane told Captain Weston as they walked one morning along the cliff path. The day was bright but very cold. Jane wore a new shawl—very thick and warm—a gift from Lady Cecily to whom she had become, in recent weeks, warmly attached.

'And I from my mother,' Captain Weston said with a laugh. 'Would it not be interesting to compare their news? I expect you know of the forthcoming nuptials of Mr Ford?'

'Indeed!' said Jane. 'Hetty says Miss Wix is a serious young woman. That will suit Mr Obadiah, I think.'

'My mother is of the same opinion. What other news does Miss Bates share?'

'Apart from a great deal about a tablecloth, which I will not bore you with, she says poor Mrs Sparks is finding it hard to feel at home at Donwell. She will not entertain at Christmas; at least, Hetty does not expect to spend Christmas there,' said Jane, thinking the while very warmly of the previous Christmas, when she had first seen and danced with the captain—then the lieutenant—in Donwell's lofty hall.

'My mother intends to invite them to dine with her—the Sparkes and your mother and sister I mean—but everyone's thoughts will be with the Knightley boys,' Captain Weston said. 'I never was more shocked or dismayed in my life when I heard about the squire's untimely death.'

'Nor I. My mama has been laid especially low by it. Hetty's report of her is—not encouraging. She and the squire were very old and intimate friends.'

'I am most conscious of it,' Captain Weston said tenderly. 'I pray that when you write to Mrs Bates you will convey my particular regards and good wishes.'

They came just then to a narrow and treacherous part of the path and were silent while they negotiated the sharp stones and muddy puddles.

'Tell me,' the captain asked when they were on safer ground, 'how do you like Brighton now the crowds are gone? Do you not miss the Assemblies and activities on the Steyne?'

Jane considered. *To everything there is a season,* she

quoted. 'I confess I enjoyed the bustle and excitement very much, the splendour of the balls, the promenades, the thrill of the races and the bizarre spectacles to be seen. Now Brighton is all but closed up I find the place has natural charms and attractions. They were obscured by all the carnival of the season but are quite as enticing. This walk, for instance, is one of my favourites. I never tire of looking at the sea and it is very pleasant to find oneself away from the crowd, one's thoughts not intruded upon.'

Her companion halted. 'Do *I* intrude, Miss Jane?'

She smiled. 'Not at all. If there is one person I would choose ...' she paused, aware that she had been about to reveal rather more of her feelings than was appropriate. 'Who else is there to remind me of home?' she concluded, avoiding his eyes.

They walked together in silence for a time. The path narrowed and they were obliged to walk in single file. Jane's next words were thrown over her shoulder. She would not be able to see Captain Weston's expression as he received them or replied, but neither would he be able to see hers. She was glad of it. She could not be sure her face would not betray her. 'Speaking of nuptials, it is very certain now that Miss Churchill will marry Mr Sealy?'

There was neither hesitation nor quaver in his voice as he replied, 'I believe so. They are in London, I think. I presume the ceremony will take place there.'

'I think so too,' Jane said, relieved beyond words, 'but I have no absolute knowledge of it. Mrs Sealy and her stepson are not close. He does not keep her informed. He has not so much as sent her a note to thank her for her great generosity to him.'

The path widened once more and Weston came up alongside her. 'That is very poor form,' he said.

Jane went on, 'Yes, and the consequences to her are legion. She has been forced to retrench. Her house will be let next season. At present she is in two minds as to whether to take a cottage—it cannot be in the fashionable streets of Brighton; the prices are prohibitive. Captain Bates, who lives a little out of town, says lodgings can be got there for a reasonable sum. But her incapacity means that no ordinary cottage will do. She must have Hardy, her maid, and Ironside, even if she has no other servants.'

'And what is her alternative course?'

'To go abroad. A villa in Italy, perhaps. One can live cheaply there, but it will have to be somewhere therapeutic aid can be got, which will not be easy to achieve, I think. Mrs Sealy depends upon the medicinal baths, you know.'

'I see her quandary. And what about you, Jane?'

They had reached the headland. A large boulder provided a convenient seat and, it being dry, Jane and the captain perched upon it. The view was quite magnificent; Brighton laid out behind them, the endless sea before, the crashing waves below.

'I do not know,' Jane said at last. 'Mrs Sealy hopes to retain me but I see that her hope is vain, based on her desire rather than on any real practicality. If her house cannot be afforded, her second carriage, her parlour maid and under-groom, how can I? I serve no practical purpose, as they do.'

'You bring her companionship and great comfort, I am sure,' the captain cried. 'I can think of no better friend for a woman like Mrs Sealy. And I am sure you do not eat much.'

'I am quite ready to take a reduction in my stipend,' Jane said. 'It is generous, considering she leaves me nothing to spend it on. I send most of it home. But,' with a sigh, 'she will not hear of it.'

Captain Weston consulted his pocket watch. 'We should turn back. It will soon be Mrs Sealy's breakfast time.'

'She breakfasts from home today. She has been invited to her friend Mrs Pelham's. The Pelhams depart Brighton tomorrow for Low Meade, their country estate. I think they are the last apart from the Fairfaxes. *They* must remain on account of Lady Cecily's health. She must not attempt the journey even as far as Woodley Court. It would be too dangerous for her. All the lodging houses are shut up but theirs.'

'If you are at liberty then, I invite you to be my guest at Mrs Kent's coffee house. She serves an excellent breakfast. You shall have a cup of chocolate, if you desire. It will be just the thing after this bracing walk.'

Jane readily acquiesced to his invitation and they began to make their way back along the cliff- top. Jane walked behind this time, admiring the set of the captain's broad shoulders, the crisp cut of his uniform, the curl of his hair on his collar. To her left the precipice of the cliff was only a step or two away. She imagined straying too close, a stumble, his swift reaction, being gathered into the safety of his strong embrace. The idea of it made her knees buckle, her heart race. In spite of the cold air, she felt her face burn.

The path widened once more and the captain stepped between her and the edge. 'Take my arm Miss Bates,' he said, 'I would have no mishap occur while I am your guardian.'

She slipped her arm into his and they walked along comfortably for a while. 'I hope you do not leave Brighton,' Weston said quietly, 'even if it is to return to Highbury. It is likely that in the spring my regiment will sail to America as part of the re-supply. Until then I would be pleased to have your companionship from time to time. If we cannot go to Highbury, then perhaps we two can bring a little of all that is special about Highbury here.'

'I would like that,' Jane said, her voice almost trembling. 'Especially because it is Christmas and *last* Christmas was so very … I mean I have particularly happy memories of it.'

He pressed her hand warmly. 'Yes. And so do I.'

Presently, emboldened, Jane said, 'You have no regret concerning Miss Churchill? Your heart is not bruised?'

Captain Weston did not laugh her question away, as she had expected him to. 'I will own to you Jane that while my heart is not wounded my pride is, a little. Louisa and I were compatible, I think. We would have made a good match. I did not allow myself to fall in love with her because I knew her brother would not allow the alliance. That is a source of disappointment to me. The disparity in our situations was a barrier *they* could not overlook.'

'Equality of rank can be a sound basis for marriage,' Jane observed, 'but I do not think it is the only one.'

'Neither do I.'

Jane took a deep breath. 'But you did not love her?'

'No,' he shook his head. 'But I could have done.'

Chapter 19

January saw a change in Jane's circumstances, but not so great a one as to cause her unhappiness. Mrs Sealy's having determined to quit Brighton for the warmer climes of Italy had been one setback, her reluctant acceptance that Jane's company was a luxury she could not now afford had been another. Neither had been unexpected, however, and Jane had been prepared for both. For a time she had anticipated a return to Highbury would be her only recourse. *That* she had viewed with no very little reluctance—to return to square one when her adventure had scarcely begun! As much as she would have been enraptured to see her mama, the idea of being again confined to Highbury was more than she could endure.

Happily, on discovering that Mrs Sealy no longer had need of Jane, Lady Cecily decided that Miss Bates was precisely the friend and companion *she* required to see her through the long, dark and lonely days of her confinement in East Street. Lady Whitby having been detained on the continent, Mr Fairfax routinely out shooting birds or riding to hounds and Dr Fairfax—

Angus now having satisfied the professional bodies that he was worthy of the prefix—absorbed by his patients amongst the fisher-folk and peasantry, Lady Cecily found the days hung heavy indeed.

'You provide the only light in my day, Jane,' she said. 'I look forward so avidly to your calls. I confess to having been quite envious of Mrs Sealy when she has kept you from me. If she can bear to release you, I will snatch you up.'

Thus, when January was half over and a break in the weather made opportunity for Mrs Sealy to cross to France, Jane packed up her valise and moved into the room her mama had vacated the previous autumn. Her situation at the Fairfaxes was quite as comfortable as it had been with Mrs Sealy but as an invalid Lady Cecily was more demanding. She had been strictly prohibited from going out; the motion of even the sturdiest carriage would be a danger. Restricted to the house she moved slowly from bed to sofa and back again, the view glimpsed from her window in passing her only experience of the outside world. She was by nature languid, with few intellectual resources to call on; she had but a passing interest in books, was not a

knitter or an embroiderer or a player of cards. She had
a fair hand at sketching and possessed many sketch
books half-filled with incomplete attempts at
portraiture, landscape and still life. But by now she
had tried studies of every table lamp, floral
arrangement and footstool in the house. Like most
ladies of rank, she played the pianoforte very prettily,
but to do so for any stretch of time made her back
ache and she was bored with the pieces on the music
stand.

Jane made valiant attempts to interest Lady Cecily in
matters Indian, since their removal to Madras at the
end of the summer was now almost a certain thing.
She had not the slightest inkling of how different life
on that far continent would be—the climate, the
culture, the food. Her understanding of the duration
and possible perils of the voyage was also vague. She
supposed there would be entertainment to while away
the hours, and, from time to time, some very fresh fish
to eat.

What Lady Cecily preferred was news; she was not
very particular concerning its nature or subject so long
as it was fresh and diverting. Jane found she best

pleased her hostess when she was able to gather plenty of it and deliver it in such a way that it brightened and hastened the day. Accordingly, she went out into the town before her mistress awoke to loiter in shops and eavesdrop in coffee houses, picking up such pieces of gossip and rumour as she felt might entertain. She befriended housekeepers and parlour maids, grooms and waiters in search of the kind of information that could only be had from these sources—often more detailed and better informed than the second and third hand, heavily redacted reports that came through polite channels. She visited the library to peruse the newspapers; anything about Court, the nobility and those known to Lady Cecily had particular interest.

The library held another interest for Jane, for she regularly encountered Dr Fairfax there. He was much occupied now that he practiced on his own account; he had a multitude of needy, grateful but impecunious patients who made great demands on his time. But was never too busy to receive a detailed synopsis of Lady Cecily's health and was rarely behindhand in calling on her. Consequently, between the house in East Street and the library, Jane found herself frequently in his company. Their better acquaintance had worked beneficially on his shyness. At first she had encouraged him to speak of his work and his patients, knowing they were topics on which his enthusiasm and passion would eradicate his inhibition. But lately she had found they could converse on any subject with ease and openness. Having Lady Cecily's health as a common concern forged a fast alliance.

'Lady Cecily complains of her ankles,' she told him one particular day. 'She says her feet will not fit inside her shoes but I don't believe she has even tried them. I think it is indicative of her general sense of discomfort and largeness.'

'I quite rely on your up-dates,' he replied. 'I find you have an intuitive understanding of her ladyship's moods.' His knowing in advance what particular inconvenience irked her was a boon; he always had the right unguent, tincture or advice to hand, as in this instance. 'I shall see if I cannot procure a large bath-tub. Immersion in water will ease her. I wish she could be conveyed to the medicinal baths but I dare not try it.'

'It is very difficult for her,' Jane sympathised, 'always

to be at home. The frost last week kept her even from the garden; the paths and steps were too slippery to be attempted.'

'She tells me *you* are always able to cheer or soothe her.'

'She says the same of you,' Jane replied happily. 'She says there is no better physician in the whole of Brighton.'

Dr Fairfax put his head on one side, 'That is quite a compliment,' he admitted. 'One quarter of the doctors in Brighton are quacks, another charlatans. Some are just sadists, I believe—they relish inflicting pain. Some are so old and palsied it is a wonder they can hold a scalpel. As for the rest—they have forgotten their oath.'

'You prove Lady Cecily's point, I believe,' Jane said brightly. 'If the rest are so inefficient, dishonest, cruel or self-interested, surely you *are* the best Brighton can offer. Indeed, if you eliminate all the rest, you are the *only* one! It is no wonder you are so busy.'

'I am never too busy for Lady Cecily, though. You must find me, when the time comes. I will walk with you now, if I may. I am at liberty for the next hour or so.'

The weather that day was bitter, a cruel wind blew off the sea and few people ventured abroad.

'I pity the poor fellows under canvas,' Dr Fairfax said as they walked across the Steyne. 'The officers are billeted in the town but the privates over there and at the camp at Wick suffer in this weather. Their conditions are intolerable. There are cases of ague and influenza. Injuries that cannot be kept dry are unlikely to heal.'

'Poor fellows. I feel very sorry for them.'

'As do I. I go this afternoon to meet with Captain Campbell, who is responsible for the men's corporal well-being. I like and admire him enormously—apart from my brother he is the man I esteem most highly, and I think the feeling is quite mutual. These past weeks we have been often in one another's company. He is a sensible, compassionate man. Mrs Campbell is just newly arrived in Brighton from the midlands; he has taken a house for her on Middle Street. I should like you to know them. Perhaps I will ask Cecily if they can call.'

'For my part I should be delighted,' said Jane, 'and any

company is welcomed by Lady Cecily.'

'Captain Campbell seeks my advice as to the conditions in the camp. I fear I will have no very reassuring counsel for him. Sick soldiers cannot fight—they would be unlikely to survive the voyage. *That,* Miss Bates, is my chief concern. Can you imagine it? A ship, hundreds of miles from land without fresh viands, its water stale and possibly contaminated. Men and animals packed together in airless compartments What if fever strikes? Pox? Cholera? A contagion aboard ship would decimate the entire ship's company. And then there are the injuries generally attendant on seafaring—cuts, fractures, falls. If the conditions are not sanitary and the ship's surgeon no more than a glorified dentist, what hope is there? If we cannot send the men off in the peak of fitness and transport them in healthy conditions under proper medical care, I ask you: what hope is there of a speedy or successful outcome to the war?'

'I am quite of your opinion. Indeed …' a little sob caught in her throat. She swallowed it back. ' … I find your picture of it very frightening. My friend Captain Weston has voiced concern for the welfare of his men.' She did not—could not, without weeping in earnest—articulate her own very pressing concern for Captain Weston himself in the scenario Dr Fairfax had created. 'He holds out no very sanguine hopes. He tells me that morale is low. I read in the newspaper that General Cornwallis' troops have been ordered to reconvene in Virginia. It sounds like a retreat to me. It sounds as though …' She found the tears would flow and she was powerless to stop them.

'My dear Miss Bates,' Dr Fairfax exclaimed, taking her hands in his and searching her face narrowly. 'Are you unwell? What has upset you?'

'Oh!' Jane said with an attempt at a smile. 'I am quite well. Where is my handkerchief? Here it is. How silly of me. How Mama would scold.'

'I am convinced she would not scold,' Dr Fairfax said, retaining one of her hands and leading her to a quiet enclave between two buildings. 'She would be most concerned—as I am—to know the import of these tears.'

'Oh well, you know,' Jane stammered, 'it is the idea of the poor soldiers … and when you speak of the conditions on board … and from what I read, the war is all but lost. What is the point of sending more men to die? Men who ought to be home and safe with their … lov … loved ones!' She looked up at Dr Fairfax, her eyes swimming with agony and apprehension.

Dr Fairfax nodded. His eyes, behind his spectacles, blinked rapidly. 'I see. Yes of course. I see,' he said, almost to himself, and then, 'I see you have a particular reason to be afraid, Miss Bates. Your friend Captain Weston. I had not realised. I upbraid myself for frightening you so thoughtlessly. There is … an understanding between you?'

Jane hesitated. She understood her own feelings very clearly. She was in love with Captain Weston and had been since the previous Christmas. She dated her love from the moment he had appeared, on foot, through a howling blizzard, to accompany her to dinner with his mother. He had gone away in January but she had thought of him often since, fondly, without any kind of hope and yet very much desirous that the basis for hope might come. It *had* come. Since Louisa Churchill's departure for London and the announcement of her engagement she had felt justified to hope. He had given her cause by seeking her out, by his conversation—free and unfettered by nicety or convention, they had enjoyed animated and honest intercourse. His smile gave her cause for hope, the warm press of his hand, the light of his countenance. And yet, in spite of all these things she could not say that she absolutely, unequivocally understood his heart. *That* he had not opened to her.

'Yes. No. That is, I do not know,' she admitted now.

Dr Fairfax nodded and took her arm. 'Let us go home,' he said. 'I will speak to my brother. He is acquainted with Captain Weston I think. In the absence of your own father or a brother, Douglas will ascertain Weston's intentions. I see this uncertainty is making you quite ill.'

'On no account,' Jane protested. 'I would not have Captain Weston coerced by any means. I do not want him brought to the point if it is not his own will and intention. And, in truth Dr Fairfax, I do believe that my acquaintance—my friendship—with him is such that if it *is* his intention, he will need no intermediary.'

Dr Fairfax hesitated. 'I will not have you unhappy, Jane.'

She smiled bravely. 'I am not unhappy. Indeed, I am

not. I had not known how my anxiety troubled me until we began to speak of the war. And surely, I am not alone in feeling anxious about that. Everyone must, even if they have no particular connection with it. America is far away but France, their ally, is close, *very* close to us here.'

'You would prefer Captain Weston not to go, though.'

'I would have every man do what he sees as his duty,' Jane replied resolutely. 'Captain Weston is an honourable man; he will do whatever he thinks is right. He relishes adventure. A voyage to America, a chance to put into practice all he has trained for, the opportunity to serve his King and his country—these are meat and drink to him. I would not deny him them.'

'Even if it breaks your heart. Are these the qualities in him you admire?'

Jane nodded. 'They are qualities we share. If I were a man, I like to think I should have been such a man as Captain Weston. Of course, *I* cannot sail across the sea or explore new countries. But if Captain Weston does it, I shall feel as though he does so on my behalf. I shall do it through him.'

Jane and Dr Fairfax had not been long back in East Street when the front door slammed and Douglas Fairfax rushed into the room. He crossed to kiss his wife before throwing a newspaper down on the table. 'I bring you news, Cecily, that you are sure to find interesting. I do not think *you* will have seen it yet Miss Bates for it is in the late edition just delivered by mail from Fleet Street.'

'Douglas, you scatter mud everywhere,' said Lady Cecily, 'have you not wiped your boots?'

'I have ridden hard from Hove where I saw the paper,' her husband cried, but nevertheless kicking off his boots.'

'What has happened, sir,' Jane enquired. 'Is it news of a military nature? Is the war over?'

Angus Fairfax rose from his seat and went to peruse the newssheet. 'Is it the headline?' he asked.

'No, just a small piece on the back. It is all up with that dog Sealy. Would I had thrashed him when I had the chance. He has absconded leaving vast debts behind him. Miss Churchill is left high and dry. If I were her brother, I would pursue him to the world's end until I got satisfaction.'

'I do not think Mr Churchill will do so. He is not the type,' observed Lady Cecily. 'Poor Louisa, she will be vexed. Mrs Churchill will be more annoyed though. The marriage was her particular scheme. I cannot say I feel very sorry for her—insufferable woman—but I do feel for Louisa, do not you, Jane?'

Jane had turned rather pale. A sort of dread gripped her heart.

'I think Miss Bates has tired herself this morning,' Dr Fairfax said. 'I recommend rest, if you can spare her Cecily? I am engaged to meet Captain Campbell in a quarter of an hour but now Douglas is home I have no concern about leaving you. He will bear you company while Jane lies down.'

'Yes,' Jane said, standing up. 'I do feel somewhat tired. I beg you will excuse me, Lady Cecily.'

'I had not thought to stay …' Douglas Fairfax began, but Jane and his brother had quit the room before he could complete his sentence.

Chapter 20

The Churchills returned to Brighton in such a hurry and in so clandestine a manner that it would not be too much to say that they took flight there. Mrs Churchill found the taint of scandal that had attached itself to them attendant on Mr Sealy's defection intolerable. While the doors of polite society were not absolutely closed to her, they were only just ajar; she found hostesses very reluctant indeed to include her in their soirees and at-homes. Her husband cringed so thoroughly at the murmurs of speculation and the sideways glances from the men at his club that he ceased to go there. Miss Churchill had not been seen in public since her fiancé had absconded. She kept to her room and would see no one. It was widely supposed her heart was broken but the supposition provoked little sympathy. How can sympathy prevail when indictment and blame ride roughshod? Her character was stained with his disgrace, his profligacy at the gaming tables and inebriation in the drinking dens were chalked up to her account. Dissatisfaction with *her*—it was speculated—could be their only excuse. A public and painfully vociferous encounter with one of Sealy's creditors proved the final straw. Under cover of darkness, so hastily that their own groom knew of it only half an hour before they bundled themselves into the carriage, they quit London.

Their suite at the Ship Hotel was small, and not as elegant as Mrs Churchill would have liked, but Brighton being empty of noble families and their having ascertained that Mrs Sealy was not in residence, they had chosen it as a temporary refuge until it could be decided what ought to be done. It would be truer to say—and, as things turned out, quite proven—that Louisa had chosen it as she chose everything—very much for her own purposes.

'I do not know why you wished to return here—full as it must be of memories that are of the utmost discomfort now,' Mrs Churchill complained.

'It is the one place where *he* will not come,' Louisa said. She sat beside the small fire, poking dispiritedly at the coals. The day was already nearing its close and the lamps had yet to be brought in. In the firelight, however, it was possible to see the scars of Louisa's treatment at the hands of Arthur Sealy. A purple bloom of bruise spread from the corner of her eye and down her cheek. An ugly scab on her lip left the horrified observer in no doubt that she had been bitten. Her arm, about the wrist, was almost black and rather swollen. Red weals marked her throat. What evidence of his brutality the remainder of her person might reveal must be left to the imagination but it was very clear that she had been subjected to an attack of the most monstrous nature.

'Will you have some tea? I could ring the bell,' Mrs Churchill said.

Louisa shook her head. 'I am heartily sick of tea.'

'You had better not have any brandy,' Mrs Churchill warned. 'You have had more than enough of that, I believe, in the past few days.'

'I have needed it. It dulls the pain.'

'Dr Chisholm said the arm was but sprained,' Mrs Churchill said, rising and ringing the bell.

'It is not my arm that pains me.'

Mrs Churchill sighed. 'Where is your brother? He is never here when he is wanted. I do not know what he finds to do in this dreadful town. Everything is closed. There is nobody here at all. We ought to have returned to Enscombe. It is what *I* urged, but, as usual, nobody listened to me.'

'*I* listened to you, Eustacia, and look at the result.'

'There now, I have been expecting that jibe. I did what I thought was right. And, I must say Louisa, since you bring the subject up, I do feel that you handled Mr Sealy most unwisely. He is jealous by nature. Gadding around London, attending balls, fraternising with other gentlemen—it was bound to upset him. I would say it was almost calculated on your part. Did you set out to annoy and frustrate him? The wedding day was set, preparations in train, untold hundreds of pounds laid out and yet you persisted in behaving like a giddy debutante. I heard Lady Hart declare with my own ears she had never seen such a determined flirt as you.'

'I did not chain him to the card table or pour liquor down his throat. I told you he had a bad reputation. We each behaved according to our characters; we could never have made each other happy.'

'I am prepared to concede as much. And naturally I do not condone his treatment of you. No provocation on earth should have incited him to such violence. A severe scolding you certainly deserved, but not more. '

Tea was brought in and in spite of what she had said earlier, Louisa accepted a cup.

'We must think of the future,' said Mrs Churchill when the girl had gone, 'though it holds no very bright prospect I am afraid. *This* will be our lot from now on; the seclusion of deserted towns, discreet lodging houses in out of the way places. Respectable doors will be closed to us; a girl who has been jilted—for whatever reason—cannot expect to be welcomed back into society.'

'*I* have done nothing wrong,' Louisa declared.

'You *have*,' griped Mrs Churchill. 'You were quite flagrant in your carelessness of him. Your determination to snub and belittle him would have tested the patience of a saint.'

'*He* is no saint.'

'Indeed not. But in cases such as this it is always the girl who gets the blame, Louisa, you know that. His debts, his drinking, and his ungentlemanly conduct— they will be passed off as high spirits, a regrettable lapse of manners. In time they will be forgotten. *You* will be tainted and I fear the disgrace will be of long duration. People will always wonder what fault in *you* caused him to behave as he did. Mark my words: no one will wish to marry you now.'

'Well …' said Louisa.

Just then the manservant brought candles and coal and Louisa retreated to the shadows while he moved around the room. 'There is a young lady below, ma'am, who begs leave to come up,' said the servant when he had mended the fire.

'We will see no one,' replied Mrs Churchill.

'Who is it?' Louisa asked.

'Miss Jane Bates, miss.'

'Please ask her to come up,' Louisa said.

A few moments and Jane stepped into the room. 'Mr Churchill called at East Street to speak with Mr Fairfax,' she said. 'I asked him if I might call and he gave me leave. Mrs Churchill, Miss Churchill, I am sorrier than I can say for your trouble.'

Louisa stepped from the shadow of the curtain into the light and seeing her—her bruises, her pale complexion, her woebegone expression—Jane could do no other than burst into tears. She threw herself into Louisa's arms. 'I blame myself,' she sobbed. 'I should have warned you.'

The two young women clung to each other and then seated themselves on a small sofa at some distance from Mrs Churchill. 'He treated you the same?' Louisa whispered.

'Not so bad. He was stopped … I was saved from further violence. Was there no one there to give *you* aid?'

Louisa shook her head. 'He took me to a room in the house where we had dined—a library, I think. I do not recall. It was dark, the fire had burned down. He locked the door and then … and then …'

'Hush,' said Jane, 'do not speak of it if it pains you.'

'I blame myself,' Louisa admitted in a low voice. 'I would not say as much to any other living soul, Jane, but I did provoke him. I behaved very badly. I played a very risky game.'

'You do not seek to excuse him?'

'No, by no means. The man is a brute. I … I have paid

a much heavier price for my conduct than I ex … than
any woman should have to bear.'

'Indeed, you have. And yet, Louisa, his character was
not unknown to you when you entered into the
engagement?'

'No. But Eustacia urged it. And … I thought it the
only way to get what I really wanted.'

Jane stared at her, at a loss to understand the import
of Louisa's words 'What you really wanted?'

Louisa glanced across the room to where her sister-in-
law sat, stabbing at a piece of embroidery on her lap.

Jane frowned. 'Do you imply that you engaged
yourself to Mr Sealy simply in order to be free of Mrs
Churchill?'

Louisa smiled. 'Oh no, Miss Bates. I sought a much
greater prize. If I gain it, even this … even what I have
endured … will be worth it. Let me pour you some
tea.'

She got up from the sofa and crossed the room
towards the tray. 'Eustacia and I were just saying,
before you came in Miss Bates, that my reputation is
probably beyond redemption. I have been ruined in

every way a woman can be ruined.'

'Louisa!' cried Mrs Churchill, 'there is no need to announce it so baldly.'

'What is the point of obfuscation? We have reached that point—I believe I quote your own words, Eustacia, when 'there isn't a man in England who will take me.' She glared at her sister-in-law, the light in her eye hectic and unnatural.

'Surely not,' said Jane, shocked, but not so much by the appalling inference of Louisa's words — the extent of Sealy's barbarous attack in the library—as by her comparative cheerfulness in declaring it. The only conclusion she could draw was that Miss Churchill's mind had been in some way unhinged by the ordeal. That would explain the impression that Louisa had in some way engineered the situation in which she now found herself. What had she called it? 'A risky game'? And she had spoken of a 'prize' as though there was something to be gained by this terrible, tragic situation.

'I am afraid it is but too true,' Mrs Churchill said, shaking her head. 'Louisa's case is entirely hopeless.'

A light tap on the door and Mr Churchill put his head into the room to say, 'Louisa, there is someone here to see you. I met him as I came from Mr Fairfax's house. He would not for the world intrude. He has been on manoeuvres these last few days and had only just heard … that you are in town. He is anxious—most anxious—to do anything he can that will assist you in this time of need.'

He opened the door a little more and Captain Weston stepped over the threshold.

Louisa Churchill's face lit up. Jane watched it illuminate with more brilliance than the fire or the smoking candles could possibly impart. The light came from within her—joy, relief, love and triumph. 'Perhaps Eustacia,' she said, 'my case is not entirely hopeless after all.'

Chapter 21

High Street

Highbury

Dear Jane,

Christmas is over and January is here. We do not have snow, as we did last year, but it rains perpetually. The leak in Mama's ceiling is worse than ever. I suggested we bring the matter up with Abel Larkins—as the Donwell steward he could surely sanction repairs to the roof. I suppose this house does still pertain to the Donwell estate. It is still a very odd thing, though, not to be able to mention these matters to Mr Knightley himself.

Our Christmas was most pleasant. Mr and Mrs Weston were so kind as to invite us to dine with them and we met Mr and Mrs Sparks there along with Master George Knightley and young John. Several members of the Weston family were present including various grandchildren—I will not enumerate them and indeed they multiply so exponentially that I begin to confuse my Johns, Toms, Jims and Tims. I must say it was most entertaining watching them play with their new toys. Master George seemed a little subdued. He feels his new position very *keenly. He made particular enquiry as to our comfort and resources—just as his father would have done—and I did just mention the difficulty at the bishop's office these past months with regard to our little pension and also the matter of the leaking roof. He seemed most concerned indeed. But Mama interrupted our discourse and bid him go and play with the other children. He is but nine years of age, after all!*

Mama seems a little more herself. She was most anxious about meeting the Sparkses — having only greeted them—and that very distantly—at church, she has had no conversation with them. I do not know why. It is most unlike her. She is generally so warm and welcoming is she not? I wonder if she expected them to be rather puffed up by their new situation. But Mrs Sparks is so very unassuming a woman and Mr Sparks has no airs whatsoever, she could not but warm to them. She is invited to Donwell—Mrs Sparks expects her daily—but so far, she has not walked that way. I think I will suggest that Mrs Sparks calls on us—then Mama will have to return the visit.

We have had no more sudden explosions of unaccountable temper or long periods of morose silence. There are many times when she does not hear me though and I continue to be uneasy about her audible range. However, I have every hope that an improvement in the weather will ameliorate her mood and if—as seems likely—spring will also bring you home to us I am quite certain of it being completely restored. I am astonished at Mrs Sealy going away without you though Jane. My understanding was that you were to have been her permanent companion. I wonder why she did not take you. Perhaps, after all, you did not suit. How happy that Lady Cecily has need of you. If she retains you until her lying-in you will avoid travelling in this terrible weather.

The Bramhalls are come to Randalls and I own myself completely mistook in my assessment of their character. They are amiable and pleasant, without airs. Mrs Bramhall was all friendliness at church and expressed interest in joining the ladies' benevolent sewing and knitting circle. General Bramhall, while of course having that military bearing and no-nonsense manner one would expect, is genial enough. They have two daughters, one married and one soon to be so, and a son still at school. He must have been a late addition to the family since the general must be sixty and his wife scarce six or seven years less.

Mama has just returned from Mrs Weston's. She sends her particular love and tells me to say she has heard the news from Mrs Weston and thinks of you most tenderly. She will write to you herself in a few days. I do not know what she can mean. I have heard no news from Mrs Weston and I was with her only yesterday. What can have happened between then and now? And why should it especially appertain to you? I am at a loss. I am avid to know but Mama is tight-lipped.

Mr Obadiah Ford and Miss Wix were married on Boxing Day. I am sorry to say the weather was dismal indeed. Rain poured from the gutters and the path to the church door was under two inches of water. No amount of sweeping by the verger could keep it away. The bride arrived attended by umbrellas and a solitary bridesmaid—her sister, an employee of the draper's in Kingston—neither of which were able to prevent her feathered headdress from becoming woefully bedraggled. The groom remained po-faced throughout the ceremony and when mounting the carriage that was to take them to their honeymoon. I must say they did not seem to be very happy. Since then, they have returned and are in the process of removing old Mr and Mrs Ford's belongings to their cottage on the outskirts of Kingston. The new Mrs Ford is an industrious and busy person. She went to no end of trouble for me the other day when I needed a pearl button to replace one I had lost from my glove. Mr Obadiah stands like a mannequin and watches all the others do the work. He would not even help her get a box down from a high shelf even though he could have done so easily and it would have saved her fetching the stool.

I have put my toe through the bedsheet. It needs turning but you know I am no seamstress and will be sure to make a terrible hash of it. I asked Martha to do it but she says she is too busy. Who will do these things for us now you are not here, Jane?

Mama must have told Abel Larkins about the leak in the roof; some men came to repair it yesterday. Also, it appears the administrative delays at the bishop's office have been untangled and our allowance has resumed. Mama needs new boots, however she insists the old ones are watertight except for at the sole, and a cobbler can put that right.

Mrs Hopley and Mrs Cropley are fast friends again and I may humbly say that I played a small part in bringing them together. I visited Mrs Wiggins as I told you I would, speaking beforehand to her housekeeper who I happen to know from being lost once in the alleyways of Kingston when she was kind enough to put me on the right path. It transpires that Mrs Wiggins has no knowledge whatsoever of preserves, has never made so much of a jar of anything in her life and never eats any when it is put on the table. She was as surprised as anyone to be asked to judge the village show. It seems Mrs Winwood asked her before quitting Highbury for the archdeaconry and would not take no for an answer. Poor Mrs Wiggins was mortified to be put on the spot but no substitute was to be found and she did the best she could. As you can imagine I hurried back to Highbury with this information and made it my business to communicate it to Mrs Cropley and Mrs Hopley as soon as may be.

I encountered Mrs Cropley first. 'Mrs Wiggins was of the opinion that your gooseberry preserve was of the ideal sweetness and firmness to be applied to a toasted muffin,' I said, as though I had no particular consciousness of the extreme delicacy of the topic. 'She told me so most particularly when I met her in Kingston and she begs you to send her a jar if you have one spare. She found Mrs Hopley's preserve to be piquant and delicious and very spreadable, the perfect filling for a sponge cake or the like. She was most angry to be asked to choose between the two for she said they ought to have been in different categories altogether. Mrs Beeston the baker's wife overheard our conversation and she is wild to secure a jar for herself for she says she has never been able to make it without lumps.'

This satisfied Mrs Cropley, and when I regaled Mrs Hopley in a similar fashion, she too was much mollified.

Since then, the ladies have both attended the benevolent ladies' sewing and knitting circle and it was universally agreed that this year we shall have two entirely separate classes for preserve and jelly, that Mrs Wiggins will by no means be invited to judge and that Mrs Winwood has a great deal to answer for in her meddling and high-handed interference.

I am extremely happy to report that the wet spring has had a most deleterious effect on the blossom and there is unlikely to be a good crop of soft fruit this year.

Mrs Cropley promises Mrs Hopley the receipt for the unguent that has had such a beneficial effect on her bunion. Mrs H suspects some rheumatism in her thumb and it is hoped that the same good result will accrue.

Work has recommenced on Abbey mill. Mr Pole, the architect who supervises Mr Woodhouse's mansion, has agreed to oversee it and has called in an engineer friend who can assemble the gears and props of the machinery. It is a positive sign, I think. Life, after all, must go on.

On the subject of Mr Woodhouse, he has been here to Highbury to look over the house, which is to be called Hartfield. He brought his wife with him, a sensible, quiet woman who commiserates with all his little ailments and indulges his whims but has absolutely no truck with them herself. They had tea here last evening. He took his customary bowl of gruel but she ate bread and butter and a large slice of Madeira cake and ignored all his cautions and prophecies of dire consequences. I liked her very much.

I sign myself as always, your affectionate sister, Hetty.

Chapter 22

Captain Weston took an extended leave of absence from his regiment and passage was booked for him and the Churchills to Italy. The atrocious weather of late January and February meant that packet ships were locked into the harbour, delaying the consummation of the Churchills' plans, but their intention did not waver. Miss Churchill would become Mrs Weston at a discreet ceremony under the campanile of a quiet Tuscan church. Thereafter it was agreed that the couples would separate. Having seen Louisa married (she could not bring herself to add the epithet 'respectably') Mrs Churchill was minded to throw her off to sink or swim as she might, so disgusted was she with what she now discerned as Louisa's reckless, calculating and thoroughly reprehensible scheme. The Churchills would return to Enscombe, the Westons would travel in Europe until such time as the consequence of Sealy's assault on Louisa—had it even occurred, Mrs Churchill harboured the gravest of doubts—could be fully understood or consigned to memory's oblivion. What the Westons did *then,* Mrs Churchill opined, with a condescending curl of her thin lip, was their own business; *she* would have no part in it. So, they waited out the storms in Brighton, very acrimoniously, with many a bitter recrimination on one side and a scornful determination to make light of every reproach on the other, as the town rallied itself for the new season's visitors. Lodging houses were repaired and painted, the Assembly rooms aired and cleaned, shopkeepers refreshed their window displays ready for Easter, when the first influx of visitors would arrive. Captain Weston and Mr Churchill took their exercise early, before the townsfolk were about, or late, as they dressed for dinner. Mrs and Miss Churchill drove out in a closed carriage and maintained a silence charged with mutual hatred, resentment and disgust.

Jane kept much indoors. Her sources of news were full of the engagement—everywhere she went for information that would divert Lady Cecily she met only with trivia attendant on Miss Churchill's triumph; the gowns that had been delivered from London, the heirloom ring released from the bank and brought by armed courier from York, the anger and dismay in

Weston's regiment, that he should be deserting them in this their time of greatest need. It was too much.

'I fear I can no longer be of any use to you,' she said tearfully to Lady Cecily one morning. 'Everywhere I go I hear only of what distresses me the most.'

Lady Cecily was sufficiently apprised of Jane's disappointment for her to be very kind. 'Do not concern yourself,' she crooned. 'We will amuse ourselves here. Mama assures me she will be back on English soil within the month. Until then, let us try that book again. You read so prettily. I am sure I do not know why I get the characters so muddled in my head.'

Jane was utterly wretched, and not just on her own account, although this was severe enough in all conscience. Her dreams of James Weston were at an end. What had begun the previous Christmas—the chance of happiness she had glimpsed with him—must now be put to one side and forgotten; it could never be. This was the dreary truth that haunted her as she lay wakeful in the night and the shock that assaulted her as she blinked at each new lacklustre day. Louisa Churchill had gambled, risking everything, but had won the prize. Perhaps she deserved it. Jane would never have placed herself in such danger, not even for James Weston. No outcome would have been worth putting herself—and him—in such an impossible position. Louisa had calculated on his good nature, his honour and his high principles—all the things Jane admired about him—and she had placed herself so far beyond the pale that only a good, honourable and principled man like James Weston could have rescued her. And she had relied on her brother to give in, as he always had. Whatever the cost might have been—what it might yet turn out to be— she had been willing to pay, and had paid, in full. In some ways Jane had to admire Miss Churchill—there was no denying the great depth of her love for Mr Weston. That he would be married to someone who loved him so completely, so desperately, ameliorated to some degree her own unfathomable sense of loss. *His* losses, though, she could not forgive. For Louisa, he had given up everything. Firstly, his duty to his superiors and to his men. There could not have been a worse time for his defection; he would feel it keenly, would berate himself, probably, for years to come. Then, his own quest for adventure—his yen to travel—the wanderlust that he and Jane had shared; that, too, now, must be given up. A stately honeymoon progress through Europe could be no substitute for the nomadic, hand-to-mouth travels he had hoped for. And last of all, his independence, the thing he had fought for, resisting his father's efforts to involve him in the family trade. Now he would be an awkward scion of the Churchill household, dependent on their wealth, branded a social climber, out of his depths in their elevated, patrician sphere.

The days passed in East Street. Rain beaded the windows, wind howled over the roofs causing soot to fall in the grates and gaps in the windows to moan and complain. Jane read aloud, page after page, chapter after chapter, absorbing nothing of what transpired in the book and often finding, on looking up, that Lady Cecily dozed. Then she would place the book aside and wander, quiet and drooping, from room to room, trying to find a place where Mrs Brigham would not come across her, where Lucy would not find the need to dust or tidy, a place where she could sit alone and mope and allow the tears to fall. It was in these places—behind the curtain in the window at the turning of the stair, before the cold grate of a room rarely used, on the chill iron of the seat beneath the naked sycamore in the stunted, bare garden—that Dr Fairfax often found her.

'How do you, today?' he would ask her, his voice very gentle, and she would pour out, without any words at all, her utter, overwhelming, immeasurable misery.

'Yes, yes,' he would say when all that day's tears were spent and she leaned against his shoulder exhausted by the fullness of all she could not even begin to articulate, 'I think I understand.'

When the weather was clement, he would lead her— she all unresisting and barely conscious of where they went—to places in the vicinity that would have no association for her with Mr Weston or Miss Churchill. He took her to the fishermen's cottages, to the tenements where the waiters and grooms and kitchen maids lived. He was very popular there, flocked around and made much of, and little gifts pressed into his hands by grateful patients who could afford no money for the treatments he offered them. Sometimes he tended the sick and wounded while she watched, mildly curious as his hands gently pressed and probed, half listening to his questions; does the cold make it worse? Does it suppurate? Are you eating green vegetables? They explored the countryside far from the sea and from the sight of the encampments where officers in red jackets would remind her of the man she had lost. One day they found themselves in a sunken lane, between hawthorn hedges and—beyond the hedges—neatly ploughed fields. Early daffodils danced along the hedgerow. The slightest possible haze of green heralded the slow awakening of new leaf.

'Does this not remind you a little of the country around Highbury?' Dr Fairfax asked her.

She looked around her. 'Yes,' she said at last, 'it does a little. But our soil is much darker—Sussex has a sandy loam, I think. Surrey soil is black. Mama had no end of trouble scrubbing it off my hands when I was little.' The memory brought a smile.

Dr Fairfax nodded. 'I am glad you mention your mama,' he said. 'Do you recall the conversation we had when Mr Knightley died?'

Jane bethought herself. At last she said, 'Yes, you said that people do not die of broken hearts. Your prognosis was that she would recover.'

'And has she?'

Jane put her head on one side. 'She is recovering. Hetty was more sanguine in her last letter.'

'I am glad to hear it. Let us walk on a little further. There is a cottage ahead. I tended the ploughman who lives there last week—he had sliced his arm while sharpening his harrow. His wife makes the most delicious shortbread I have ever tasted. Let us prevail on her to serve us some with a cup of tea.'

On another day he said to her, 'Come with me, Miss Bates. I am summoned to the lying in of Mrs Mason, the harbour-master's wife. If you are to assist Lady Cecily when the time comes you had better know what to expect.'

For those hours, in the cramped gloom of the harbour-master's cottage, Jane forgot Mr Weston, Miss Churchill and her own unhappiness in the woman's travails, Dr Fairfax's patience and gentleness and at last in the squalling, squirming infant she could place in the exhausted woman's arms.

'You did very well today, Jane,' Dr Fairfax said as they

walked home through the blue dawn air. 'You were not frightened or repulsed?'

'I have seen lambs and calves born by the score,' she told him, 'and I helped Mama at Mrs Tremble's last confinement although she did not allow me to be present at the moment of the birth. I found the experience at Mrs Mason's house to be extraordinary and … most wonderful!'

'You would make a good nurse, Jane. Indeed, it may be profanity to say it but you would make a good doctor!'

He walked her to the door of his brother's house and bid her farewell, but, on the point of leaving her, turned back. 'I forgot to say. Mrs Campbell invites you to call on her this afternoon. Would you like me to tell her you are too fatigued? The call can easily be made another day.'

'By no means,' Jane replied. 'When I have slept a little and refreshed myself I will be delighted to attend her.'

'Excellent,' Dr Fairfax smiled. 'I am eager for you to know her—to know them both. I will call on you at noon then, and we will go there together.'

The call to Mrs Campbell was duly made and, Captain Campbell also being at home, Jane was introduced to both. They were a merry couple, the lady displaying a lively wit, very ready to laugh, he rather more staid but often moved to smile by his wife's high spirits. It was immediately manifest to Jane that both held Angus Fairfax in very high esteem.

'I shall not be satisfied until I have Dr Fairfax enlisted as my company surgeon,' Captain Campbell said, 'He revolutionises matters at the encampment, he is quite a force of nature. What could I not achieve with a man like him on my staff! Not but what he doesn't cause me considerable trouble. The tents must be larger, with ventilation to admit air but not rain—how can *that* be achieved, I ask you? But he says it must be so. The men's cots must be spaced farther apart, the slop-buckets emptied thrice daily. *Thrice* daily, mark you …'

'I am sure Miss Bates has not the least interest in slop-buckets, my dear,' interjected his wife. She was a petite, pretty woman with an elfin face and very fine almond-shaped eyes. Her hair was only brown but abundantly curled, her figure of pleasing plumpness. 'I must confess to you that even I find my interest waning on occasion.' She turned to Jane and added in a voice that was low but fully intended to carry to her husband, 'The difficulties we have had instituting the new slop-bucket emptying detail Miss Bates,' she rolled her eyes comically, 'you *cannot* imagine!'

'My dear,' boomed her husband, 'I do not think I have troubled you with it, have I?'

'Other than speaking of it morning, noon and night for the past fortnight, no, not at all. Now Miss Bates, let me take you into the parlour. You will forgive our state of disorganisation. We had just unpacked at our house in Burton when the captain was transferred here so you see we are all packing cases and pictures swathed in cotton sheeting. No doubt I will but just get things to rights here before we will be off again.' She spoke so cheerfully, though, that no one could infer that she was anything other than delighted to be wherever her husband was posted.

The room they entered was certainly in some disarray; boxes half unpacked, mirrors and pictures leaning against each other, rugs as yet unrolled and stacked in corners. But a table and chairs had been assembled and cups and saucers unearthed from a box of straw wadding.

'This is but the second-best set,' Mrs Campbell lamented as she wiped a saucer with her handkerchief, 'and we have not even had the chance to wash them. I do hope you'll forgive me. I don't know where the best tea service might be. Knowing myself as I do, I have probably left it behind in Burton!'

'Miss Bates is the last person to care about china,' Angus Fairfax said. 'She drank her tea last week out of the humblest earthenware and made not the least remark or shudder at it.'

'Good heavens, Angus!' Mrs Campbell cried, 'where on earth did you take her?'

'We visited one of Dr Fairfax's patients,' Jane replied, 'a ploughman with a nasty laceration. His wife served us tea. But I am quite used to it. My papa's ministry took us to houses high and low, great mansions and leaky shacks. He taught us not to differentiate but to accept with grace whatever we were offered.'

'Most laudable,' Captain Campbell said. 'I hope Betsey will not be long bringing the tea. There is some business I wish to discuss with the doctor and you know he is always called away to some emergency or other as soon as ever he gets here.'

No emergency arose however and after tea the two gentlemen retired to the captain's study leaving Jane alone with Mrs Campbell.

'You do not mind the itinerant nature of your situation then, ma'am?' Jane asked.

'It cannot be otherwise when one is married to an army captain,' said Mrs Campbell. Her hand flew to her mouth. 'I am so sorry my dear. That was a most unfeeling remark, in the circumstances.'

Jane blushed. 'Dr Fairfax has told you of my troubles, then?'

'The merest hint. He has been most concerned about you and confided in me. I am sorry, it was tactless of me to make mention of any subject that would distress you, and now I have betrayed his confidence also.' She looked genuinely dismayed. 'My mouth *will* run away with me.'

Jane smiled. 'Do not concern yourself. I have a sister with the same affliction.'

'Indeed? I would be delighted to hear about her. But as to the moving—I do not mind it. I am delighted by

307

new places—can settle as easily in one place as in another. I have a facility for forming acquaintance wherever I go. What I do *not* like is when the captain is obliged to go away without me. He is but a poor correspondent and the weeks pass without any news at all. I begin to wonder if I will ever see him again and then, without warning, the door opens and there he is.'

'I had not considered …' Jane faltered, 'that one would not *always* be able to accompany …'

'Oh no. One is more often left behind than able to go. The captain's *next* posting—as soon as May, I fear— will be without me. It is likely to be in the Americas.'

'And officers' wives are not permitted to accompany their husbands there?'

'*Some* naval officers' wives are, but not army wives unless there is a particularly pressing need. A chaplain may take his wife, I believe, because she may be of some use. But for the rest of us, we must stay at home and wait, and pray. But my dear I want to know all about you. You say you have a sister? I always longed for a sister but I have only brothers …' Mrs Campbell turned the conversation and Jane found herself speaking of Highbury.

The time passed pleasantly. Dr Fairfax and the captain took leave. 'You will not mind making your own way home?' Dr Fairfax enquired. 'We find nothing will do but we must visit the camp and pace things out properly. I am convinced that by a rearrangement of the tents and re-siting the latrines we can make better provision for the men but the captain does not agree with me.'

'And while we are there I will see if I cannot get him to take the King's shilling,' boomed Captain Campbell. 'The more I see of him the more certain I am that he is indispensable to the war effort.'

'I can walk home perfectly well,' Jane said.

'Very well,' said Dr Fairfax, 'but be sure to do so before the evening closes in Jane. I would not have you abroad after dark.'

Accordingly, an hour later, Jane set off from Middle Street with an invitation to return at any time, and began the short walk home. Deciding to go via the seafront she found her steps passed the end of East Street and took the way along the sea-wall towards the cliff path she had walked with Captain Weston some few weeks before. The light was already fading, a bluish twilight creeping in from the east, swallowing up the headland before her. The wind blew strong but for that day the incessant rain had ceased. It was pleasant to be out of doors and Jane felt reluctant to return home immediately. She loitered a while by the wall, looking at the surging sea, feeling the wind and spray on her face, finding herself nearer and nearer to the narrow cliff path.

A footstep. A soft voice behind her. 'Jane, you will not walk the cliff path now?'

She turned, startled. 'Captain Weston!'

He looked past her, at the cliff path, 'It is too dark to walk this way. You will allow me to accompany you home?'

'Perhaps.' Jane looked down, unable to meet his eye or look upon his face. Even to hear his voice caused her exquisite pain.

He gently took her arm. 'Jane,' he said, 'I hope we may speak to each other as of old. I am the same, and you are the same. We have enjoyed such open, unfettered discourse in the past. With you I have felt … entirely free. May we not be friends, as we have always been?'

'I do not know,' said Jane. 'Things are *not* as they were.'

'Because I am engaged? Why should that change things between us?'

'Because … because,' Jane struggled, 'because it makes me fear that you are not the person I thought. You have given up all that made you … all that made me like you so much.'

'What have I given up?'

'Your duty. Who can lead your men as you would have done? Who knows them like you do?'

'Ah yes. You are right Jane. That was very hard. Some of them wept. *I* wept.'

Somehow his pain made it easier for Jane. At least he had not abandoned his brigade lightly. 'Of course,' she said softly.

They walked for a few moments, back towards the town. Shops were closing. The men refurbishing lodging houses were packing away their tools.

'And what else?' Weston asked.

'Your dreams of travel. The Indies, the Holy Land— the places you spoke of with such warmth and excitement. They are to be given up for Yorkshire.'

'It is not fixed that we shall settle in Yorkshire,' Captain Weston demurred, 'perhaps we shall return to Highbury. But you are right, Jane, it will be tame in comparison.'

'And for a woman who—by your own admission— you do not love! She has manipulated and connived to get everyone to do what she wants. You *do* know, don't you?'

'Of course. She has confessed all. I am sure a more devious and Machiavellian scheme has never been conceived. I almost—*almost*—feel sorry for Sealy. He has been her hapless foil and in consideration of that, if I ever meet him, I shall thrash him only to within an inch of his life. She used him shamefully, but he used her worse. She did not expect him to take such a terrible revenge on her. *That* was not part of her plan. But she did intend to sufficiently enrage him to make him break with her, to render her unmarriageable by anyone else.'

'Except for you.'

'Except for me. I had nothing to lose and everything to gain. And you see Jane, it counts for much when you consider that she did it *all*—endured abuse and unspeakable brutality—for *me*.'

'You were flattered.'

'Of course I was. I *am*. Louisa is determined. She has decided that she will be my wife. It is pointless to stand in her way and I find … I find I do not wish to.'

Their path had brought them to East Street. 'You sail for the continent very soon, I suppose,' Jane said, removing her arm from where it lay on Weston's.

'Next week. We remove to Dover tomorrow and wait for a suitable tide.'

'So this is our farewell. Goodbye Mr Weston. I wish you happiness.'

He bowed, and, taking up her hand, kissed it. 'Goodbye Jane. I will always remember you.'

He stepped away and Jane began to mount the steps to the front door. 'Mr Weston,' she called, turning to see him one last time. 'You did not have 'nothing to lose'.'

But he had crossed the street, and did not hear her.

Chapter 23

'How one is thrown about,' complained Mrs Churchill. 'I hope the seas will not continue to be as rough as this. One will be black and blue by the time we reach Calais.'

She perched on a narrow bunk surrounded by trunks and boxes, the portmanteau containing her jewels clasped firmly on her lap. The cabin was small with a low beamed ceiling. A tallow lantern on a hook gave the only light apart from the very small amount that came through a grimy porthole.

'My dear,' said her husband, 'we have hardly left the dock. I fear you must brace yourself for far more motion than this.'

'The crossing is short, ma'am,' Captain Weston said. 'But a very few hours will see us safe on French soil. I shall spend most of the passage on deck and I recommend you do the same. The motion of the ship is always worse below decks.'

Mrs Churchill made no acknowledgement to Captain Weston's remark.

'I shall come with you, James,' Louisa declared, tying her bonnet ribbons more tightly under her chin. 'It is the only way I can prevent you from being drawn into conversation with sailors and merchants. You were almost rude at the inn yesterday—it nearly seemed that you preferred that fellow's company to mine.'

'He was most interesting—just returned from the Canaries. I have been there and …'

'But I have not,' Louisa pouted, 'so his news is of no interest to me.'

'I shall stay below,' declared Mrs Churchill, 'and I suggest you do the same, Louisa. The sailors are uncouth. Their language as we boarded! I have never been so insulted.'

Mr Churchill crossed the cabin to peer from the tiny porthole. 'You did shriek at him rather, Eustacia. I am sure he would not have dropped your trunk. It is not for a lady to dress down a man like that. You should have left it to me.'

'You would have said nothing if my gowns had disappeared to the bottom of the dock,' Mrs Churchill grumbled. 'I wonder if any tea could be got.'

'Brandy, ma'am would settle you better,' Captain Weston said. 'I hope you ate a good breakfast. That too is efficacious against sea-sickness.'

'I ate no breakfast—it was impossible to eat at such an early hour,' Mrs Churchill returned. 'But I shall not suffer from sea-sickness; I have a most robust constitution. I consider myself an excellent traveller.'

'That is happy indeed,' Captain Weston said. 'But if you do feel the least queasy, there is a bucket under the bunk.'

'A bucket?' cried Mrs Churchill. 'I assure you I will have no need of a bucket. Sir, if you think I am the kind of lady who will have recourse to a bucket you mistake my character entirely. I never have sullied my hands with one and do not intend to start now.'

'Ma'am, I do apprehend my error,' Captain Weston said.

Louisa stifled a giggle. Mr Churchill consulted his pocket watch.

'This cabin is intolerably small, Charles,' his wife said. 'Could not a better be secured? My seat is unconscionably hard—barely any padding whatsoever.

And the floor is filthy. All in all, it is a disgrace.'

'These are the captain's quarters, Eustacia. He gave them up to us as a particular favour. You can be sure there are no better on the ship.'

Mrs Churchill sniffed. 'I am glad our crossing is to be of brief duration. Thankfully,' she added, with an attempt at levity, 'we do not go to the Azores!'

'Where *are* the Azores?' Louisa asked mischievously.

'I understand they are a great distance. In the Indies.'

The other three passengers exchanged a look, but no one contradicted Mrs Churchill.

'I will find tea and brandy,' Captain Weston said. 'I shall be but a few moments. The galley cannot be far away.'

'Be sure you do not get distracted,' Louisa called after him.

The ship gave a decided lurch. Mrs Churchill was thrown against the bulkhead. The trunks shifted and slid towards the cabin door. 'Oh Charles,' shrieked Mrs Churchill, grasping her husband's arm. 'I am sure we are going to sink! Speak to the captain. It is not safe, we ought to turn back.'

'Do not distress yourself, Eustacia. All is well. We have but just left the shelter of the harbour I believe.'

A few moments passed. The ship's timbers began to creak as the vessel rolled from side to side and also rose and plunged in turn as it rode the waves. Mrs Churchill was repeatedly thrown forward and back, now against the wall and now almost off the bunk. 'Oh dear,' she gasped, 'oh dear Charles, I fear … that is I feel …'

'I wonder what the food will be like on the continent,' mused Louisa. 'I am quite wild to try all the delicacies, are not you, Eustacia?'

'I shall require proper English food,' Mrs Churchill replied faintly, 'particularly in France. To eat French food would be unpatriotic. I hope we will travel through France very quickly. One is quite in fear of being clapped in irons. We are at war, after all.'

'Very likely they will think us spies,' Louisa agreed.

Mrs Churchill made no rejoinder but pressed her lips firmly together. She was very pale.

'Oh no, I shall not eat a morsel of anything that is not authentically French,' Louisa went on. 'Frogs' legs and snails …'

Mrs Churchill's pallor turned greenish.

'Let me hand you the bucket,' said Louisa. 'I shall follow James on deck. If we shall not have refreshment at least I shall enjoy the fresh air and the view.'

She found him at the stern rail, looking back at the white cliffs with an air of thoughtfulness. 'There you are,' she almost scolded him. 'I told you not to be away long and now I have had to come and look for you.'

'Did the tea not arrive? The steward said he would take it directly,' Weston said, pulling her arm through his. 'I am just looking at England. Is she not very beautiful?'

'I like to think there is *more* beauty closer to you,' Louisa said coyly.

'Ah yes.' Weston slipped his arm around her waist. 'You are indeed very beautiful Louisa. I am a lucky man.'

Presently she said, 'I do so wish to make you happy, James. I will try. Only you must let me have all my own way. It is what I am used to, you know.'

320

Lady Whitby did not arrive in time to be present at the birth of her grandchild, a girl, who was to be named Juliette. Dr Fairfax and Jane assisted at the birth, which was comparatively easy, the usually lethargic Lady Cecily exerting herself to a strenuous degree for the speedy delivery of the child into the world.

'You did very well, *very* well my dear,' said a delighted Mr Fairfax when he was at last admitted to the chamber and allowed to see his daughter. 'Angus says you are quite a natural. And next time …'

Lady Cecily held up her hand. 'Do not speak to me of next time, Douglas. I shall not contemplate more children for a very long time.'

Douglas Fairfax laughed heartily. 'That is just what Angus predicted you would say, but he told me to pay no heed. *All* new mothers are of the same opinion but soon change their minds.'

'I wish to ask Jane to be god-mother,' Lady Cecily murmured. 'She has been such a stalwart friend. I do not know how I would have managed without her.'

'Very well my dear, it shall be so. And Angus shall be God-father shall he not?

Lady Cecily nodded but her eyes were closed and she was close to sleep.

'Very well my dear, you rest now,' said Douglas. 'Juliette and I will stand here by the window and look upon the garden. I doubt not that when Lady Whitby arrives, she will be taken off me and I shall not see her again until we sail for Madras.'

April had brought weather that was bright and promising, all vestiges of the rain-sodden winter erased. The leaves on the sycamore gave shade to the seat beneath. Tulips and anemones gave way to peonies and freesia. The lodging houses of Brighton were freshly painted, linen aired and covers removed. The Assemblies at the Crown and the Ship began once more and new visitors flocked to pay their subscriptions and be introduced to the master of ceremonies. On the Steyne the regiments paraded, trumpets blared and drums beat.

'So, little girl,' Douglas Fairfax said to his daughter. 'We are to go to Madras. How shall you like being the daughter of the special attaché to the Governor of the

East India Company? What sights you shall see! I shall buy you your very own elephant.'

Over the next fortnight, as Lady Cecily regained her strength, the Fairfax household began its preparations for departure. The family would return to Woodley Court for a few weeks and then set sail for Madras. Jane watched them with dismay; she longed to be asked to accompany them. *She* had devoured what literature she could find on the Indian sub-continent with pleasure and interest although she had signally failed to engage Lady Cecily's curiosity in the smallest detail. She would have travelled as companion, nurse, even as lady's maid. But no invitation was forthcoming and she could not bring herself to ask.

There had been some suggestion that Mrs Sealy might send for her once she was established in Italy, and for a while Jane had held out hope of a letter, but no word had come. Captain Bates, though, was preparing his own departure and removal to Italy—an enormous logistical undertaking; he had employed a full-time secretary to arrange every detail of conveyance and accommodation. His purpose in putting himself through such upheaval and inconvenience was clear to see; he made for no other place than the little coastal resort where Mrs Sealy had ensconced herself. No vertiginous hill or narrow cobbled alley would deter him from placing himself under that lady's eye and thereafter into her embrace and neither, he had decided, would a reduction in her capital. Having conceived the idea of marrying her he found he could not rid himself of it; his ardour was as strong if the pecuniary argument was weaker. Put simply, he missed her; she was as necessary to his happiness as foie gras and Madagascan vanilla, more beautiful than any trinket in his comprehensive collection and he owed it to himself to garner her into his compendium of recompense.

With him Jane would not have chosen to travel, even if it had taken her to Mrs Sealy. His transportation to Italy would be as burdensome and tricky as carrying a large tureen of soup thither, the consummation of his hopes was almost as difficult to contemplate; she had no desire to be part of either.

Captain Bates sent for her to bid her farewell. *He* was extremely sanguine about both his journey and its terminus. 'Italian weddings,' he said, with a lewd wink that made her feel ill as well as wretched, 'are all the rage, you know.' He did not omit to press her once more about the Bates family finances. 'Are you certain that your mama would not conjoin with me to fathom brother Edgar's larcenous dealings? Together, you know I think we might do something.'

But Jane shook her head and took her leave.

She saw nothing of Dr Fairfax for some time. When he was not attending his patients he was busy at the army encampment, ordering supplies and instituting improvements that would alleviate the suffering of the enlisted men. Jane missed him. She would have liked to have consulted him about the possibility of taking up nursing. How did one gain an entrance to such a career? And although the worst bitterness of her disappointment over Captain Weston had eased, she still thought of Dr Fairfax as a sympathetic confidant. *He* understood those periods when she was too swamped with gloom and hopelessness to maintain a façade of cheer. In the absence of any opportunity forthcoming from Mrs Sealy or the Fairfaxes, or the occasion to consult Dr Fairfax, Jane set about making enquiries on her own account for an alternative situation—as a companion or a governess, even as a housekeeper, but it seemed there were no openings—she was met with refusal at every turn.

'I fear I shall have to return to Highbury,' she confided to her friend Mrs Campbell one afternoon as they strolled on the Steyne. 'I have been but eight months from home. To return so soon would feel like surrender.'

'An honourable one, though my dear,' Mrs Campbell replied. 'Many girls would not have done as much as you have.'

'It is so very little, though.'

Jane looked around her. It seemed to her that Brighton was filled with strangers. The Pooles, she had heard, would not return this year, their daughter having engaged herself during the London season to an under-secretary at the Treasury. The Pelhams had determined to try the bathing at Bath. The Cumberlands and the Abergavenneys had as yet made no appearance; their houses remained closed up. In place of these familiar families, new ones occupied the lodging houses, thronged the Steyne and danced across the parquet of the Assembly room floors. Jane was on the outside, set apart, with no role to play and almost no right to be there at all.

There was to be a horse race on the Steyne that afternoon and the master of ceremonies was busy overseeing the arrangement of the course. 'Good day Miss Bates,' he said as they passed him. 'I believe I have yet to receive your subscription to the Assembly. I trust there will be no difficulty?'

'No, sir … that is, I do not anticipate … My plans are not yet fixed,' she got out at last. When he had gone, she said to Mrs Campbell, 'I feel quite an alien here.'

'Well, *here* are two to whom you are very familiar and very dear,' Mrs Campbell said gaily, indicating two officers striding towards them from the direction of the encampment. Jane looked in the direction she indicated and saw Captain Campbell and Dr Fairfax— the doctor in a red jacket and with all the regalia of a Captain's rank.

'So, Augustus,' Mrs Campbell said to her husband as they drew near, 'you have got your way at last and persuaded Dr Fairfax to enlist! Bravo! I shall feel so much happier knowing he is at hand.'

'Yes indeed,' Captain Campbell replied, clapping the

doctor on the back, 'and does he not look the part? What say you, Miss Bates? Do you not think he looks exceeding handsome?'

Jane could hardly reply. She felt as though she, Brighton, the whole of England had been swallowed into an abyss. She stared at Dr Fairfax as though he was an apparition, or as though he had dressed up for some joke. Surely, he could not really be going away? Was it possible that he, too, would desert the ones who depended on him most? How would his patients fare without him? How—it crashed upon her with the shock of a cold wave—would she?

Dr Fairfax gave a nervous laugh. 'Miss Bates cannot tell a lie,' he said falteringly. 'I fear no amount of scarlet wool or gold braid can improve my inherent plainness.'

'Forgive me,' said Jane at last, 'I am just … you have taken me by surprise.'

'You are pleased, though?' Dr Fairfax asked earnestly.

Jane was at a loss. 'I do not know,' she said.

'Let us walk a little,' Captain Campbell said, drawing his wife's arm through his. They strolled across the

Steyne and towards the sea wall, the Campbells walking a little apart from Jane and the doctor. The shingle was full of fishing boats, nets and tackle. Further along, the bathing machines were busy. There was plenty to observe and for a time the party occupied itself with the sights and sounds around them. Presently Captain and Mrs Campbell bade them adieu and made their way back in the direction of the town.

'Do you not have duties elsewhere?' Jane asked dully.

'No, not at present. Will you walk further with me? Shall we take the path to the headland?'

The beginning of the ascent was very close to them. It snaked up the slope of close-cropped turf, twisting between outcrops of rock and little plantations of gorse. She had not walked that way since the day she had done so with Mr Weston. There had been something sacred and also something strangely dangerous about it. She did not feel its sanctity now, but its danger—the closeness of the path to the cliff edge, the strong gusts of wind that could catch a lady's skirts and pull her about, the sharp stones that might cause a stumble—these had an appeal that was powerful and disturbing.

'Very well,' she said, and they began to climb.

'I see you are determined not to ask me about my decision to enlist,' Angus said. 'I own to you I am a little disappointed Miss Bates. I thought you would be pleased.'

Jane stopped and turned to him. 'Did you? Pleased that you would desert your patients here? Do you feel that the enlisted men and officers have a greater claim on your duty?'

He considered. 'Not a greater claim, but a more urgent one. A state of war calls for surgeons with extraordinary skills and exceptional compassion. Campbell has convinced me that I can be useful and … and *you,* Jane, made me consider whether I could not rise to the challenge.'

'I?'

'Yes. I do not generally wish to make a name for myself—with *one* exception. Amongst the men I treat I hope to be a figure of reassurance and balm, of course. If, in the midst of a storm at sea, when they are as wretched as can be, or in the hurly-burly of battle when they face death itself, if at those times I can provide calm and kindness and assuage their suffering, I want to do so.'

They came to that part of the path that was too narrow for two to walk together. Down below the sea looked speciously benign, smooth as a bolt of sky-blue silk fringed with a spume of lace where it met the foot of the cliff. But above, where they stood, the wind had power, Jane felt it worry and tug at her skirts. Some veiled import behind Dr Fairfax's meaning agitated Jane's thoughts with quite as much force as the wind. She faltered, almost stumbled.

'Do not look down, Jane,' Dr Fairfax said. 'Fix your eyes on my back and follow in my footsteps.' He put out his hand and grasping hold of hers, led Jane between the rocks and the grassy precipice.

'I do admire your humanity,' Jane said faintly when they could walk side by side again. He retained her hand in his and she did not withdraw it.

'And here too is an opportunity to see the world,' Angus went on. 'I never looked for it before—I think you know that I am not wealthy. My parents have not the means to send me abroad. Douglas has paid for my training that I might be equipped to earn my own living. I never thought to ask him to provide money for idle travel. But *this* will not be idle. The travel costs me nothing and I use the skills I have acquired to do good.'

'It is a happy arrangement,' Jane conceded. 'But I was not aware that you were so desirous to explore the world.'

'I was not, until you told me that *you* wished to.'

There it was again, the suggestion that she was in some way behind his decision. It was beyond Jane's ability to fathom—that she had somehow encouraged him to this course that would leave her more alone—more bereft—than she had ever been before.

They reached the summit. The boulder afforded a seat and a place from which to admire the view. Angus handed Jane to a comfortable place and stood beside her. The sea sparkled in the spring sunshine, the horizon lay, like a lip on the world, before them.

'You must forgive me Dr Fairfax,' said Jane after a while. 'I have been selfish and very ungenerous towards you. Your intentions are most honourable, I see that now; I admire your desire to do good. I would on no account discourage you from your intention. If I am a little envious of the opportunities your enlistment brings it is only because my own future is unclear to me.'

'Is it, Jane? Can you see no glimmer of what it might be?'

'You are right, I dissimulate. It is not unclear. I see it precisely and, in truth, I do not like it.'

'What is it that you see?' he asked slowly.

'I must return to Highbury. I alone, of all my little circle of acquaintance in Brighton, must return to my point of origin. Your brother and Lady Cecily will sail to Madras. Mrs Sealy, Miss Churchill and Captain Weston are in Italy, and my uncle goes there also. You and Captain Campbell will depart for the Americas. *I* must go home to the sleepiest and most parochial village in the country, where the pinnacle of the week is an invitation to tea at the vicarage and one looks forward to the ladies' benevolent sewing and knitting circle because the calendar is empty of all else. While you meet with the indigenous peoples of Virginia, I shall meet the miller's wife and discuss the state of her bunion. Lady Cecily will concern herself with exquisite silks and exotic perfumes while I turn sheets and hem handkerchiefs. Mr Fairfax will arbitrate in matters of politics but my lot is to mediate between two housewives over the consistency of a jar of gooseberry jam. You see why I am envious, Dr Fairfax? Do you wonder at it? I thought Captain Weston betrayed me when he went away, but now I see that it is my destiny to be left—because I am poor and a woman, it is my fate. Mrs Sealy left me, Lady Cecily will follow and so will you. But you are worse than them. They follow their own dreams but you … you follow mine.' She looked up at him, astonished at her own outburst, to find him regarding her with great intensity but no trace of dismay. 'I suppose I shock you,' she concluded.

'No,' he said, 'you do not.'

They looked out together over the vista before them.

'You have not asked me in what ways *you* have influenced my decision,' he said.

'No,' she agreed. 'I wonder at it but I cannot conceive how I might have done so. However it was I regret it bitterly. Why did I put such an idea in your head? I wish with all my heart I could pluck it out again.'

'You will not, when you hear it. It is simply this: I

recalled your words about Captain Weston—how you admired him because he was honourable and did his duty. You did not know *then* that other duties would take precedence. And you spoke of his spirit of adventure—you thoroughly approved of it. In fact you said—and your words have stayed with me—that Captain Weston was the kind of man *you* would have been if you had been a man.'

'I did say that,' Jane recalled. 'But I was mistaken in Captain Weston. He was not the man I thought he was.'

'Perhaps, but that does not mean the epitome of manhood as you perceive it cannot exist.'

'I suppose not,' she shook her head, 'but I do begin to doubt.'

'Oh Jane,' Dr Fairfax burst out, 'do not doubt. Do not doubt your hopes and dreams and do not doubt me. *I* aspire to be that man—your ideal of manhood. You have inspired me to be a better iteration of myself, the man that you seek to be—the man you *would* have been but for the accident of birth.'

She avoided looking at him. 'As far as that goes,' she said, 'you are; you are that and more. How much more bitter, then, that you will do as Captain Weston did.'

He said, 'I am not like Weston.'

'In that you go away and leave me behind, you are,' she said brokenly.

He knelt down on the grass and took her hands. 'May I ask you—is it my going away that gives you pain, or the being left behind?'

She did not reply, but in her heart she knew that it was the loss of him she could not bear, his going, his not being where she was.

'Well, Jane,' he said, when she made no answer, 'I do not go away and leave you behind, not if you do not wish it.'

She frowned. 'You would stay, then, if I asked?'

He nodded. 'Yes, if you asked I would.'

She sighed. 'But I will not ask you. I will not deny you.'

'I am glad of that, for I am going to ask you for my heart's desire and if you say yes, I believe we shall both have our dreams fulfilled.'

'I ... I do not understand,' she said.

He lifted her hands and kissed them. 'Darling Jane,' he said. 'I did not enlist as army surgeon without ascertaining to a certainty that I may take my wife with me wheresoever I may be posted. Where I go, so you shall go. If you wish it, dear Jane. If you will consent to be my wife.'

Jane found she could not quite see him; the lowering sun cast his face in shadow, her eyes swam. She loosed her hands from his and reached for his face—his dear, beautiful face. He stood and drew her to her feet, his arms around her, bending his head down to hers. 'You must say it, Jane. You must say the word.'

'Oh yes,' she said, looking now at him and now at the glorious expanse of sea and sky before them. 'Yes.'

Great was the rejoicing in East Street when the couple returned there, although naturally their return was not soon, Jane and Angus finding that they had much to discuss—confidences to exchange, hearts to open and minds to understand—before they could include others in their delightful new accord. Lady Cecily roused herself from the sofa and embraced Jane with as much affection as a sister still recovering from the exertions of lying-in could muster. Baby Juliette was declared to be delighted that her godmother and god-father should be even more closely connected than through their duty to her, and indeed her little face did seem to crease into something that might have been a smile. Douglas shook his brother most heartily by the hand and sent for a bottle of champagne. If he lamented Jane's lack of a dowry or a title he gave no voice to it—his brother's happiness was what he most desired and the manifest joy of Angus' countenance was all the proof of it he needed. Concerning Angus' enlistment he was less sanguine. The war in America went very ill—he could see no satisfactory outcome from it. He would much rather have included Angus in the delegation to Madras where he could have acted officially as medical overseer or unofficially as private physician, whichever suited Lord Macartney and the East India Company. But what was done was done. Douglas was acquainted with Captain Campbell and felt that if he had to entrust his brother to someone's care, he could do no better. Accordingly, a messenger was dispatched to Middle Street and Captain and Mrs Campbell summoned to join the celebrations, which they did with all alacrity, hurrying round to add their good wishes to the general, joyous clamour.

Dinner was announced before the first bottle was empty, and two or three more consumed during the course of that celebratory meal. Afterwards, at Angus' urging, Jane went upstairs to dress. He would see her dance at the Assembly and, more than that, although being no great dancer himself he would do himself the honour of leading her to the set so that all of Brighton might see what a luminary had been amongst them all along. Lady Cecily sent her own maid to have the arranging of Jane's hair and costume and the girl who descended the stairs could have stood beside any lady of even the highest rank without a blush of shame. Angus Fairfax stepped forward to offer his arm and hand her into the carriage. Jane felt as though she floated on air.

Later, her feet aching and her head a-buzz with the music, Jane sat down at the little desk in her room to write to her mama. She had so much to say! So much to tell! Her heart fairly burst with joy and pride, her fingers itched to take up the pen and let her love for Angus pour out in ink as the tears of gladness poured from her eyes. She so wished to decant it all onto the page but some inner sensibility held her hand. Firstly, a question of constancy. Would she seem fickle, having loved Captain Weston so lately now to engage herself to another? And secondly, her poor mama. Would not news of another's passion, in all its ardency and hopefulness, simply revive all *her* heartache? Would not talk of a marriage—places, people and dates and all the silly fripperies attendant on it— double the wound she already bore so stoically? What agony would it cause her to see her daughter walk down the aisle *she* was to have travelled, with the self- same guests and onlookers that would have attended *her*, and witness the gladness which had been denied her? She should have been married by now, ensconced at Donwell Abbey, the most respected lady in the area and from that elevated position able to shower good onto all who had any kind of need. But fate had dealt with her otherwise; the joy of love had turned to bitterness in her mouth and Jane found she could not add to it. She would have plainly explained her reservations to Marie if she could have been sure of Hetty's not overlooking them, would have described with just what tenderness and compassion she considered her mother's feelings in all her own hopes and arrangements but that it would expose her to Hetty's well-meaning but blundering care.

After much thought she wrote:

East Street

Brighton

Dear Mama,

It is very late—indeed, almost morning—but I could not retire without writing some lines. The most extraordinary thing has occurred. It has taken me by as much surprise as it will cause you and yet I would have you know that although the outcome has been sudden its evolvement has not been. Now that it has happened it feels right to me; the entirely natural result of the previous months. I would not have you think that I have by any means stumbled into my new circumstances or that it relates in any way to previous reversals or disappointments. This is a new plant that has grown independently with its own integrity but that has been unseen simply because other plants have distracted the eye. Now I see it, and it has its own unique and wonderful beauty and lustre. I hope you will comprehend my meaning Mama.

Dr Fairfax has asked me to be his wife and I have agreed. He is enlisted as army surgeon to Captain Campbell's regiment and we will both sail to Virginia in the next few weeks. Your being acquainted with Dr Fairfax is a great comfort to me. I know you esteem his character and his family, which counts for much. The life he offers me will not be one of luxury but it will be one I relish. You of all people will understand the appeal of being a husband's helpmate, to serve alongside him, facing the same trials and sharing his triumphs, to participate equally and to be equal in all things. You will understand me, Mama, and believe me when I say that no one could be more conscious than I of how my news and my future may revive the sadness of losses past. I would do anything rather than inflame past wounds particularly in one who is so very dear to me as you are.

Accordingly, Angus and I feel that a quiet ceremony here in Brighton will be the best course to pursue. Naturally I would like you and Hetty to attend and Lady Cecily has been so good as to offer to remain here until after the marriage that she might offer you her hospitality, although I know it is her dearest wish to return to Woodley Court for a few weeks until their departure for Madras. If you feel, however, that the travel would be too much for you or that for any other reason you are not equal to attending, I will quite understand. As excited and happy as I am, dear Mama, be assured that you—your feelings and peace of mind—are uppermost in the heart of

Your affectionate daughter

Jane.

The letter, when received at Highbury, was exclaimed and wept over but not greeted by quite that degree of surprise that Jane had anticipated. The short time Marie had spent with Dr Fairfax had amply convinced her of his goodness and she had perceived a partiality for Jane in his manner when he spoke of her—which was often—that had prepared her for just such an outcome. Marie fully appreciated Jane's delicacy of feeling and naturally did not begrudge her daughter's happiness but found that her own wound was still too raw to contemplate a local wedding. A Highbury wedding, and one so nearly touching her, risked the pain of private associations becoming all-too public. Therefore, she gently encouraged Jane to marry at Brighton, telling Mrs Cole—who could be relied upon to tell everyone else—that demands on Dr Fairfax's time from his patients and his responsibilities towards the regiment precluded any possibility of the nuptials taking place in Highbury. The marriage of Captain Weston and Louisa Churchill also having taken place at a distance created a useful precedent and no one remarked on the matter to any particular degree. Congratulations were expressed and good wishes sent even by young George Knightley, who received the news of Jane's engagement with glassy eyes and a trembling lip but stoutly declared himself happy for her.

Hetty enjoyed the novelty of the idea—her younger sister married and transported to the Americas—and the source it provided for erroneous conjecture, interminable reminiscence and lurid hyperbole. She spoke with great energy about it in every farmhouse kitchen and elegant drawing room that would admit her, mingling dread and dire prophecy with extreme—perhaps unfounded—confidence for the length and utter happiness of the union. The voyage alone would be a test of endurance *she* would not like to undertake and one read such frightening things about the terrain—completely unlike the environs of Highbury, and what good could come of *that*? Not that but she supposed there were some pretty enough spots in America and she knew some who found great solace in tobacco, so to be sure it was not all bad and she expected Jane would make the best of it even if it was just a liking for tobacco smoke. *She* had met the doctor and liked him well enough, but could not contemplate marrying a man who wore eyeglasses or had red hair—not that any had asked her to marry them, or were likely to (with a self-deprecating smile) no, no, she did not expect any such thing to occur *now* and indeed, on the whole, she did not wish for it, really … She had quite a horror of a doctor's occupation—to be for ever delivering grim prognoses, prodding and poking and asking intimate questions. She doubted it was the profession for a gentleman but then recollected Mr Perry, who was as good as—in some ways, no doubt, a good deal better than—a physician. *He* was undoubtedly a gentleman and had treated young Lilly Tremble's quinsy with great sagacity and patience when really all hope had been lost, turning out at all hours of the night. Now if *that* was not the sign of a gentleman, she did not know what was. Weddings of course were very happy occasions but she did not know that Highbury had seen sufficient of them for the time being. Hermia Winwood's had been celebrated in Highbury—not in actuality—but in so far as avid interest in every detail was concerned; she was sure she had described it a hundred times without at all slaking the Highbury thirst for every flounce and sweetmeat. Mr Obadiah Ford's wedding had been something of a washout, she had to admit. One never could legislate for the rain and it was as likely to be wet in Highbury as to be dry. Who was to say that Jane's wedding, if it *had* taken place in Highbury, would have been any better (except for in the matter of smiles, she was sure that Jane and Dr Fairfax would have done better than Mr Obadiah and Miss Wix, who had scarce managed a glimmer of one between them either on their marriage day or since). Her own journey to Brighton, their accommodations, her choice of bonnet—Mrs Obadiah Ford had been so kind as to offer to refresh the trimmings on an old one—and her likely role in the ceremony, if any (one could not hope to be bridesmaid *twice* in a twelvemonth even though one did, perhaps, almost expect that one's sister, one's *only* sister …), the likelihood of their attending the Assembly, or not, dresses (unsuitability of, possible improvements to) … All this fuelled Hetty's conversation and occupied both her waking and her slumbering hours until an unhappy stumble over the notorious step at the dark and treacherous turn in the passageway caused her to twist her ankle. The injury was of such a severe degree that all the Bates' plans to travel to Brighton had to be given up.

Dr and Mrs Fairfax were quietly married before May became June and if the absence of Jane's mama and sister was much lamented it was in some degree compensated for by the presence of the Fairfaxes, who attended with their trunks literally packed and their horses all but put to for their return to Woodley Court. The honeymoon was of short duration and the couple were soon aboard Admiral Hood's vessel that led the re-supply mission to Yorktown. That Mrs Fairfax was an indispensable aid to her husband during the voyage and in the military engagements that followed may be safely assumed. Captain—later Colonel—Campbell by no means regretted giving way to Angus Fairfax's adamantine condition for his enlistment—that his wife should be permitted to accompany him. She was worth the interminable hours of bureaucracy and the heated arguments with his superiors which—all unbeknownst to her—paved her path to embarkation. She was valued and loved by the soldiers of Captain Campbell's regiment, as wholly respected and treasured a member of the company as the doctor himself. To Dr Fairfax the colonel had particular reason to become peculiarly and personally grateful. A terrible camp-fever assailed him and only the doctor's care and expertise pulled him through. The true depth and enduring nature of Colonel Campbell's esteem for both Dr and Mrs Fairfax was to be signally proved in due course.

No girl from Highbury had ever travelled so far from home; Jane was quite the talk of the little town. Mrs Goddard placed a globe in the classroom whereon the wanderings of the Highbury phenomenon might be plotted, and enjoined her little pupils to take note that so long as they be not immodest, a girl could harbour dreams and achieve them, too. Reverend Paling mentioned Dr and Mrs Fairfax in his prayers although the majority of his parishioners had but a very vague notion of the location of the exotic places they were known to have served. Mrs Cropley declared to anyone who would listen that her bunion had never once troubled her since Dr Fairfax's treatment of it. Jane's letters were perused a hundred times by her sister and read aloud to her mama even though Marie would much have preferred to read them herself. They were passed around and discussed at the ladies' benevolent knitting and sewing circle, shared with any who showed the least interest, looked upon, treasured, touched and prized until they disintegrated into dust.

Dr and Mrs Fairfax were happy for the relatively short time providence allowed them, whether aboard ship or on dry land, walking tropical sands or climbing forested mountains, tending the men of their regiment or the indigenous peoples who shyly came to request their healing aid. They were all in all to each other for so long as they lived—which was not long. Dr Fairfax perished during a skirmish on foreign soil whilst administering aid to a fallen comrade. Jane buried him, weeping an ocean of tears, and then took passage as she could, making her way back to England with her infant daughter. She returned at last to Highbury, to be cosseted and cared for by her affectionate mother and well-meaning sister until grief and a consumption of the lungs took her to that far country from which there is no return.

Captain and Mrs Weston returned from an extended tour of Europe, their fears of a premature addition to their family proving without substance. Although

Enscombe afforded plentiful accommodations within its vast and ancient walls, and alternative eminently suitable properties existed in its extensive curtilage, none were offered to the Westons, and they settled in London. The captain transferred his posting to a neighbouring militia and took up a soldier's life once more, as much liked and respected by his new comrades as he had been by the old. Society welcomed them; they were popular. The spirit of Mrs Weston caused remembrance of her former shame to dim, the affability of her husband made up for his less than unobjectionable birth. The Westons lived well—and well beyond their means, Louisa feeling that all that had been enjoyed by Miss Churchill should not be denied Mrs James Weston. She bought clothes and drove carriages and entertained as she always had done without at all admitting that a captain's stipend could not by any means equal the contribution her brother had always made to her personal allowance. Application for funds made to Enscombe were ignored, likewise letters of affronted entreaty, stiff-necked apology and angry recrimination. The Churchills had thrown them off and could be looked to neither for financial aid nor familial affection.

Captain Weston quailed at the negative balance that accrued daily to their account, but could not persuade his wife to retrench. If only the deposits of gratitude he poured into the coffers of their marriage could have made good the deficit! He remained grateful—grateful and amazed—that a lady like Miss Churchill should have loved him and determined to have him even at such personal cost. But gratitude is not love and it cannot pay the milliner's bill or feed the horses. The Westons continued to live well, but not happily.

A child was born however, a little boy doted on by both. He mended matters between his parents temporarily at least, and when a lingering illness claimed his mother it was concern for *his* future that brought the Churchills from their stronghold of disdain to her bedside. Charles Churchill wept over the diminished form of his sister—it had never been *his* will that they should be estranged of course, *that* had all been Mrs Churchill's doing. Mrs Churchill snatched the infant into her arms and took him, more wholly and unreservedly than she had ever taken anyone, into her heart. He was to be all the children she had not borne, the fulfilment of every disappointed hope. Louisa faded day by day and finally slipped away when her little son was barely three years of age. Captain Weston was bereft, considerably worse off than he had been before his marriage, and with a child to support. The Churchills offered to take the child, to educate and care for him and, in due course, to make him their heir. Relieved of the responsibility of little Frank, although lamenting very much the necessity of their separation, Weston quit the militia and joined his brothers in business, making for himself a not inconsiderable fortune. In time, he returned to Highbury.

Captain Bates' dreams of happiness were also to founder. He traversed Europe in quest of Mrs Sealy's hand, enduring indignity and discomfiture of a nature too extreme and painful to recount, to find her gone. She had removed to a mountain eyrie accessed by a perilous and vertiginous hairpin path. Only very dogged donkeys and mountain goats could negotiate it in any degree of safety. Her chattels had been carried up by local porters, Mrs Sealy herself following in the reliable arms of Ironside, her arms around his neck, her head resting prettily on his shoulder. It was beyond any possibility of doubt unreachable by Captain Bates; no harness, hoist, litter or conveyance of any type ever conceived could carry him there. Her villa was remote, shaded by olive groves, watered by a mountain stream and provisioned by the monks of a monastery that stood on the other side of the lofty Alpine peak. What occurred there, unseen by any eye, may only be imagined. But the tolling of the monastery bell towards the end of August brought meaningful nods from the aged populace of the little village below. 'A wedding,' they said, through knowing, toothless smiles.

Jane Fairfax, orphaned at the age of three, spends her early years as the darling of her grandmamma and aunt Hetty in Highbury. She seems likely to remain there permanently, with only her own pleasing person and good understanding to augment what their limited means and middling connections can provide. But the return from overseas of Colonel Campbell, with every reason of duty and gratitude to take up the daughter of his fallen friend, changes Jane's circumstances—and her destiny. At eight years of age she is adopted into the Campbell family. Though brought up as a second daughter and given every advantage of education, culture and accomplishment that wealth and affection can supply, the colonel's provision cannot extend further. Jane is destined at last to earn her own independence as a governess until a holiday in Weymouth throws her plans into disarray and tests her character and loyalty to breaking point.

Jane Fairfax's early years get only a few paragraphs in Jane Austen's *Emma* and what really occurred in Weymouth is left largely for Emma Woodhouse to speculate upon. What was the real nature of the relationship between Mr Dixon and Miss Fairfax? *Did* he transfer his affections to Miss Campbell?

This novel answers those questions and more. What was it like for Jane to live in the household of the Campbells, the eternal guest who must never allow herself to outshine their mousey and dull-witted daughter? How would knowing that she must quit the luxury and affection of the Campbells to earn her own competency taint her enjoyment of them while they lasted? What on earth would make a sensible girl like Jane engage herself, in secret, to a feckless and unreliable man like Frank Churchill?

THANKYOU

Thank you for reading this book. I really hope you enjoyed it. As a self-published author I don't have the support of an agent or a huge marketing department behind me. I rely on my readers to spread the word about my books. Please would you consider returning to your purchase platform and leaving a short review? Just a few words to accompany your star rating would mean so much to me.

You could connect with me via Facebook or visit my website at www.allie-cresswell.com where you will find details of my other books and have the opportunity to sign up to receive news and special offers. If you don't live too far away from me I would be happy to visit your reading club, WI or creative writing group to give a short talk or a reading.

I can supply questions to guide your reading group discussions about any of my books.

BIBLIOGRAPHY

Of course Jane Austen's Emma has been my main inspiration for this trilogy of Highbury novels.

In addition I benefitted from the wealth of information in:

Georgian Brighton by Sue Berry published by Phillimore & Co Ltd.,

The Georgian Seaside by Louise Allen

ABOUT THE AUTHOR

Allie Cresswell was born in Stockport, UK and began writing fiction as soon as she could hold a pencil.

She did a BA in English Literature at Birmingham University and an MA at Queen Mary College, London.

She has been a print-buyer, a pub landlady, a book-keeper, run a B & B and a group of boutique holiday cottages. Nowadays Allie writes full time having retired from teaching literature to lifelong learners.

She has two grown-up children, two granddaughters, two grandsons and two cockapoos but just one husband – Tim. They live in Cumbria, NW England.

The Other Miss Bates is her eighth novel.

You can contact her via her website at www.allie-cresswell.com or find her on Facebook

ALSO IN LARGE PRINT BY ALLIE CRESSWELL

The Talbot Saga (so far) comprising

The House in the Hollow

The Lady in the Veil

Tall Chimneys

The Highbury Trilogy inspired by Jane Austen's *Emma*, comprising:

Mrs Bates of Highbury

The Other Miss Bates

Dear Jane